D0883583

The Book of Nights

The Book of Nights

A NOVEL BY

Sylvie Germain

✜

TRANSLATED FROM THE FRENCH BY

Christine Donougher

Verba Mundi

DAVID R. GODINE · PUBLISHER

BOSTON

First published in the U.S. in 1993 by
DAVID R. GODINE, PUBLISHER, INC.
Horticultural Hall
300 Massachusetts Avenue
Boston, Massachusetts 02115

Originally published in French in 1985 as *Le Livre des nuits*
by Editions Gallimard. This translation was first published
in Great Britain in 1992 by Dedalus Ltd.

Library of Congress Cataloging-in-Publication Data

Germain, Sylvie, 1954–
[Livre des nuits.   English]
The book of nights : a novel / by Sylvie Germain ;
translated from the French by Christine Donougher. — 1st ed.
p.   cm.
I. Title.
PQ2667.E6845L513   1992   823'.914 — dc20
93-27128   CIP

ISBN 0-87923-975-1

First edition
Printed and bound in the United States of America

TO HENRIETTE AND ROMAIN GERMAIN

NON est mon nom
NON NON le nom
NON NON le NON
  René Daumal, *Le Contre-Ciel*

And the angel of the Lord said unto him:
Wherefore askest thou after my name,
seeing it is wonderful.
                    Judges, 13, xviii

The Book of Nights

"With his mother's cry,
Night took possession of his childhood
one September evening,
rushing into his heart with a taste
of ashes, and salt, and blood, never again
to leave him, running through his life
from age to age — and speaking its name
in the face of history."

But the night that seized him, forever racking his memory with terror and anticipation, and the cry that entered his flesh, there to take root and there to bring conflict, came from infinitely further back.

Oceanic night of his ancestors in which all his people had risen, generation upon generation, in which they had lost themselves, had lived, loved, fought, been wounded, lain down. Had cried out. And fallen silent.

For this cry too originated from further back than his madness. It came from the depths of time, an ever-surgent echo — ever on the way, ever resounding — of a manifold, unassignable cry.

Cry and night had torn him from childhood, alienated him from his own, smitten him with solitude. But thereby made him irremissibly at one with all his people.

Mouths of night and cry confounded, open wounds across faces

3

that in a violent fit of forgetfulness suddenly remember another night, another cry — even older than the world.

Night out of time that presided over the emergence of the world, and cry of unearthly silence that opened the history of the world like a great book of flesh leafed through by wind and fire.

Charles-Victor Peniel, called Night-of-amber, destined to fight to the midnight of night.

~ I ~

Night of Water

IN THOSE DAYS the Peniels were still freshwater people. Going with the almost currentless flow of the canals, they spent their lives on the horizontal of a world leveled by the grayness of the sky and overwhelmed with silence. They knew nothing of the earth but these banks edged by towpaths, bordered with alders, willows, birches, and white poplars. The earth around them lay open like the palm of a hand, incredibly flat, flush against the sky, in a waiting gesture of infinite patience. And likewise were their hearts surrendered to the sky, somber hearts, full of endurance.

The earth to them was an eternal horizon, a land always slipping away on their line of vision, always receding on the skyline, always skimming their hearts without ever seizing them. The earth was a domain of open fields stretching to infinity, of forests, marshes, and plains steeped in the milt of mists and rain; drifting landscapes, strangely distant and familiar, with rivers threading through them — and following the course of these slow waters, they lived out their lives more slowly still.

They knew nothing of the towns but their names, legends, markets, and festivals, as reported by the land-dwellers they encountered where their boats put in.

They knew the outlines of these towns, fantastic engravings etched on a background of sky and light in perpetual metamorphosis, set against fields of flax, corn, bluebells, straw, and hops. Mining towns, cloth manufacturing towns, towns of craftsmen and commerce, rearing their towers and belfries in the wind that blew in from the sea yonder, and testifying themselves in the face of history — and of God — to be cities of serious and hard-working men. And so did their hearts rear up, straight out of the immensity of the present.

They knew nothing of men but those they met on the reaches, at the locks, and on the wharfs, exchanging with them only simple words squared like stone through usage and necessity — words forged in keeping with the water, barges, coal, the wind, and their lives.

They knew nothing of men but what they knew of themselves — the rough lightward-turned surfaces of face and body, reversed out of impenetrable shadow. Among themselves, they spoke even less, and to themselves not at all, so much did the words always reverberate with the dissonant echo of a silence too profound.

But they had a better knowledge than anyone else of the light and dark of the sky, of the wind's moods and the rain's texture, of the earth's smells and the rhythm of the stars.

In their own company, freshwater people were more apt to call themselves by the names of their boats than by their family names. There were the folk on the *Justine*, the *Saint Eloi*, the *Liberty*, the *Bel-Amour*, the *Angelus*, the *Swallow*, the *Marie-Rose*, the *Heart of Flanders*, the *Good News*, or the *Mayflower*. The Peniels had the *Mercy of God*.

I

Vitalie Peniel had brought seven children into the world, but the world had chosen only one — the last. All the others had died on the day they were born, without even taking the time to utter a cry.

As for the seventh, he cried even before his birth. During the night preceding her confinement, Vitalie experienced a sharp pain such as she had never known before, and a tremendous cry resounded in her womb — like the cry in the mist from the boats returning from fishing on the high seas. She knew this cry, having heard it so often in the past, when she stood clutching her mother on the beach, watching for the return of the *Northern Rose* and the *Lamb of God,* on which her father and brothers had gone fishing. Yes, she was well acquainted with that cry rising from the mists, having twice waited for so long to hear it, and having met with it, beyond all expectation, only in the fantastic echo inside her mother's frantic body. But she had left the world of those too-violent waters to follow a freshwater man, and she had driven those cries from her memory. Yet now a new echo had just risen up again from the depths of her body and her forgetting, a great sea-in-springtide cry, and she knew that this time her child would live.

"Listen," she said to her husband asleep at her side, "the child has just cried. It's going to be born and wants to live!"

"Don't talk nonsense, poor woman," replied the man, turning to the wall, "your womb's but a grave that can give birth to nothing!"

At daybreak, while her husband was already up attending to the horses, Vitalie bore her child, all alone, at the rear of the cabin, propped up against the pillows. It was a son. He cried louder than the day before as he emerged from his mother's body, and his cry terrified the horses standing huddled together on the bank in the lingering darkness. The father, on hearing this cry, sank down on his knees and began to weep. Seven times the child cried, and seven times the horses reared, lifting their necks to the sky and swaying their heads. The father wept all the while, and seven times he felt his heart stop.

When he got to his feet again and returned to the cabin, he saw his wife's body gleaming in the semidarkness with a chalky white brilliance, and the child laid between her knees, still dripping with water and blood. He went over to the bed and caressed Vitalie's face, a face overcome with tiredness, pain, and joy. This face he scarcely recognized. It seemed to have become detached from itself, raised by an onslaught of light that welled up from the depths of her body, and dissolved into a smile more ethereal and palely illuminant than the light of a half-moon. Then he took his son in his arms; the little naked body was an immense weight. The weight of the world and of mercy.

But he found not a single word to say, to mother or child, as though the tears he had just shed had washed him clean of all language. And from that day forth he never spoke again.

Vitalie crossed herself, then made the same sign all over the newborn baby's body, to ward off misfortune from every scrap of her son's flesh. She remembered the ceremony for the christening of boats, in the course of which the priest, dressed in white surplice and gilt stole, sprinkled the new boat with holy water, even in its least recesses, so that death should find no hold when the sea swelled up against it. But while she was recalling these rites celebrated on the strand of her native village, lulled by memory, she gently drifted off to sleep and her hand fell back before it had finished tracing a final sign of the cross over the child's forehead.

So did the last born of the Peniels take his share of life, and in exchange he received the name of Theodore-Faustin.

Actually, the child seemed to have taken more than his share, as though he mustered in himself all the strength stolen from his brothers, and he grew with the vigor of a young tree.

At first he became a boatman as all his paternal ancestors had been, spending his days on the barge and on the banks, between the luminous smile of his mother and the impregnable silence of his father. This silence was stamped with such great calmness and such gentleness that at his side the child learned to speak the way a person learns to sing. His voice modulated itself against the background of this silence, taking on a timbre at once low-pitched and light, and with inflections similar to the water's undulations. His voice seemed always on the point of falling silent, of dying away in the murmur of his own breath, and it had strange resonance. Whenever he finished speaking, the last words he had just uttered persisted for a few moments more as an imperceptible echo that seven times rippled the silence.

He liked to play at the bow of the boat, where he sat facing the water, with whose lights and shadows he was more familiar than with anything else. He would make paper birds that he colored in bright hues, then launched into the air. They would wheel around for a moment before falling onto the water, where their wings collapsed and their colors bled away in trickles of pink, blue, green, orange. He also carved little barges out of pieces of bark and branches gathered on the banks; he would stick a big mast in them, to which he tied a handkerchief, and then he cast his boats into the current, loading their empty holds with the weight of all his dreams.

Vitalie was never again with child. Every night her husband held her close and joined with her, dazzled by the whiteness of her body that had become all smiles and happiness. He would fall asleep inside her, into a sleep deep as oblivion, absolved of dreams and thoughts. And dawn always came upon him like a renaissance of his own body merged with his wife's, whose breasts since the birth of their son had unstintingly produced milk with a taste of quince and vanilla. And of this milk he drank deeply.

The father remained at the helm, and Theodore-Faustin minded the horses. There was Tallow-coat, the big black mare that always swung her head as she walked, and two rust-colored horses named One-eyed-red and Greedy-red. Well before daybreak Theodore-Faustin would come and feed them, then until evening he accompanied them along the towpath. When they stopped at locks or loading stations, he would venture a little among the land-people, the lock keepers, café owners, and traders, but he never mixed with them, always held back by some obscure fear relating to all human beings. He dared not talk to them, so much did the strange intonations of his voice surprise those who heard it, and who then made fun of him to protect themselves against the vague disquiet they felt at the sound of it. During rest stops, he would stay with his beasts, whose heavy heads and silken-lidded eyes he liked to stroke. The enormous globes of their eyes, which took fright at the slightest thing, rested upon him a gaze infinitely more gentle than that of any of the land-people he had encountered — excepting his father's, and his mother's smile. Their eyes had the mattness of metal and frosted glass, at once translucent and without transparency. His own gaze could plunge and penetrate deep into theirs, but could distinguish nothing there: he became lost in the precipitate of sand-choked light, of muddy water and smoky wind that had accumulated within them in a lustrous bronze-brown silt. There, for him, lay the hidden face of the world, the mystery part of life where it meets death, and the seat of God — a haven of beauty, calm, and happiness.

His father died at the helm of the new barge he had bought a few months earlier. This was the first boat of his own on which he was not just working. And it was he who had chosen the name inscribed in large letters on the barge's prow: *Mercy of God*.

Death entered his heart suddenly, without warning, making no sound. So unobtrusively did it steal upon him that he did not even start. He remained standing upright, facing the Scheldt, his hands on the wheel, his eyes wide open. Theodore-Faustin, who was leading the horses on the bank alongside, did not notice anything. Yet there was that strange behavior of the three animals: together, they stopped for a moment and turned their heads toward their master, but when Theodore-Faustin looked over in that direction he saw nothing out of the ordinary. His father was, as usual, on duty at the helm. It was Vitalie who noticed: she was at the stern of the boat at the time, busy wringing out some washing that had been left to soak in a large bowl. It was her body that registered alarm. An intense coldness suddenly came over her and penetrated her flesh to the bone. Her breasts froze. She jumped up and rushed toward the bow, colliding with everything that lay in her way, like a blind woman. Her breasts hurt, she was short of breath, and she could not call out her husband's name. At last she got to him, but was stopped short the moment she placed her hand on his shoulder. She had just seen the still man's body, as though caught in a flash of lightning, blaze in dazzling transparency at the touch of her hand. And through this body, like some tall windowpane, she saw her son beyond, farther along the towpath, leading the horses at a slow steady pace. Then darkness descended and the man's body was steeped in shadow. He collapsed then with a subdued rustle and landed, as he fell, in Vitalie's arms. This body seemed to her to be heavy with the accumulated weight of all those nights during which he had lain upon her, embracing her and binding himself to her with his every limb. The weight of a whole lifetime, of so much desire, of all their love, suddenly brought down in a cold inert mass. She was borne under by his fall and collapsed beneath him. She tried to alert her son, but already her tears prevented her from calling out. White tears, with a taste of quince and vanilla.

When Theodore-Faustin came running onto the barge, he found the two bodies of his parents intertwined on the barge as though in a silent and desperate struggle, and entirely bathed in milk. He separated these two bodies of fearsome heaviness, then stretched them out side by side.

"Mother," he said at last, "you must get up. Don't stay lying there, like father."

Vitalie obeyed the voice of her son and let him carry the body into the cabin, where he laid it on the bed. At last she followed him back to the cabin and shut herself inside on her own for a while to lay out the dead man. It was in the milk of her tears that she washed him, then she dressed him, crossed his hands on his chest, lit four candles around the bed, and called her son back.

As soon as he entered the room, in which his mother had put a drape over the window, Theodore-Faustin was overcome by the almost nauseating smell of sweetness that hung in the semidarkness. There was a strong trace of tart quinces and vanilla in that closed atmosphere. This smell deeply disturbed Theodore-Faustin, who experienced the taste of it even in his very flesh, and inside his mouth. And this taste, at once strange and so violently familiar, scared him as much as it delighted him, stirring within him a rush of obscure desires. He tried to call to his mother, but his cry was choked in the spate of milky saliva that suddenly filled his mouth. Vitalie sat next to the bed, perfectly erect upon her chair, her hands laid flat on her knees, which were closed together. Her chest scarcely moved, although her breathing made curious hoarse and spasmodic hissing sounds. Her face, in the dancing light of the candles, emerged only sporadically and partially, with its surfaces unequally lit. This fragmentary face seemed not so much to be made of flesh and skin as to result from the shifting play of bits of paper cut up and stuck down this way and that, and it suddenly put Theodore-Faustin in mind of the paper birds he used to make as a child and then throw upon the water. But this bird profile was capable of neither flight nor fall and was completely colorless; it was in a very still state of repose, on the verge of absence.

He finally came up to the bed and leaned toward his father to kiss his brow, but as he bent down he was arrested by the recumbent man's eyes, which remained half-open. His father's gaze more than ever resembled that of the horses — the glow of the candle flames penetrated deep into the amber brown of the irises, but was not reflected in them; they were illuminated from within. Fossil light, stratified water, a still, ashy wind. And the vista thus glimpsed, through the slit of his eyes, reached ad infinitum into the invisible and the mysterious. Was this, then, where the seat of God lay, in the throes of gentleness, silence, and absence? Theodore-Faustin kissed his father's face three times, on the eyelids and on his lips, and placed another four kisses on his shoulders and hands. Then he came and knelt beside his mother, and resting his forehead on her lap, he began to weep quietly into the folds of her skirt.

2

From that day Theodore-Faustin took his father's place at the helm of the barge, and Vitalie replaced her son leading the horses. But he alone continued to feed them and tend them, ever seeking in their eyes the reflection of his father's gaze.

He was just fifteen, and already the responsibility had fallen to him of being master aboard the *Mercy of God*, that heavy lighter, its holds filled with coal, gliding imperturbably all along the Scheldt. But this boat was not just his; it remained his father's. It was even his father's second body — an immense posthumous body, its sides filled with black concretions torn from the bowels of the earth like so many residues of millennial dreams. And these blocks of dreams he delivered to the fires of the land-dwellers, those strangers isolated in their stone houses, over there.

He could not yet be the master, he was only a ferryman whose job was the perpetual towing of a body grown fantastic, on the surface of the water, flush with the sky, in the bosom of the earth — at the terrifying mercy of God.

So the days, months, and years passed. One evening at dinner, Vitalie said to her son, speaking to him in profile: "Now, haven't you ever thought of taking a wife? The time has come for you to marry, to build your own family. I'm already getting old, and soon I shall be good for nothing."

The son did not reply, but the mother well knew what his thoughts were. She had been aware for some time of a new unrest within him, and she had heard him murmur in his sleep a woman's name.

She knew this woman: she was eldest of the eleven daughters of the bargeman on the *Saint André*. She must have been coming up to seventeen; she was blonde and astonishingly pale in all seasons, as fragile and slender as the reeds standing by the banks, but she was hard working and knew the work well. She was said to be dreamy and even inclined to melancholy, unlike her sisters, but gentler and more silent than all of them. Which was surely why this girl had been able to touch her son's inward heart. And Vitalie had no doubt that his feelings were fully reciprocated.

Yet, what she could have no inkling of was the strength those feelings had gained in her son's too-long-unclaimed heart. From a succession of chance meetings at locks and at various waterman's locations, Theodore-Faustin had allowed himself to be surprised, then charmed, and in the end tormented even to pleasure and pain by the young girl's image. This image was so inwardly engraved upon him that he carried it even within his gaze, and he could not open or close his eyes without seeing it transparent in all things, even in darkness. This image had melted through his flesh, and every night he felt his skin burning and his whole body maddened with irrepressible desire. And now, with his horses, he sought less to penetrate the mystery of their eyes than to rub his head, aching from love, against their blood-warm, blood-sonorous necks.

"You see," Vitalie went on after a period of silence, "I know the girl you'd like to take as your wife. I like her very much, too, and I'd be happy for her to come and live with us. So why wait to go and ask to marry her?"

Theodore-Faustin squeezed the glass in his hand so tightly that he shattered it and cut his palm. When his mother saw the blood running onto the wood of the table she stood up and came over to him.

"You've cut yourself, your hand needs bandaging," she said, but he gently pushed her away.

"Leave it," he said, "it's nothing. All I ask of you is not to mention that woman's name until the day when she's finally mine." He surprised himself by this ban he had just imposed, more than he did Vitalie, who acquiesced without surprise.

"Very well," she said, "I shan't mention her name so long as she's not one of us."

Theodore-Faustin made his marriage proposal several weeks later, one day when his barge, heading downstream, passed the *Saint André* on its way up the Scheldt. As soon as the barge came into view, he immediately left the helm, dived into the cabin, quickly put on the shirt he kept for special occasions, crossed himself seven times before opening the door again, and waited for the *Saint André* to skim past the side of his boat. As the two barges passed each other, he jumped overboard onto the *Saint André's* bridge and walked straight up to old Orflamme, who was standing at the helm, his short black pipe stuck in his mouth like a duck's beak.

"Nicolas Orflamme," said Theodore-Faustin, without further preamble, "I've come to ask for your daughter's hand."

"Which daughter?" said the old man, tightly screwing up his eyes. "I've eleven, you know!"

"Your eldest daughter," he replied.

The old man seemed to consider this for a moment before remarking simply, "That's fair. The first should come first." Then he immersed himself in his pipe smoke again, as though nothing had happened.

"So?" said Theodore-Faustin anxiously. "Do you agree?"

"The fact is that I'll miss her, my firstborn," sighed old Orflamme after a moment's reflection. "She's probably the shyest and dreamiest of my daughters, but she's also the most loving. Yes, indeed, I shall miss her . . ."

The *Saint André* sailed on, gliding upon the purple- and silver-glinting water caught in the light of the bright March sun, slowly moving away from the *Mercy of God,* which continued on its course in the opposite direction.

"You haven't answered me," said Theodore-Faustin, rooted to

the spot, and only three paces from Nicolas Orflamme.

"The fact is that it's not up to me to answer," said the other. "So go and ask her."

She was already there. He had not heard her approach. He saw her as he turned around. She seemed more absent than ever as she fixed her tranquil gaze upon him. He lowered his head, not knowing what more to say, and his eyes were absorbed in the dazzling whiteness of his own shirt. He did not know what to do with his hands, which weighed terribly on the ends of his numb arms. They dangled pitifully in space, like dead poultry hung up on butchers' stalls. His eyes traveled along the deck of the bridge, then fixed upon the young girl's feet. They were bare, powdered all over with coal dust, on which the light caused minute watery reflections to sparkle purplish black. And he was seized with a violent desire for those thin sparkling feet. He clenched his fists, then let his gaze rise over her dark dress, girded with an apron patterned with tiny squares that covered the girl's belly in a dizzying checkered labyrinth. And so he reached her shoulders, where his eyes finally came to rest, incapable of meeting the sight of her face.

"Help me . . ." he murmured at last, his voice almost imploring her.

"I'm here," she said simply.

Then he lifted his head and dared to look at her. But once again words failed him. He slowly raised his frozen hands toward her face and lightly touched her hair. She smiled with such gentleness that he was overwhelmed by it.

Her father, who still had his back to them, suddenly cried out, "It sure is silent, that marriage proposal of yours! Have you lost your tongue, you great oaf? How do you expect her to answer if you don't say anything, blockhead?"

"I certainly can answer him," said the girl. "And my answer is yes."

This "yes" reverberated in Theodore-Faustin's dazed head with more resonance than the chimes of bells pealing out in celebration of a holiday. He seized her hands and squeezed them hard in his.

"And your boat, you useless fellow," said Nicolas Orflamme, "look at it floating off downstream with no master aboard!" Theodore-Faustin turned to him. "Maybe, but the master who's about to return to it is the happiest man on earth!" he cried. And he jumped overboard again, onto the bank, without even saying good-bye, and ran until he was breathless after his drifting barge.

When Vitalie saw her son arrive, his face all flushed and his eyes sparkling, she asked him, laughing: "So, may we say your beloved's name now?"

"You may say it and shout it!" replied Theodore-Faustin, completely out of breath.

3

The marriage was celebrated about mid-June. It was a very simple wedding, with the festivities held at an inn on the banks of the Scheldt, upstream of Cambrai. Noemie wore an ivory white dress trimmed with lace around the neck and wrists, and she had pinned to her belt a tulle rose with silver pearls at the heart of the flower. In her hand she held a long bouquet of eleven stems of cotton grass, which her sisters had picked for her. Theodore-Faustin had plaited his horses' tails with ribbons of white gauze and decorated the mast of his barge like a maypole. At about midday it started to rain, but the rain did not drive away the sun. It skipped in the light, in fine sparkling drops, the color of melted amber. Nicolas Orflamme raised his glass to the health of bride and groom and cried out merrily, "Sun and rain! But it's the devil marrying his daughter!"

That day Noemie forsook the name of Orflamme for that of Peniel, and forsook her father and mother, her ten sisters, and her childhood, to become Theodore-Faustin's wife. She felt light, infinitely light, although an invincible melancholy still tormented her in some indefinable way. What it was that she loved in the man she had just chosen for her husband, she would not have been able to say. All she knew was that to live apart from this man would surely have driven her mad.

Vitalie beheld her daughter-in-law seated at her son's side with a secret happiness mingled with surprise and gratitude. Here at last was the daughter she had never had, and this girl, she thought, was too pure to be in any danger of being blighted by the curse with which she herself must have been afflicted to give birth to so many stillborn sons. For the first time, too, she considered the cold barrenness of her widow's solitude, and her body, already old, quaked at the knowledge of now being excluded from the wild season of love. She thought of those nights of long ago, so vivid in her memory and still fierce upon her flesh, when her body, buried beneath her husband's, whitened under the sheets, like a big bath of milk tasting of quince and vanilla.

Theodore-Faustin himself was not thinking of anything. He sat very close to Noemie, trying to hold pace with her heart, which he sensed beating imperceptibly at his side. He listened, beyond the clamor of the guests' voices, laughter, and songs to the high-pitched whistles of the black-necked grebes and the strangely resonant hooting of the bitterns rising from the banks of the Scheldt in the warmness of the evening. And for the first time he realized how greatly his father's silence had marked his heart and shaped his own voice into a tremulous plaint of exquisite silence. Then he thought of those days long ago when he used to walk with the horses along the towpath, beneath the gaze of that father who had never spoken to him, and his body, momentarily exulting in desire, began to shudder with emptiness upon hearing the distant cries of the birds nesting by the river, as though through them his father were expressing his absence. He suddenly seized Noemie's hand and squeezed it so tightly he almost hurt her. She lowered her eyes, but when she looked up again a smile full of calm and trust lit her face. And at once he forgot his anguish and recovered both his strength as a man and a childlike happiness.

Early the following spring Noemie gave birth to a son. He was called Honoré-Firmin and he took his place aboard the *Mercy of God* with radiant ease. He was a quiet and happy child, who seemed to have no knowledge of anger or sorrow. Everything, to him, was happiness and enjoyment. He learned to sing even before he could talk and to dance before he could walk. He put so much fervor into living that all around him experienced the passing of the days as so many promises of joy fulfilled by each evening. Then came a little girl, whom they called Herminie-Victoire. She had her mother's gentleness, in fact she resembled her in every respect, but her brother always knew how to distract her from her cares and fears.

They both loved the fantastic stories that Vitalie would tell them in the evening, before going to sleep. There was the story of Jean-the-bearcub, son of Gay-the-Gaylon, who set off through the forest to rescue the king's three daughters held prisoner by the terrible Little-old-Bidoux; and the story of Jean Hullos, known as the Marmot, who, deep underground, came upon the stone that burns; and the misfortunes of the lovely Emergaert, imprisoned by cruel-hearted Phinaert; and then the thousand and one adventures of Till Eulenspiegel and his fellow beggars . . .

When Vitalie recounted these legends peopled with fairies, ogres, devils and giants, water sprites and wood sprites, the two children would see the face of their grandmother, who sat by the bed on which they were huddled up together, suddenly shed upon their cot a subdued chalk-white glow. And their very own grandmother seemed to them to be endowed with strange and terrifying powers — an immortal old woman hailing from the mouths of the Scheldt.

Sometimes, too, she told them stories of fishermen lost on the high seas on flaming ships; or catching in their nets fabulous fish that sang with women's voices; and stories of drowned men returning from the bottom of the ocean to visit the living, bringing to the just pearls of sunlight and rings of moon- and star-dust and

casting fearful spells on the wicked. All these stories had a resonance that persisted long afterward in their sleep, sweeping their
dreams into eddies of crazy images, and the world upon their waking seemed a mystery that both captivated their hearts and terrified them. Herminie-Victoire was glad she was a river child and
that her home was not among those mysterious land folk, always
battling with some demon or cruel and jealous giant, nor among
those other, yet wilder, folk of the seashore. But two stories in particular distressed her: there was the story of tall Halevyn, singing
in a marvelous voice as he rode through a forest bathed in moonlight, amid the frail bodies of long-haired virgins hanged from the
branches of the trees; and that of young Kinkamor, who ran all
over the world, and other worlds besides, in order to escape Death,
who nevertheless followed him every step of the way, wearing out
thousands of shoes in this chase. She decided she did not want to
grow up. "That way," she said to herself, "I shall always pass unnoticed. I shall remain small, I shall even make myself smaller and
smaller — so tiny and discreet that not even Death will ever be able
to find me, no matter how many shoes it might put on to pursue
me. And no wicked fiancé will ever be able to find me either. In
any case, I shall stay right here. I shall never leave this barge. Death
will never catch me if even Life doesn't know I exist!" And she
locked herself up in her childhood, as within a chestnut burr of
everlastingness and invisibility.

Honoré-Firmin, by contrast, burned with the desire to leave the
boards of this floating stage where nothing ever happened, to set
out to travel the world and sail the seas. He wanted to visit all those
towns raised in stone, reaching to the skies, their streets swarming
with people; he wanted to travel through those forests haunted by
wild animals and wicked ogres of which he was not afraid. The
too-slowly flowing waters of these canals and rivers in flat countryside bored him. He dreamed of sailing in enormous ships, their
sides crammed not with cheerless coal but with spices, fruit, dazzling textiles, weapons, and gold — and slaves, too. He pictured

himself entering ports, rowdy with the sounds of men, horns, and birds, in the red glow of sunset. And, like Jan-the-Great-Bell-ringer, he was willing to sell his soul to the devil in order to see his wishes gloriously come true.

4

But the devil had no time for the souls of children thirsting for adventure; mankind itself had just initiated its witches' Sabbath in honor of gods that were faceless and nameless, though equipped with dauntless mouths and maws. The maws of these gods rang hollow, and in their lairs the roars of hunger suddenly began to resound with much rolling of drums and blaring of bugles. And so Theodore-Faustin was asked to leave his excessively quiet boat in order to take his place at the emperor's board. Long ago, when he came of age to do military service, he had had the incredible good fortune to draw a lucky number. But, as he was so poor, he had not even appreciated the enormity of this kindness of fate, so overwhelmed was he at the time by another happiness. He had merely said to himself that it was the very strength of his love that had protected him. And he had settled himself into the magic of this love with equal ease and confidence. But all at once this luck he had thought eternal had run out — not that his love had lost any of its strength, quite the contrary, but very simply because the lottery wheel had now gone into a spin, promiscuously naming those who had already been called up and those who had been forgotten, those in love and those not in love, the happy and the despairing.

And then he was gone, off to war, without even time to await the arrival of his third child, although soon to be born; and above all, not understanding in the least the part that, without warning and without recourse, he had just been assigned to play, in red trousers and pompomed kepi.

The very next day after his departure, Noemie took to her bed.

Vitalie thought her daughter-in-law was going to give birth within the next few days, if not hours, for her time had come. But neither within hours nor days was the young woman delivered. And weeks passed and nothing happened. Noemie remained imperturbably confined to her bed, lying inert beneath the weight of her enormous belly. She was heard crying all night and all day long, but there was no sign of her tears; only the faint murmur of an incessant inward trickling could be heard when passing close to her. Soon her belly seemed swollen with emptiness; it had the hollow resonance of a cast-iron cistern with water dripping into it with owl-like hoots.

Honoré-Firmin came into his own having to stand in for his absent father. Although only thirteen, he managed from the outset to show authority and competence. As for Vitalie and Herminie-Victoire, they each in their own way had to forget their age. One forced her body to rediscover vigor and endurance, the other was unable any longer to shrink into her childhood. And so the *Mercy of God* continued to observe its routine while father fought at the front, far away in the hinterland, and mother lay in the semidarkness of the cabin, desperately holding back inside her frozen body the child she was carrying.

Theodore-Faustin marched for a long time, loaded up with all his campaign equipment and his bayonet rifle, which hurt his shoulder and banged against his side. He marched for so long his legs trembled. It seemed to him, when at last he took brief rests at halting places, that the flesh on his calves and thighs had caught fire and that his knees had become soft and spongy. He trod the ground as he had never yet trodden it, crossing towns, fields, bridges, and forests that he was seeing for the first time, with vague surprise mingled with fear. It was summer, the weather was fine, the ripe corn swayed alongside the paths, and the banks around the meadows were all spangled with pretty, brightly colored flowers; the earth smelled good, his companions sang funny songs full of verve, but he himself was so sad at heart that he could not laugh, or sing, or even talk. He felt as though he was dragging around a body that was not his own, and his name at roll call rang so false that he never recognized it. He thought of his family, and particularly his wife, who must have already given birth to their last child. It was surely a son, for lately Noemie's body had had that same smell of ivy and tree bark as when she was expecting Honoré-Firmin; when she was pregnant with Herminie-Victoire, her skin had had the flavor of rye and honey. To this new son he would give his father's name, for the boy would be the child of their reunion and of a new beginning.

The nights especially were painful to him, so unused had he become to sleeping alone after all these years. Noemie's body kept tormenting his dreams; he saw it getting bigger, turning and twisting around him; he felt it panting, slipping into his arms, but he was never able to embrace it. And he would wake up sweating, haggard, among those hundreds of strange men lying around him, men who themselves tossed and moaned in their sleep.

He had not been gone two weeks and already he was scared by the length of his exile, and he wondered whether, through solitude, his body, like his mother's after his father died, would end up becoming hard and rugged like stone. But the war was well under way and the enemy so close that soon Theodore-Faustin lost the thread of his thoughts and of his homesickness in lieu of other thoughts. These, moreover, gathered day by day into one single thought, as compact and cutting as a steel breakwater, which he was continually slamming against. The fear of death, of his own death, had just reared up inside him, all at once reducing to dust his memory, dreams, and desires. The enemy was at hand, closing its grip ever more tightly around the camp. Already all the peasants in the area had fled, abandoning their farms and fields, taking their chances and disappearing into the depths of the forest, carrying away in their jolting carts their shabby furniture, their plates and dishes, bundles of linen, and their children and old folk squashed in among all this bric-a-brac. But he could not flee; he was caught in the heart of the battle, and for days already he had been living in a state of constant alarm, not even distinguishing between night and day any more, so much had the fires and blood and cries that kept rising from every corner of an ever more closed-in horizon transformed space, time, sky, and earth into an enormous mire. Great storms, such as the high temperatures of August bring, sometimes broke toward evening, with purplish glimmerings and bright yellow flashes, the spattering of rain mingling with that of machine guns and the explosions of thunder with those of shells. The world's state of confusion then reached its apogee, throwing men, horses, trees, and the elements pell-mell into the same inextricable debacle.

When he was called, Theodore-Faustin no longer heard his name as an incongruous sound but as a terrifying word of danger, for each time it seemed to him that he was being called to Death. And he responded with extraordinary alacrity, without even taking time to think, so preventing his name from being uttered twice and Death from taking note of it.

Now, again, someone called him. "Peniel!"

He came running, prepared to do anything to silence that intolerable cry. "Peniel," the fellow repeated, "it's your turn. Water fatigue. Take these canteens and get a move on. Don't come back unless they're filled."

He tied the bunch of canteens to his belt and with them jangling from his waist he set off in search of water that he stood little chance of finding. The battle all around was raging, the wells were filled with mud or corpses, and the river secure behind enemy lines. For a long time he crawled blindly among the bodies lying everywhere strewn on the ground. Bullets kept whistling past him, but none of them hit him. This went on for so long that he completely lost all notion of time. Then suddenly a fantastic silence spread over the battlefield. He stopped, holding his breath the better to listen to this miracle of silence. Death rattles and cries still rose on all sides, and he even heard sobs. But this sound of moaning and of the suffering of countless dying soldiers served only to heighten the silence even more relentlessly.

The experience of being unhurt, without even a scratch, and so alone amid these hundreds of dead and wounded, suddenly overwhelmed him with amazement and happiness, an amazement and happiness so great, so savage, that he started to laugh, to laugh to the point of insanity. He could not stop. He rolled onto his back and let his exhausted body draw renewed strength from those peals of uncontrollable laughter. He laughed into the vast August sky flashing above him, drunk with the smell rising from the earth that was all churned up and gorged with the blood of men and horses. He laughed louder than the dying men shrieked or sobbed.

Was that the sound of his laughter galloping back from the river like that, like an echo? Maybe this careering laughter was going to bring him some water. The galloping sound drew nearer, ever nearer, punctuated by another very regular sound, a swift whistling that on each occasion expired in a soft thud. It all came so fast — as fast as his laughter.

He saw passing over him the sweat-glistening belly of a dapple gray horse and a body that leaned from his mount's flank with extraordinary suppleness. He also saw the gesture — so assured and full of grace — that the horseman made with his arm. This arm seemed amazing to him, it was so long and curved. How that arm sliced the air and how his gesture accentuated the youth and animation of the horseman's handsome face. Theodore-Faustin, still in the grip of laughter, noticed all this in a flash. He even noticed that the horseman was smiling — a vague, rather absent-minded smile, like that of an adolescent lost in a daydream — and that this smile raised the fine tips of his blond mustache. He noticed, too, that the horse had turned its head toward him and that its enormous globulous eye was lowering over him, but this eye was just a big unseeing ball, rolling loose. He heard the air whistle above his head and almost immediately afterward heard the whistling expire in a soft thud. Already horse and rider had disappeared. In fact everything had just disappeared, even the sky, suddenly submerged in a rush of blood.

Theodore-Faustin instantly stopped laughing; the sky in spate was pouring blood, filling his eyes and mouth. He felt a word no sooner rise to his mouth than drown in it. It was his father's name, the name he wanted to cry out to Noemie to give their son. The horseman rode straight on, still dancing lithely in his saddle with tireless ample gestures accompanied by those whistling sounds.

So the war ended for Soldier Peniel. It had lasted less than a month. But then it established itself within its victim's very body, where it carried on for nearly a year. Theodore-Faustin remained for so long with eyes closed, limbs inert, lying on an iron bedstead at the far end of a room, that when he finally got up he had to learn to walk again. Indeed, he had to relearn everything, starting with himself. Everything about him had changed, especially his voice. It had lost its deep timbre and those very soft inflections. He now spoke in a screeching jerky voice, with accents that were harsh and overforceful. He spoke with effort, constantly searching for words that he then cast into disjointed, almost incoherent sentences. Worse still, he spoke with violence, hurling his broken sentences like fistfuls of pebbles at those he addressed. But worst of all was his laughter — an evil laughter that seized him seven times a day, shaking his body to deformity. It was more like the grating of a rusty pulley than a laugh, and during every one of these fits his features were twisted in wrinkles and grimaces — his entire countenance, even in repose, was in any case disfigured. The uhlan's saber stroke had shattered half his skull and face, and an enormous scar diagonally scored his flesh from the top of his head to his chin, dividing his face into two mismatching sections. This wound formed a strange tonsure on the top of his skull, and at every fit of laughter the too-tender skin could be seen bulging and quivering like a piece of soft wax.

He was congratulated, and even decorated. He was allowed to go home. It was the height of summer. He went back across the countryside he had come through a year before. The fields were laid to waste, the bridges were in ruins, the villages reduced to ashes, the towns occupied, and the people everywhere seemed mistrustful, withdrawn, nursing their griefs and shame with hunted looks.

He came back alone. Of all his companions who went with him, there was not one left; most were dead, the others had long since returned to their families. He came back alone, and late. But he felt no joy nor any hurry to get back. He was indifferent. This delay was one he could never make up. It was too late, now and forever.

5

He did not even greet his family when he returned to them. And they did not recognize him. When they saw him arrive, they instinctively huddled together, without a word, seized with terror at the sight of that man with convulsive gestures, his face split in two and so crudely sewn back together. Vitalie stood between the children, and all three of them observed in silence this stranger they had yet so eagerly awaited. Herminie-Victoire suddenly began to cry. Her father stared at her viciously and, stamping his foot, shouted, "Stop that noise, you silly girl!"

Honoré-Firmin took his sister in his arms and held her close. Vitalie finally approached her son, but she did not know what to say. She held out her hands in an awkward, almost suppliant gesture. Theodore-Faustin turned away and asked in his shrill yelping voice, "Noemie. The child. Where are they?"

Vitalie recoiled, the two children jumped, less at the question, dreaded though it was, than at that awful yapping. At last Honoré-Firmin found the strength to reply and confront his father. "She's there, in the cabin. She's not been up since you left." Then after a moment he added, "She's not given birth." Without any further questions, Theodore-Faustin went into the cabin. He found Noemie lying still on the bed. Her entire body had grown terribly thin around that distended belly. She stared vacantly at the ceiling, her eyes wide open and ringed with large purplish shadows. She did not emit any particular smell other than a vague whiff of salt-peter. All of a sudden Theodore-Faustin felt the blood rush to his head and the pain with which it so often throbbed immediately became acute. Then he was seized with a frightful burst of laughter.

Noemie slowly turned her head toward this noise, for a long time regarding the person laughing so with total impassiveness, before she showed the slightest reaction. And this reaction was actually expressed by her belly rather than her face. She was soon seized with sudden convulsions. But her belly seemed to be a part of her body that was foreign to the rest of it; it labored alone, while her head and limbs remained inert, as though too weak to participate in the effort of giving birth.

Theodore-Faustin himself, who on the first two occasions had helped to deliver his wife, did not stir, nor come to her aid. This scene did not concern him; it was taking place too close to him, or too far away, for him to intervene, and he remained entrenched in a corner of the bedroom, rooted to the spot by his laughter and the pain in his head.

After nearly two years' gestation the child came out without difficulty, despite its mother's extremely feeble state. It was Vitalie who presided over the birth on her own. In fact she had very little to do, it all happened so fast. Only what came out of Noemie's womb was not a child any more but a little salt statue. The newborn creature, still all curled up, was entirely encased in a thick salt crust. Its mother paid no attention to what was happening; she seemed not even to have noticed that she had given birth. The skin of her belly, for so long distended, subsided with a sound of dry cloth. She had lost neither any blood nor her waters.

Understanding none of this, Vitalie held the strange human-shaped thing in her hands. She looked at the bowl of clear water and the linen laid ready to wash and swaddle the baby, as if they were ludicrous things. Yet she very gently began to rock that completely rigid, crystallized little body in her arms, and started singing a lullaby under her breath, the same one she had so often sung in the past for her stillborn sons. All at once Theodore-Faustin woke from his stupor and emerged from his retreat. He came over to Vitalie and snatched the child from her arms, then held it up in the air. The little salt body became iridescent with light and for a moment was almost transparent. Theodore-Faustin brutally dashed his last born to the ground. The child-statue broke cleanly into seven pieces of salt crystal. Seated on the edge of Noemie's bed, Vitalie went on singing her lullaby for dead children, but it was no more than a very faint murmur. "You see," Theodore-Faustin cried out at last, turning to her abruptly, "I wanted to give him Father's name. But Father wants to remain with the dead, he wants to remain there, in oblivion; he didn't want to give his name back to the living. And he's quite right!"

Since Vitalie seemed not to be listening to him, he flew at her and began to shake her by the shoulders. Then, shouting in her face, he repeated, "Yes, he's right! And do you know why, tell me, do you know why he wants to keep his name in oblivion and silence? Well, it's because he knows. He knows that God doesn't exist. And there's worse still! He knows that God is silent and wicked! Father's dead, completely dead, and his name, too, is dead. So it mustn't be mentioned, otherwise it brings bad luck. Only Death knows his name, that's why Death took it back as soon as it was given away again. And do you know what? There's no mercy of God. No. There's nothing but the wrath of God. Wrath, that's all!" Then he fell at his mother's feet, and letting his head roll on her lap, he began to sob into the folds of her skirt.

Noemie recovered neither her reason nor her health. She lay on her bed, absent from everyone and from herself. Vitalie spoon-fed her, like a sick animal, but she seemed beyond the reach of any food and any care. Soon, strange black purplish bruises began to appear on Noemie's skin. Then these bruises burst and filled with a viscous soft-green liquid. This spread all over her body, which blossomed with flowers of flavescent flesh whose centers went deeper and deeper, emitting a putrid and compelling smell. Despite the impossibility of keeping the bedridden woman aboard the barge any longer, Theodore-Faustin adamantly refused to leave the boat in order to take her ashore to some place for the dying. This stubbornness of his, in wanting to keep his wife, thus imposing on everyone the noxious smell of her body that death was ransacking alive without being in any hurry to make an end of, resulted less from the desire to remain with the woman he had so loved than from an irrepressible rage. Since the world was just some dark nether region in which God took pleasure in seeing men flounder and suffer, he was duty bound to denounce to all and sundry this divine wickedness and everywhere to protest the human stench.

He was no longer master of the *Mercy of God*; he was now the ferryman of God's wrath and cruelty.

Increasingly violent conflicts soon broke out between Honoré-Firmin and his father, whose whims, rages and, above all, fits of manic laughter the son could not bear. There came a day when the two men came to blows. Honoré-Firmin was remarkably tall and strong for his age and he quickly got the better of his father, whom he managed to throw to the ground, then tie to the foot of the mainmast. After that, he went into the cabin, pushed aside Vitalie, who was busy nursing the bedridden woman, rolled his mother's body in a blanket and picked her up in his arms, then left the barge.

•

They never knew where Honoré-Firmin had gone, nor what he had done with his mother's body. He disappeared. He had probably set out at last to discover a wider and more adventurous world to match his eagerness for life.

For a long time Herminie-Victoire mourned her brother's departure, but she was much too afraid of the land-dwellers to dare venture off in search of him. Her imagination, fed only by the tales her grandmother had told her and by vague rumors picked up along the canal, and now struck by the terrible transformation her father had undergone during a year spent far from his family, so tortured her that she was incapable of distinguishing reality from the most fantastic dream. In a world in which the grace of God could, from one day to the next, turn into relentless wrath, in which the body of a young woman started rotting like an old carcass without even taking the time to die, in which a father who was full of love and blessed with a low sweet voice disappeared and came back a violent squawking stranger — in a such a world everything seemed possible to her, starting with the worst.

Yet a certain calm had returned to the Peniels' lives. Following his son's departure and Noemie's disappearance, Theodore-Faustin was less aggressive, less touchy and forbidding. In fact he paid no attention to the two women around him and practically never spoke to them beyond the verbal exchanges the work required. On the other hand, he very often talked to himself. At least, that was what one might have thought, catching him talking alone throughout the day. But in truth it was not so much to himself that he spoke as to another self. The scar that zigzagged across his face seemed to correspond to a much deeper wound that must have sliced through his very being, and he was now two persons in one. There was Theodore and Faustin, without the hyphen any more, and these two fragments confronted each other in continuous dialogue. Moreover, this dialogue never came to anything, it drew so much on absurdity and contradiction; but it was regularly punctuated with peals of manic laughter that obliterated the discussion. And this laughter seemed to spring from yet a third part of himself.

6

It was after lunch on a fine spring day, when they were stopped for a rest. The reed buntings' brief whistles and the chirping of siskins nesting in the alders could be heard rising from the banks. A smell of soft grass and of flowering brushwood hung in the air. With his back against the cabin door, busy filling his pipe, Theodore Faustin viewed this resurgence of greenness and life that was once again coming over the earth. Herminie-Victoire sat on the bank by the horses, mending a sheet stretched out on her lap. All at once the image of the young girl grew distorted and leapt at Theodore Faustin's eyes, momentarily blinded by the flame he had just lit in the bowl of his pipe. The flame died, but the image continued to leap at him, to waver, to burn his face and hands. A mad desire to possess the young girl suddenly overcame Theodore Faustin. He stood up, left the barge, and walked straight toward Herminie-Victoire without taking his eyes off her for an instant. The whiteness of the sheet spread around her reflected an almost bluish brightness on her face and neck.

She had not heard her father's approach, so she started when she saw him suddenly standing there in front of her. He stood very erect and seemed taller than usual. He stared at her with a look so intense and transfixing it unnerved her. She sat there openmouthed, watching him, with one hand held lightly in the air, drawing into space the thread at the end of her shiny needle. He dropped his pipe in the grass, then kneeling before his daughter, he grabbed her by the shoulders, forced back her head, and kissed her. She wanted to cry out, to call Vitalie, but a force greater than her fear restrained her, and even made her yield to her father's desire without further resistance. He had thrown the sheet over them, and it was in this milky shade, lying upon the damp soil, that he took his daughter. The more she thought to fight against her father's embraces, the more she surrendered to them with an obscure joy that frightened her as much as it delighted her.

She remained lying on the grass, wrapped up in the sheet for some while longer after Theodore Faustin had gone. She felt a strange emptiness gaping inside her, and this emptiness was wonderfully sweet to her — she had lost her fear. It was Vitalie who got her up. Coming out of the cabin where she had just been taking an afternoon nap, she noticed the young girl lying on the grass, coiled in the earth- and blood-stained sheet, and rushed to her at once.

"Herminie, my little one, what's wrong? Have you hurt yourself?"

The girl suddenly sprang up, like a jack-in-a-box, and looking at her grandmother brightly, she rejoined, "No, I've become my father's wife!"

Vitalie was so amazed by this response and the impudent tone in which Herminie-Victoire had just spoken to her that she was dumbfounded at first. Then she said, "Whatever are you talking about? What do you mean?"

"It's none of your business!" retorted the girl, and gathering up the sheet in a ball under her arm, she promptly returned to the barge.

Vitalie could only wail, "Poor child! Poor wretched child!"

From that day Herminie-Victoire actually considered herself her father's wife, and every night took her place in his bed. It was during one of these nights that she conceived a child, and she carried it with pride and joy. She suddenly felt so strong, so truly and fully alive. As for Theodore Faustin, he learned with total indifference the result of his couplings with his daughter. Only Vitalie took alarm: she feared the fruits of such barbarous lovemaking.

Herminie-Victoire gave birth one winter's night. Outside it

was glacial, and the cold seemed to have petrified the sky that loomed like a vast black window frosted with tiny stars of dazzling gold. The birth promised to be so difficult that Vitalie sent Theodore Faustin to fetch a doctor from the nearest village. She remained by herself with Herminie-Victoire, trying to calm the dread that had all of a sudden assailed the poor girl again. For fear had just returned to reassert its rights over her with exceptional violence. The child she had been so proud and happy to carry, now suddenly, when it was time to give birth, scared her witless. And in her fear and pain she called on her mother, she begged her to come and rescue her, to comfort her. She even begged her mother to come and take her place again, the place that she had usurped. She watched the stars twinkling through the window, and her gaze came to rest upon one of them, which appeared to be racing toward her and at the same time retreating to the far side of the night.

The child was born before the father's return. It was so big it tore its mother's body coming out. It was a boy. As soon as he was born he bawled himself breathless, and waved his arms so vigorously that he broke the umbilical cord himself. He had an impressive crop of hair, of a magnificent red-brown, that was all tousled. This child, thought Vitalie as she dipped him in the water, is made to live at least a hundred years. And she thought, too, that he must have taken more than his share, as Theodore Faustin had done so once already, and this presaged many misfortunes and vicissitudes, but perhaps, too, she said to herself, some great joys. As she dwelt thus on her thoughts and memories, she suddenly felt for the newborn babe an overwhelming rush of love such as she had never felt before, not even for her own son. She gazed at the infant in amazement, wondering, not to say marveling, at the charm radiated from the outset by this little creature, only just come into being.

When Theodore Faustin finally came back with the doctor, he found the baby already wrapped up, lying next to its young mother. She had lost so much blood that she lay there unconscious, and the doctor held out little hope for her recovery. And the more blood she lost, the blacker the blood became — a glossy shining black. It could have been a blood-flux of night itself, spangled with clouds of stars. She did once reopen her eyes, but did not turn her gaze upon her child. She was the child, the only child on this earth. She strained to look up at the window: all those tiny stars shining above! So were those the thousands of shoes that Death had worn out and thrown away in pursuit of her? She gave a faint smile. Death had put on some very pretty gold shoes, real dancing shoes, to catch up with her and invite her to come following after. So dying was not as bad as all that. Her eyelids closed, and as she shut them she murmured faintly, "And now I'm going to dance bare-foot . . ."

Theodore Faustin took the baby in his arms with latent hostil-ity, but as soon as he lifted into the air this oddly disheveled little creature, all at once he lost his anger and felt captivated by a pro-found charm. And for the first time in years he began to smile.

Herminie-Victoire died before daybreak, without having seen the child she had brought into the world. It seemed to Theodore Faustin that his daughter had never looked so beautiful as she did then. She retained a wonderful smile in death, and her barely showing teeth gleamed with a greater brilliance than during those nights when her mouth opened to his kisses. She had just been gathered to her death cloaked in the same fantastic charm that her son had donned to enter upon life.

And her supreme and peaceful beauty was such that it barred the pain of bereavement. Herminie-Victoire seemed not so much dead as sleeping a marvelous sleep, of the world, the night, and the stars, of the waters of the Scheldt and the soil of Flanders.

Holding his son in his arms, Theodore Faustin on this occasion, too, came to Vitalie, seated at Herminie-Victoire's bedside, to set-tle at her feet, and with his head resting on her lap, he remained there, watching his little girl, whom he had taken for his wife, keeping silent vigil over her strange slumber.

7

This last Peniel son received the name of Victor-Flandrin. His always unkempt, thick mop of hair had the sheen of copper, and his blue-black eyes had the peculiarity of being differentiated from each other by the remarkable fleck of gold making half his left eye iridescent. So bright was this fleck that it glittered even in the night and allowed the child to see in the darkest obscurity just as well as in broad daylight.

Theodore Faustin circled around his son as a hunted animal circles around a house in which it is unsure whether it will at last find refuge or yet another trap. For though he could not escape the child's charm, neither did he dare to surrender to that surge of love he felt throbbing inside him, for fear of having cause once again to suffer by it. All those he had loved had died or disappeared, apart from his mother, who was already no more than a shadow of herself, and furthermore, the love he had borne them had always become a curse. The war had turned him into a kind of monster branded with so much suffering and despair that he could no longer approach anything without in turn destroying it, as though the uhlan's saber cut rebounded without end.

But that war could start again. In a few years' time new emperors could call his son to their battlefields. This thought tormented Theodore Faustin and became an obsession. He kept thinking of how to save his son, so that he might never become a soldier.

And in the end the boy's father had to steel himself to carry out his terrible measure of protection.

Victor-Flandrin was then just five years old. As soon as his father called he came skipping up to him. They both left the barge and walked for a while on a muddy path running alongside a field of flax strewn with dark sheaves. The child was happy to be out in the countryside with his father, like this, and he gamboled around him, chattering constantly.

When they came to a big stone jutting out onto the path, Theodore Faustin stopped, then crouching down in front of his son, and squeezing the boy's hands very tightly in his own, he said to him, "My little one, my one and only, what I'm about to do is going to seem terrible to you, and it will hurt. But it's for your sake that I'm going to do it, to save you from wars, from the madness of emperors and the cruelty of uhlans. Later on, you'll understand, and perhaps then you'll forgive me."

The child listened without understanding a word of this, while his father's face for the first time appeared terrifying to him. Releasing his grip, Theodore Faustin laid his son's little round hands on his own flattened palms and suddenly began tearfully to cover the boy's fingers with kisses. The child dared not move nor take his hands away; he stiffened to prevent himself from crying, too. Then the father abruptly stood up, dragged Victor-Flandrin over to the stone, seized his right hand, folding back all but his son's first two fingers, which he rested on the stone, and then, swiftly drawing a hatchet from his pocket, chopped them off.

At first the stupefied child remained rooted to the spot, before the stone, as though his fist were welded to it. Then he jumped back, and fled across the field, screaming. Theodore Faustin could not run after his son. A violent pain had just shot through his head, and where his tonsure was, the suddenly puffed-up skin throbbed violently. He collapsed against the stone, stricken with a tremendous fit of laughter.

Victor-Flandrin did not come back until evening, brought home by a peasant who had found him unconscious in his field. His wounds had been cauterized and he held his bandaged hand close to his chest. The child had refused to say a single word, and the peasant had spent all day trying to find out where he came from. As soon as the man was gone, Vitalie flew to the youngster, but he

37

would not say anything to her either, and he pushed her away when she asked to see his injured hand. He kept his hand pressed to his heart and stood there motionless in the middle of the room, with his head lowered, his eyes pinned to the ground. Vitalie fretted, not understanding what had happened, and she reeled across the room, whimpering, bumping into all the furniture.

Theodore Faustin stood with his back to the wall, facing his son, just as stiff and silent as the boy, with his arms dangling beside his body. His head was bandaged. Eventually Vitalie turned to him, to ask him to question the child, but as soon as she looked up at her son she abandoned all thought of speaking to him. She had suddenly understood. There was nothing more to say. She felt a grayness veil her eyes.

From that day, silence and loneliness resumed full powers aboard the *Wrath of God,* an old barge whose master no longer took any care of it whatsoever. Of the Peniels there now survived only a few scattered remains. Vitalie sank ever deeper into the darkness engulfing her eyes, and the present, now almost invisible to her, frayed as it faded, allowing the memory of ever yet more distant days to resurface. Every day she went further back down the slow waters of the Scheldt in order to throw herself into the vast gray sea, far beyond. She returned to the empty beach where her mother's skirts flapped in the cold wind as she waited. And every evening, seated at her grandson's bedside, Vitalie invited the child to accompany her down the twisting paths of memory, a memory crowded with faces full of radiance and names abounding with fabulous echoes. And in these folds of memory, soft and silky as still water thick with mud and steeped in sunshine, the child would fall asleep. A woman always appeared in his sleep, a woman who was both mother and sister, blessed with a lovely smile that made him smile back as he slept.

This smile was all that remained to Theodore Faustin, who came to watch him every night. In cutting off his son's two fingers he had in the same fell swoop, and irretrievably, cut away the child's love and trust in him. All day long Victor-Flandrin would avoid his father's gaze, and he never spoke to him. He obeyed his orders and did the work required of him without saying a word and without raising his eyes to his father's face. But as soon as his father moved away or turned his back, the child would then glare at him with extreme violence. Theodore Faustin was aware of this look, though he could never meet it. He was aware of it just from feeling it in his flesh each time, like a blow coming from behind, then shooting sharply through his head, reviving the pain of his incurable injury. For that matter, he always wore a bandage around his brow now.

Yet Theodore Faustin never turned around to confront the child, to chase him away or force him to stop — he was too afraid he might then see the face of the uhlan with the fine blond mustache appear in his son's very own eyes. For that was where the seat of God lay, in the crazed eyes of men full of hatred and violence. Then he would start to laugh, a piercing convulsive laugh that terrified the child just as much as it gave him a sense of power and pleasure.

But at night, softened by sleep, the child's face opened up with a smile filled with wonder, and Theodore Faustin glimpsed, stealing into that smile, the ghostly profiles of Noemie, Honoré-Firmin, and Herminie-Victoire, and sometimes even that of his father. And so he spent his nights, huddled in the dark by his sleeping son's bed, watching the passing of bygone days, the passing of forgetfulness, and sometimes he lightly touched the child's copper-colored tousled hair and with trembling fingertips stroked his face.

The Peniels had to abandon the *Wrath of God* in the end. In fact, though it had long eluded God's mercy, it was no longer answerable even to his wrath; it had forsaken everything and was simply rusting away, to God's and man's indifference.

They then moved into a little lockkeeper's house. While they were not really freshwater people any more, by no means were they land people yet. They were waterside people, with no roots on that bit of bank where they dwelt uneasily, feeling the burden of that undue immobility to which they were not accustomed, and, above all, for which they had no taste. They were people on the edge of land and water, on the farthest fringes of everything, and it was as though they lived at the world's end.

It was at the lock gates that, in the year after adopting this settled life, Theodore Faustin killed himself. His body was found in the morning, tossed up against the lock gates by the greenish water, like an empty barrel. The way he was lying horizontal in the water, he seemed to be trying to keep those gates forever closed, to halt right there, at the zero-point of his body, the progress of all those barges, if not that of the world.

It was Victor-Flandrin who found the body. He immediately went to tell Vitalie, who was still asleep. He came into her room, stood by her bed, and gently shaking her by the shoulder, he broke the news to her in an emotionless voice, "Grandmother, wake up. Father's drowned."

When they brought back her son's body and laid it on the bed, as once before, when her husband died, Vitalie asked to be left alone. Her eyes could no longer see anything, but her hands were still better able to see than her eyes had ever been, and it was by an extraordinarily skillful touch that she laid out the dead man. To wash the body of this only son of hers to be born alive, she rediscovered the same gestures she had used more than forty years ago. And she forgot everything, the entire burden of the years, her bereavements, the war, those other births — she remembered only that splendid night when the child had cried in her womb and that dawn when she had seen emerge from her body, brought to term at last, the fruit of her love, desire, and faith. How he had cried, seven times, and how strangely his cries had resounded! Could it be that the echo of such cries might fall silent? This could not, nor would not, be for as long as she lived. For she still felt vibrating within her, deep in her womb and in her heart, the fabulous echo of the life born to her, a life, although departing the world, that had its place somewhere in eternity.

And she did not mourn her son, for on the threshold where she herself now stood, she knew that tears and lamentations simply disturb the dead and delay them in their already very difficult passage to the other side. She thought of this passage as similar to the progress the barges make along the canals, gliding from lock to lock; and just like these boats, the dead had to be towed; you had to accompany them, walking slowly along the bank, to lead them to that elsewhere awaiting them, yet vaster and more uncharted than the sea.

This was how Victor-Flandrin found his grandmother when he came back to the room — sitting on the bed, with her son's head in her lap. He was surprised to see the old woman so calm and resolute. She sat with her face turned toward the open window, where homeward migrating birds kept up their fluted chirping. The room was bathed in a very bright luminous atmosphere. Vitalie smiled into space, imperceptibly swaying her head; she was singing a song under her breath, in a light, almost playful tone. It was her lullaby for dead babies. He thought that perhaps nothing had actually happened, that his father was not really dead but simply resting there, on his mother's lap. And for the first time in years, he called to him: "Papa!"

He had the impression his grandmother's smile was reflected on his father's face, upon whose mouth in turn a similar smile gradually appeared. And when he came closer to the bed, he saw seven tears the color of milk trickle from the dead man's closed eyes and settle on his face. "Papa," he said again. But neither his father nor Vitalie seemed to notice his presence. He then reached out his hand toward his father's face to wipe away his tears, but as soon as he touched it the seven tears rolled off and fell to the ground, where they bounced with a tinkling of glass.

He gathered them up into the hollow of his hand. They were

little pearls of nacreous white, very smooth and cold to touch, that gave off a vague smell of quince and vanilla.

Victor-Flandrin was still too young and Vitalie much too old for the pair of them to be able to continue looking after the lock by themselves. So once again they had to leave, to move farther away from the water, to venture deeper inland.

They did more than just venture inland — they penetrated the interior. They exiled themselves to those black towns that in the past they had only approached from a distance, to load their barge with the coal extracted from the towns' mysterious terrain. But the terrain that now revealed its mystery to them was just a terrible dark and grimy warren.

Victor-Flandrin was already a tall, strong lad, and he lied about his age. So, despite his mutilated hand, he was taken on in the mine. He was not yet twelve.

He started out screening, spending his days sorting the coal, with which he filled an endless number of tip trucks. Then he became a pit boy, spending his days scuttling like a rat into every nook of the endlessly winding galleries, scrambling up narrow sloping passages carrying pieces of wood, tools, and air pipes. Then he became a hauler, spending his days shoveling coal onto an endless number of skips that he pushed and pulled, now full, now empty. Then he worked as a mine builder, spending his days excavating, timbering, cutting out the coal, endlessly battling away, deep in the earth's darkness.

Meanwhile, Vitalie remained in the rooms they rented on the mezzanine floor of a small terraced house in an endless row of small houses at the foot of the spoil heaps. She kept some poultry at the far end of a little bit of garden behind the house and tried as best she could to help Victor-Flandrin.

She had not relinquished her smile or her calm since the death of Theodore Faustin. Victor-Flandrin suspected that she did not sleep any more but spent her nights awake. And this was true: Vitalie no longer slept, she now inhabited the night so fully that she herself had become an extension of the sweet and gentle darkness, where patience stayed awhile, incessantly murmuring her lullaby for dead babies.

One evening when he came home from the mine, Victor-Flandrin noticed that his grandmother's smile played on her face with greater expansiveness and brightness than usual. She was sitting at the table, peeling apples. He came and sat down opposite her, and taking her hands, silently clasped them in his own. He did not know what to say before such a smile, in which Vitalie seemed to be taking refuge ever more, to the point of almost dissolving into it. It was she who spoke after a moment.

"Tomorrow," she said to him, "you're not to go to the mine. You're never to go back there. You must leave, and get away from this place. Go wherever you please, but leave, you must. The land is vast, and surely somewhere there's a place where you can build your life and your happiness. Maybe it's very close by, maybe it's far away.

"You see, we have nothing. The little I once had, I've lost. There's nothing I can give you, except the little that will remain of me after my death — the shadow of my smile. Take it, take the shadow with you, it's light and won't weigh you down. That way, I'll never leave you, and I'll remain your truest love. And I bequeath to you this love; it's so much greater, so much vaster than me. It contains the sea, the rivers, and the canals, and so many people, men and women, and children, too. This evening they're all here, you know. I sense them around me." Then she fell silent, suddenly distracted by some invisible presence, and she wandered off into that peculiar smile of hers as though she had not said anything, as though nothing had happened.

Victor-Flandrin wanted to detain her, to question her, for he did not understand these strange words she had just spoken to him in a voice at once very tender and distant, as though saying goodbye — but he felt overcome by an irresistible drowsiness and he slumped heavily onto the table, his head rolling among the apple peelings, his hands still holding his grandmother's. When he awoke, he was alone. Where Vitalie had been, there was a quivering glow, airy as a mist gilded by the rising sun. As soon as he rose from his chair and called out to his grandmother, the glow of light stole across the floor, and circling around the room, came and melted into his shadow.

Victor-Flandrin did as Vitalie had asked him. He did not return to the mine. He set off, not knowing where, walking straight ahead, cross-country. He took with him as sole inheritance his father's seven tears and his grandmother's smile that lightened his shadow. In his face, still ingrained with coal dust, glistened the brilliant fleck of gold, like a star in his left eye, that wherever he went earned him the name Night-of-gold.

◠ II ◠

Night of Earth

IN THOSE DAYS wolves still roamed the countryside on frosty winter nights and came right into the villages looking for food, killing donkeys, cows, or pigs, as well as poultry, goats, and sheep. For want of anything better, they sometimes devoured dogs and cats, but whenever the opportunity presented itself they very happily feasted on human fare. Indeed, they seemed especially fond of children and women, whose more tender flesh gratified their hunger. And their hunger was truly prodigious, only increasing with the cold, famine, and war, to seem then the ultimate echo and the most insolent expression of these.

So it was that some landsmen lived in a state of ever-renewed fear of this insatiable hunger, and they gave the wolves a single name that consecrated both their fear and their enemies — they called them "the Beast."

This multibodied Beast was said to be the work of the Devil, sent into this world to try the poor. Some maintained that it was the vengeful soul of a man doomed to the torments of damnation for having dared to defy the world order, or else the guise of some bloodthirsty, evil sorcerer. Others went so far as to see in it the very finger of God, raised in anger against men, whom He was thereby punishing, even in this world, for their disobedience and sins. So when the peasants went beating to track down the Beast, they loaded their guns, which were blessed on the church steps, with bullets cast from the metal of medals of the Virgin and saints.

But the Beast managed to remain out of sight, beyond the

hunters' range. It lurked in the most densely wooded shadows of the forests, which sometimes resounded with low snarls, and appeared only to those its hunger had selected.

Occasionally some of its victims would be found still alive, but the least bite from the Beast seemed to doom to death anyone who was bitten. It was useless treating the casualties by rubbing their wounds with cloves of garlic steeped in vinegar to draw the blood, or by placing poultices upon them made of chopped onion mixed with honey, salt, and urine, and covering their bodies with amulets; they died all the same, sooner or later, in the most atrocious agony.

The closer they came to dying, the more these victims of the Beast seemed to turn into wolves themselves, so terrible did the violence that possessed them become, kindling a blaze in their eyes, like that in the Beast's slanting eyes, and twisting their nails and teeth into claws and fangs always ready to attack. It was not unusual then for the relatives of the crazed victim to put an end to this appalling metamorphosis by smothering the poor dying wretch, foaming with madness, between two mattresses. After which, they put the body back in bed to lie there quietly and kept vigil in true Christian fashion, so that his soul should not go straying into the woods, where the Beast reigned, and then come back to prowl around their house with muted howls.

To ward off such returns and above all to keep the Beast away from their farms, it was usual among the peasants, when they finally succeeded in shooting a wolf, to hang the animal's paws, or even its head or tail, on barn doors. For the Beast had to be kept from coming anywhere near the living. It was said, in fact, that even a glimpse of its eyes alone was enough to rob men of their voices and power of movement, and above all, the putrid stench of its breath was likely to poison anyone who smelled it. Furthermore, it was said that the gypsies, so like wolves themselves, who sometimes came and pitched their camps on the outskirts of the villages, used tobacco mixed with wolf's liver, dried over the fire, to smoke in their long pipes, so as to frighten the dogs guarding the animals with this foul smell.

Such were the real ogres that haunted the forests in those days, terrorizing the land-dwellers; these ogres were called the Beast and they were even more fearsome than the hobgoblins, giants, and dragons of legends and fairy tales.

But as for Victor-Flandrin, at that time his only memory was of the slow gentle waters of the canals on which he had spent his childhood and of the earth's black entrails into which he had had to descend for seven years.

I

Victor-Flandrin walked for a long time, following the same path his father had taken more than twenty years ago, the path that had irremediably separated Theodore Faustin from his family. But Victor-Flandrin had no companions with him, he did not carry a gun over his shoulder, and he was not pining with homesickness. He could never be separated from the two people who had been his whole family. His grandmother's smile followed his every footstep, indissolubly bound to his shadow, and his father's tears hung around his neck, strung on a bootlace under his shirt.

He crossed towns, fields, bridges, and forests, the same ones that his father had encountered long ago, but they caused him no surprise or fear. It was winter, and the weather was so cold that the branches of the trees snapped like glass with a very dry sound that for a long time afterward reverberated in the silence. The stick he was holding sparkled with frost and made a curious sound on the icy roads. He felt lighthearted; not that he was happy, but he was now so alone that this deserted world, opening out in front of him as far as the eye could see, was sweetly comforting in its strangeness.

The snow was so dense and hard packed that no footprints were left in it, and when toward midday the sun broke through, a paler yellow than sand, all the countryside was resplendent in its featurelessness. In this dazzling emptiness and silence Victor-Flandrin felt his body grow in strength and presence, for at last he was experiencing in complete freedom the vigor of his youth. He did not feel the cold, although it made the bridges crack and the ground hard and drove the ravenously hungry wolves out of the forests.

He came to the foot of a hill covered with oaks, beeches, and fir trees; a north wind swept across the surface of the snow with shrill whistlings. He climbed the narrow, increasingly twisting road that wound its way up the hillside. It was impossible to keep any sense of direction in this forest transformed into a vast snowdrift, where only a dim light penetrated, and through which Victor-Flandrin advanced with difficulty.

He finally became so breathless that he sat down for a moment on a rock jutting out on the edge of a clearing. Evening was beginning to draw in, and for the first time since he set out, Victor-Flandrin wondered uneasily where he would sleep when darkness fell. He was completely lost, imprisoned in this soughing labyrinth.

The noise made by the wind was in fact very strange; it sounded like the voice of a man in distress, screaming frantically, and Victor-Flandrin suddenly shuddered, so similar were the strains of that voice to his father's pain-filled laughter.

And now this wind began to prowl around the clearing, imperceptibly closing in. He sat there, lodged on his stone, not daring to move or even look around. The gloom had turned to darkness, night had already fallen, and the slender crescent moon shining very high in the sky, like a tiny white comma among the stars, lit only the middle of the clearing. But Victor-Flandrin was drawn to this small amount of light; he finally rose from the stone, upon which he was beginning to grow numb, and walked toward it as though that poor patch of moonshine could offer him a safer refuge. Two other gleams pierced the darkness. He noticed them as he moved toward the halo of moonlight; they were still at some distance, but he was able to discern them, thanks to the fleck of gold that gave him a cat's keenness of vision in his left eye. They were two thin slanting gleams of dazzling yellow that seemed to be staring at him. His steps slowed, and his heart, too, slowed its pace. The creature finally emerged from the darkness, but did not make straight for Victor-Flandrin; it began to circle around the edge of the clearing without taking its eyes off him. It had a great suppleness of movement that emphasized the narrowness of its back. Its chest, by contrast, was broad and round, where its gray coat, silvered by the frost, bristled lighter.

Victor-Flandrin did the same as the animal and began to circle around, holding its gaze with his own, and soon he answered its growls with sounds just as raucous. This circumambulation went on for a long time, then the wolf made a sudden feint, which Victor-Flandrin immediately imitated. So before long the two of them were very close to each other, moving in ever-narrowing circles.

They were now right inside the ring of moonlight and mirroring each other's movements so closely that their shadows brushed. The circling stopped when the wolf placed its paw on Victor-Flandrin's shadow. The animal immediately stood still and, uttering a sharp cry, it crouched down, with its ears flattened against its head. Victor-Flandrin took his belt and buckled it around the trembling beast's neck, then attached the strap of his bag to it. The wolf meekly allowed itself to be put on a leash.

Victor-Flandrin felt not the least fear — which seemed to have transferred entirely into the body of the animal lying at his feet. But he felt a great weariness and he decided to wait till daybreak before continuing on his way. So he wrapped himself in his cloak and, lying down on the snow, he snuggled up against the wolf and fell asleep in its warmth.

He had a dream, unless it was the wolf dreaming through him. He dreamed of the forest: he was walking through it, and soon the trees began to mobilize, covering themselves in shining metal armor; in these carapaces the trees slowly began to move, reaching out with armlike branches, twisting them in every direction. Then they grew heads — very round and ungainly helmeted heads, which they rolled from one shoulder to the other. They painfully tore themselves from the soil's embrace and began to march. They seemed to be advancing against the wind, so bowed were they, using their arms like swimmers.

The trees in their armor were now seated in long flat-bottomed boats, descending a gray river with red gleams in its depths. Other men, who were bareheaded, were walking underwater, against the stream, carrying torches.

The trees must have left the boats, for they were now advancing toward a very long, low building; the closer they got to it, the bluer it became. They tried to enter this house, but as soon as they crossed the threshold they disappeared, as though dissolved in the deep gloom within its walls.

An empty room: the wind blows in through the open windows and twists the curtains. In the middle of the room is a big iron bed. In the middle of the bed is a woman in a white nightgown. Her belly is enormous, all swollen, ready to give birth. A fantastic noise erupts. The woman, still lying on her back, slowly rises in the air and starts to float about the room. She arches her back until she can hold her ankles. She is carried by the wind out of the window.

The roofs of a town, all gray and black, are drawn against a murky sky. Among the remarkably tall chimneys two eyes suddenly appear. They are very black, with bluish rings around them, and they shine with a muted brilliance. The town gently starts to drift, riding at eye level. Still swimming through the air with their long arms, the trees enter the town and penetrate those eyes.

The eyes are just two big fish now, gliding through the houses, whose walls turn to liquid as they pass.

A wolf is sitting at the end of a bridge, playing a musical saw, its head turned to the river.

Over on the other side, along the embankment, a window opens in the front of a house. Someone leans out, throws a rug over the sill, and starts to shake it out. There is a design printed on the rug — it seems to be a face. Through being shaken like that, the face comes away from the rug and falls into the river.

The wolf has disappeared, but the saw, left standing at the end of the bridge, continues to vibrate and sound its melody.

Victor-Flandrin awoke with the first light of dawn. The wind was whistling with high-pitched sighs. The wolf had not stirred. The sky was clear and the forest seemed less closed in upon itself. Victor-Flandrin hesitated for a moment, then decided to veer left. He rose and the wolf also got up. Then they both set off.

After walking through the forest for a long time, they came to a vast expanse of fields; on the far side was a row of houses. The marshes and pools of water that looked like holes in the country-side were frozen and took on a metallic sheen in the rising sun. At the far end of the valley the broad winding loops of a river were traced in ashy gray. Victor-Flandrin felt calmed by the sight of this hamlet lying scattered at the bottom of the fields. He liked this place for its simplicity and its severity. He liked its loneliness, the same as the loneliness of canals. Although firmly anchored in the soil, the farms, crouched over there like dogs guarding the fields and watching the forests, seemed to drift at sky level. And their drift was infinitely slower than that of barges.

He watched the thin wisps of milky gray smoke unfurl over the rooftops, then become ruffled by the wind. While he considered this, Vitalie's words came back to him: "The land is vast, and surely somewhere there's a place where you can build your life and your happiness. Maybe it's very close, maybe it's far away."

This place was neither close nor far, it was nowhere. It was blessed with neither the splendor of sea-sculpted shores, nor the architectural majesty of mountain landscapes, nor the magnifi-cence of deserts leveled by the light and the wind.

It was one of those places perched on territorial borders that, like all frontier zones, seems to be at the ends of the earth, lost in indifference and oblivion — except when the masters of kingdoms play at war and then decree them to be sacred battle stakes.

2

Victor-Flandrin was roused from his reverie by the wolf, tugging on its leash, whining. He gazed at the animal in front of him and suddenly made up his mind to let it go free. For a moment the animal did not move, then it rose and, standing up on its hind legs, placed its two front paws on Victor-Flandrin's chest.

The wolf's muzzle and the man's face were very close together, squarely confronting each other. Then very gently the wolf began to lick Victor-Flandrin's face, as though licking an open wound on its own body, then it dropped down on all fours, turned, and slowly went back along the forest path. Victor-Flandrin watched the animal until it disappeared, and then he, too, continued on his way.

When he reached the hamlet the sun was already high. He had not yet encountered a living soul. He examined the place: with a sweeping glance he took stock of the houses around. He counted seventeen, but more than half seemed abandoned. He noticed that one of them, the biggest of all, was set very far back from the others. It stood on the hillside between two groves of fir trees. But the land here was so rocky that no two houses were built on the same level. He went and sat on the edge of a well at the center of a group of five houses. He was hungry. He searched in his rucksack, but found only a piece of completely stale bread. A dog began to bark, then others soon echoed it. A man finally came out of one of these houses. He passed close to the well, but pretended not to notice Victor-Flandrin, although he stole a curious glance at him. Victor-Flandrin called out to him. The other turned with a slowness bordering on ponderousness. Victor-Flandrin asked him what the village was called and whether he might find some work to do hereabouts. While continuing to give him sidelong looks, with a mistrust fueled by the stranger's accent, the other replied, saying that in Blackland, in winter, there was no work, but that he could always go and try the Valcourts, over there, at Upper Farm. Victor-Flandrin looked in the direction the man was pointing: it was the big house between the groves of fir trees. He immediately started out for the farm.

It was farther than he had thought. The road went on and on, perhaps because it zigzagged endlessly. It was actually not so much a road as a strangely snaking path, all twists and turns. He even stopped for a rest on the way. His hunger pangs increased.

When he finally reached the farm and entered the big deserted yard, he was greeted by another outburst of barking, as though there were dogs hidden in every corner. He walked into the middle of the yard and called out in a loud voice, "Hello! Is there anyone here?" The barking increased, but no one responded. The dogs then began to whine as though they could detect the smell of wolf on the intruder.

After a while a woman finally appeared. He would not have been able to say how old she was, she was so muffled up in thick woolen garments. He could just see her eyes — narrow and gleaming black, like apple pips, they darted keen glances. Without saying a word, the woman let Victor-Flandrin introduce himself and explain himself, then, turning abruptly on her heel, she walked off toward the central building. At the threshold she turned back and shouted, "Well, come on, then!"

The kitchen was filled with a moist heat saturated with the smell of cabbage, lard, and fried onions. The woman invited him to sit at a table, to which she gave a quick wipe with a cloth, and then took a seat opposite him, having removed her big shawl. Victor-Flandrin was then able to see that she was young and sturdy. She must have been about twenty-five; she was very dark, with a completely rounded face, high prominent cheekbones, and a pretty mouth with full red lips like strawberries.

They regarded each other in silence for a while. The woman kept looking at Victor-Flandrin's eyes, staring at his left eye in particular. Because of the gold fleck, he thought. Eventually he dropped his gaze, not so much embarrassed by his hostess's intense scrutiny as gradually overcome with drowsiness brought on by the heat and by his hunger. When the woman at last decided to break the silence, he almost jumped in his seat, in which his body was now completely slumped.

"So, you're looking for work?" she said.

He stared at her in amazement, as though he did not understand her question.

"And what can you do?" she went on.

Victor-Flandrin found the woman's voice as rounded as her face; he had the impression that the words she uttered were rolling in the air like big balls of fresh bread crumbs, and his only response was to smile.

"You are strange," remarked the woman.

"I'm very tired," he said by way of apology. "I've walked a long way and I've had nothing to eat since yesterday." Then he added, "But I can do a lot of things. I'm used to hard work."

The woman rose from the table, busied herself for a while in a corner of the kitchen at a big bread box made of dark wood, and came back with a loaf as big as a grindstone for sharpening knives, a lump of cheese, and a piece of sausage, which she placed in front of Victor-Flandrin. Then she sat down again and watched him eat.

"The truth is, there's plenty of work," she said, having made her decision. "And it's still winter. But Father's ill, he's all bent over now, he walks like an old man. We have two hands, mind you, but they're not much use." Then she told him how many head of cows, bullocks, and pigs they had, and how many fields and meadows they owned. The Valcourts' farm was the biggest in Blackland, but it needed to be properly run if it was not to fall into decline as had already happened to so many other farms here. Then she told how, more than twenty years ago, the war had passed through Blackland, laying everything to waste. Farms had burned down, fields had been pillaged, and so many men killed that now there were just a few old men left. More than half the houses in the village were deserted.

"I counted seventeen houses," remarked Victor-Flandrin. The woman started at this figure as though he had just said something foolish. Faced with this surprised reaction, he added, "Perhaps I miscounted . . ."

"No," she eventually replied. "It's just that . . ." She did not finish her sentence.

"Well?" Victor-Flandrin prompted her.

"The flecks in your eye . . ." Again she broke off.

This time it was Victor-Flandrin who seemed surprised. "The flecks?" he repeated, automatically raising his hand to his eyes like a mirror, "but there's only one."

The woman simply shook her head in denial, then rose again, left the room, and came back with a mirror that she held out to Victor-Flandrin. But he had no sooner raised the mirror to the level of his face than it clouded and became completely dull, as though it had just lost all its silvering. Victor-Flandrin laid it down on the table. Until his dying day he would never again be able to look upon his own face, and for the rest of his life he was mirrored only in the eyes of others.

But Melanie Valcourt was not a woman to be frightened by such things. She took away the mirror and shoved it in the table drawer, which she banged shut. Her movements were as keen and precise as the looks darted by her little apple-pip eyes. From the moment she had encountered in the yard this stranger with a blackened face and an eye sprinkled with gold dust, her decision had been made — she would keep this man and contrive to make him hers, were he to tarnish every mirror on the farm. In any case, her own eyes were in no danger of being deceived; they were clear-sighted and able to weigh up and assess the value of everything, especially men, in the twinkling of an eye. This fellow was young and full of strength, and he had the beauty of a starry winter's night. So it was that Victor-Flandrin was hired that very day at Upper Farm. In fact this hiring was only of short duration, for by the very next day he knew that he would be master there, which he was not long in actually becoming.

His wanderings had lasted only the length of a season; he was to remain settled here for close to a century.

3

Old Valcourt was indeed so stooped now that his hands almost touched the ground when he walked. But in fact, he did not so much walk as totter, propped up by a walking stick as gnarled and twisted as himself. Most of the time he remained seated, all huddled up and dozy; he only emerged from his torpor when he recalled the Emperor. He had seen him, even spoken to him, and the very next day had shared with him the humiliation of defeat. It was at Sedan, more than twenty years ago, and in his increasingly crazed imagination, the years had transformed that lamentable battle into the stuff of the Golden Legend and his fallen Emperor into a hero. The more he burnished his legend of Napoleon III, the more he blackened the account of old Wilhelm, that wretched villain whose head the Devil himself, he declared, cursing and banging his stick on the ground, had made pointed, the better to rend the good Lord's sky, and that of France, which to his mind, moreover, came to the same thing.

Victor-Flandrin refrained from making any comment whenever the old man, with great vociferousness, displayed to him his military hardware in all its glory; for his own part, the imagery of that war came down to the picture of his father's face, which the Devil had not made pointed but simply carved up.

As for the two other men employed on the farm — Blotchy-

Matthew and Jean-François-Iron-rod — they were of such inde-
terminate age they could just as easily have been thirty as over sixty.
They both looked as though they had been roughly hacked out of
some piece of dead wood, one sideways, the other lengthways.
And this dead wood continued to warp and become all blotched
with purplish stains, like the inside of a barrel filled for too long
with old wine.

Both lived on the farm, Blotchy-Matthew in the hayloft, in the
cow shed, and Jean-François-Iron-rod in a lean-to beside the
barn. Neither of them wanted to live anywhere else, and especially not Blotchy-Matthew, although he was worse off. He loved
the damp smell of urine-sodden straw, cow dung, and spilled
milk. By way of a woman, a breed that in fact he had never gone
near, he treated himself to several in the truncated but adequate
form of holes in the walls of his lair. Not a day went by without
his coupling with one of these stone sexes cut to his size and all
mossy with soft mildew. In the spring he would copulate with the
softened earth covered with young grass. As for Jean-François-
Iron-rod, the butting a goat had given him one day, right in the
groin, had resolved the question of his sexual activities by neu-
tralizing them forever.

Such were the two companions allotted to Victor-Flandrin. He
himself on the first evening was allocated a closet in a corner of the
kitchen; but already by the second evening he was offered a much
bigger, cozier bed: Melanie's. And her body — exulting in all its
rosy, delectable flesh that had for so long been biding time — at last
found pleasure and fulfillment.

Victor-Flandrin had known only two women until then. The
first he had met at the mine, where she was a sorter. Her name was
Solange. She was quite gaunt, and her lips and hands so rough
that her kisses and caresses were never anything but rasping. The
second he had met at a dance. He had desired her for her pale
complexion and her big eyes always shadowed with blue rings
around them. But this one put so little energy and enthusiasm into

love-making, that she fell asleep as soon as she lay down, as though overcome with lethargy by the first kisses. In fact, he could not even remember her name, which she surely could never have mentioned without yawning.

So, with Melanie, Victor-Flandrin discovered at last the true taste of love, a bitter sweetness to madden the body forever.

Old Valcourt died with a cry of "Long live the Emperor!" In fact he did not complete his vivat; death cut him short. "Long live the Emp . . ." he barked. But his jaw dropped, and he collapsed open-mouthed. The time of delusion was over.

Melanie respected her father's last wish to be buried in his soldier's uniform with his rifle and all his kit. But the old infantryman's body was so crippled with rheumatism that it was impossible to dress him in his old uniform. So Melanie undertook to unpick it all and sew it up again on her father's body, which was curled up like some big half-mummified insect. However, it turned out to have been a waste of effort, when they came to put the dead man in his coffin, for in order to lay him in it properly, they then had to break all his bones with an iron bar, which immediately made all the uniform's seams rip. Be that as it may, the good soldier Valcourt, loyal to his Emperor to the end, was buried in his battle dress, which was reduced to shreds, stiffened to attention within his four planks of wood, with his old rusted rifle rattling at his side.

Shortly afterward, Blotchy-Matthew followed his master's example. Death caught him, too, right in the middle of his favorite activity. Jean-François-Iron-rod found him one morning beneath the rafters of the cow shed, standing motionless, face to the wall, with his arms dangling against his body, and his trousers down over his clogs. He had to call Victor-Flandrin to the rescue, to tear Matthew from the wall's embrace. Since Blotchy-Matthew's last paramour stubbornly refused to let go of her lover, they had to resort to the saw. So he was buried having been relieved of the only part of himself in which he had ever shown interest. It remained enshrined in the wall of the cow shed, where, as Jean-François-Iron-rod remarked as he filled in the hole with a bit of plaster in order to protect his companion's relic, it was actually much better off than under the cold earth where the rest of the body lay.

From season to season, Victor-Flandrin acquired a taste for the land. When the snows melted, he laid eyes on the waterlogged fields and meadows that surrounded the farm, as well as the ponds, streams, and marshes to which the flocks of birds driven away by winter slowly returned.

The Valcourts owned the largest of the fields in Blackland, which was in one of the best positions. It was called Blue-grease field, so rich was the soil that the furrows gleamed in the light after plowing, as though lubricated by the sun.

At Blackland there was not an acre of land that did not have a name to define its nature and its history. Thus, there was Moon Pond, Wolf Bath, Smoking Pool, Boar Well, Capricious Brook. The parts of the forest that came close to the houses were called Love-in-the-open Wood, Little-morning Wood, and Dead-echoes Wood. It was in the last, the densest and deepest of the three, that Victor-Flandrin had encountered the wolf. Each of the seventeen houses also had a name, even those of which there remained nothing but ruins. As for the inhabitants of all these places, they nearly all had some tag attached to their name, if not a nickname. Having been the home of Valcourt-Long-live-the-Emperor, Upper Farm became that of Peniel known by the name of Night-of-gold.

Night-of-gold saw the land stretch out around him, more silent and slow paced than the fresh water of the canals, as austere and harsh as the mine in the struggle that had daily to be waged against it. But all the fruits he learned to wrest from this land were his, and he extracted them from the darkness of the soil and brought them to the light.

Victor-Flandrin never spoke to Melanie of his past, and it was as a stranger that he settled into her life. And she never asked him any questions, although she wondered that his shadow was so light and that he wore around his neck that strange necklace of seven milky white pearls, which remained perpetually cold. But she suspected that a man who tarnishes mirrors with a mere look could only give to these questions even stranger responses. And in any case, what did it matter to her to know where this man came from? What counted was that he should be here, at present, beside her. With him she saw her farm revive, her livestock and her land prosper, and her own body become fertile. For just now, at last, there was a stirring in her womb.

4

It was on a summer's day that it reappeared. No one could understand why it had left the forest at such a time of year to venture into the village in the middle of the afternoon. As it came through the streets of Blackland, the peasants, initially terrified, shut away their children and animals safe inside the farmyards, then armed themselves with pitchforks, axes, and scythes, and escorted by their dogs set off in pursuit of the Beast. But the wolf kept going straight on, without seeking food in the pastures and farmyards, without paying attention to the rabble of men and dogs that hurried after it, yelling and barking. It moved so fast that none could catch up with it, and by the time it reached Upper Farm, having cut across the fields, its pursuers were still jostling at the foot of the hill.

Victor-Flandrin immediately recognized the wolf's cry. But this time the animal's cry was not so much a mad painful laugh as a long-drawn-out moan.

The wolf came to rest in the middle of the yard, and there Victor-Flandrin found it, lying on its side. He felt neither fear nor surprise upon seeing it, although more than two years had passed since his night in the forest. He crouched down beside the animal and gently raised its head to his face.

The wolf had ceased moaning, and all that could be heard now was the irregular beating of its heart, as its panting grew ever quieter. Victor-Flandrin saw the light in the animal's eyes flare brightly, then very slowly die away into the black hole of the pupil, like a will-o'-the-wisp disappearing into the night, and soon all light had gone. A thin trickle of tears seeped from the wolf's eyes, and Victor-Flandrin, hugging the animal's head closer, licked those tears that had a taste as strong as it was bitter. The wolf's head sank onto his thighs.

When he noticed the horde of hunters storming his farm, Victor-Flandrin seized the animal around the middle and carried it into the barn and locked it up inside.

All the men from the village were there, some even had their wives with them, and as soon as they came into the yard Night-of-gold went to meet them and told them the wolf was dead and they could go home. But they wanted to see the dead Beast and throw its carcass to the dogs. Night-of-gold refused, and said the time had not yet come to show them the wolf. Then he chased them out of his yard.

Some time later, long after nightfall, a great commotion was suddenly heard on the road leading to Upper Farm. It was a cacophony of kettles and pots and pans being banged together, the shouts of men and women interspersed with discordant singing, the stamping of feet, and ugly laughter. It swelled like a wave bearing down on the farm, coming ever closer, ever threatening.

The dogs began to bark, and soon the cattle joined in, adding an undertone of lowing to all the barking. Melanie, who was already big with child, sat up in bed and pressed her hands to her belly. "They're coming to put us to shame!" she cried in fear. "They want to punish us."

Night-of-gold did not immediately understand the meaning of this. "But what have we done?" he asked.

"They don't like us," she said simply. "You're a stranger and you married me. That's not done. And then there's the matter of the wolf . . ."

Victor-Flandrin got up, dressed, and said, "You stay here. I'm going to talk to them."

"It's impossible," replied Melanie. "They've been drinking, and they're the worse for it, full of anger and hatred. They won't listen to you. Stay with me, I'm scared . . ."

"No. I'm not scared. I'll go."

The tumultuous crowd surged into the yard, redoubling its uproar, and chanting to scurrilous tunes words of abuse and mockery directed against Night-of-gold and Melanie. They then started throwing stones at the walls, the door, and the windows, and making threats, brandishing their torches. In the midst of their band was an old donkey with an effigy of Peniel made of straw and rags mounted on its rump, turned to its tail. "Hey! Wolf-face!" they cried, banging their pans. "Come out so that we can thrash you, you filthy beast, so that we can tame you like an old shrew. Hey! Hey! Wolf-face!"

The door opened and Night-of-gold appeared on the threshold. Over his shoulders he wore the wolf's pelt, which covered him down to his calves. "Here I am!" he said.

At this sight everyone fell silent, then the clamor resumed, even more hostile and frightening. "It's a werewolf!" some cried, falling back.

Night-of-gold advanced toward them. "What do you want?" he asked.

But the only response he got was a welter of abuse.

"On the donkey! On the donkey!" someone shouted.

"Smear him with dung and feather him!"

"Hey, here's your hat!" shrieked yet another, offering him an old straw basket all stained with filth.

"Demon! Werewolf! Let's burn him! Let's burn him!" a few then shouted out, and soon they all took up these cries in chorus.

But as the men approached him, their faces distorted by the light of their torches, the donkey rushed into their midst, unseating the effigy, which rolled to the ground. Then having circled around Night-of-gold, it bolted, and no one could catch it.

"Accursed dog!" they shouted at him. "Even the beasts are afraid of you!" But his assailants were now unable to close in upon him. The ring the donkey had just run around him before bolting seemed to have traced an invisible circle that was impossible to enter. No matter how much they stamped their feet, shook their fists, or threw themselves at him, no one succeeded in entering the circle and laying hands on him. Then all the more angry, they turned on the effigy that had rolled to the ground, picked it up, and stuck it bolt upright on a pitchfork, which they planted in the middle of the yard, then set fire to it.

The straw figure at once burst into flames to the great joy of those present. But as the fire was already burning out, seven slender flames of a yellow that was almost white suddenly blazed from the pile of ashes, rose to the height of a man, remained poised, then died down again and rapidly scattered like will-o'-the-wisps in the night.

The peasants' anger died like the flames, and they were gripped with fear. They moved off slowly, backing away, murmuring. And it was in silence that they all left Upper Farm to return to their homes.

From that day forward no rumpus was ever drummed up against Victor-Flandrin again, but to his nickname Night-of-gold was now added the more ignominious epithet Wolf-face.

Melanie gave birth in the autumn. It happened one evening, twice over. Throughout her confinement, Victor-Flandrin remained standing behind the bedroom door, Melanie having agreed to have with her only the three women from the village who came to assist her in labor. All he could hear were these women, who, sometimes in a loud voice, sometimes in an undertone, continuously gave orders, advice, and uttered strange sounds; and along with their voices came the sound of their movements and footsteps. Melanie alone said nothing. So in the end Victor-Flandrin had the impression that these women were busying themselves in vain around an empty bed, and he waited so long in the dark on the landing, he even began to think that Melanie had fallen victim to three witches who were contriving to make her vanish by some magic spells. He started to bang violently on the door, ordering the women to open up, but they did not let him in.

He could no longer bear this silence and these misgivings that oppressed him more than any cries of pain, and in the end he felt in his own belly the suffering to which Melanie refused to give utterance. And it was he who began to scream, to scream louder than any woman in childbirth has ever screamed, to scream so loud, indeed, that all who heard him, man as well as beast, felt seized with anguish. He did not stop until there came the cry of the firstborn. Then, for the first time, he gave way to tears, weeping simultaneously from exhaustion, relief, and happiness. At the cry of the secondborn he began to smile and felt himself a child once more.

The world suddenly became infinitely light to him, as though everything, himself included, were made of paper. He rediscovered the taste the wind once used to have, blowing up the Scheldt, and the smell of the earth when evening fell, in a quivering pink haze, on the riverbanks in springtime. He pictured himself running along the towpaths strewn with horses' dung, which the flies in summer clustered upon in bluish green swarms. And he felt again Vitalie's hands gently brush his cheek as she pulled the sheets up over him, so that he might sleep snugly amid the sweet dreams she prepared for him every evening by telling him stories. He felt, too, the gentle touch of something yet less palpable that seemed to rise from within his very own body. It was like the gaze of someone unknown and yet terribly close to him, which had stolen in to explore his sleep and caress his dreams. But he was unable to define this gaze, which he sensed to be that of his mother and sister, come to visit him, and at the same time he suspected it of being his father's, spying on him without his knowledge.

When the women finally left the bedroom and let him in, he was still lost in reverie and amazement.

Melanie was lying in the middle of the bed, with her head tipped back against the pillows on which her loosened hair lay spread. He went nearer and for a long time looked upon his sleeping wife, who held the two sons she had just brought into the world clasped against her. He found her to be almost terrifyingly beautiful, with her blanched face, her eyes circled with bluish gray, and her parted mouth whose lips, fuller than usual, were the translucent red of red currants. Her hair, still damp with sweat, radiated around her face in long wavy tresses, and in the light of the setting sun took on a reddish tint. Then he looked at the children tucked in the crooks of her arms; they were absolutely identical. Melanie's body thus seemed to be a mirror reflecting a single child, and he in turn sought his own image in this reflecting body. But he came up against the same opacity he encountered in all mirrors and felt excluded from that triple body deep in a common sleep. So not being able to share this sleep, he sat on the side of the bed and remained there, watching over it.

5

While Victor-Flandrin never managed to catch his own reflection, he did leave traces of himself scattered all around. Thus his light-shadow often lingered in his wake long after he had passed, and when the people of Blackland came upon it lying in their way, they were always very careful to give it a wide berth. They made sure never to walk in the shadow of Night-of-gold-Wolf-face, which they all feared even more than his presence.

He also left the trace of his golden night in the eyes of his sons, Augustin and Mathurin. They each of them had a fleck of gold in their left eye. And this fleck was to distinguish the whole line of children that he fathered, as they were also to be distinguished by all being born twins or triplets.

For his sons he exerted even more energy and vigor, gradually making himself master of the fields, woods, and moors of Blackland. And soon his fame spread to the villages around about and even to the town where the monthly market was held. But like his shadow and his wolf's pelt, this fame inspired as much wariness as respect, and its aura had the same unsettling effect as an invisible sun, hung low in a winter sky, dissolving its light into the dazzling whiteness of the clouds.

No one really knew where he came from, or why or how he had come to be there. The wildest stories and rumors circulated regarding the color of his skin, blackened by coal dust; the gold flecks in his eye that he passed on to his offspring; his light-shadow that haunted paths all on its own; his intimacy with wolves; his voice, whose accent differed from that of the region; his gaze that was capable of dulling mirrors; and his mutilated hand.

He was not from their parts, and though he contrived to conquer the land and impose himself as master, he never would, were he to live there for centuries. For everybody, he remained ever the stranger.

But he traversed the seasons and his land at a calm and steady pace, and his heart, long enveloped in gloom, slowly opened to the cold and pure light of day. And the love he bore his wife and sons, his farm, his fields, herds, and woods, grew like the dense rank grass in the meadows. Were he to have given Upper Farm another name, it would not be what his grandfather and father had called their barges — neither the *Mercy of God* nor the *Wrath of God,* but *In the Sight of God*.

His faith was actually devoid of all imagery and sentiment. Besides, he understood nothing of the mysteries of religion and the church's rites and stories. For him, one thing was certain: God could not possibly have become a child and come into the world, for in that case the world, no longer being suspended vertically from its point of fixture, would have collapsed and fallen into chaos. And anyway a God, even as a child, was too heavy to come down to earth: He would not have been able to tread the ground without crushing everything in His path.

Cleaving to this idea, he went to Mass only once a year, which did not fail to fuel spiteful tongues against him. Night-of-gold-Wolf-face was considered a nonbeliever.

The only feast day of the year on which he attended mass was Pentecost. He went to church on that day because the sole gesture that he recognized as worthy of God was commemorated then — when "there came from heaven a sound as of the rushing of a mighty wind, and it filled all the house where they were sitting. And there appeared unto them tongues parting asunder, like as of fire; and it sat upon each one of them. And they were all filled with the Holy Spirit, and began to speak with other tongues, as the Spirit gave them utterance."

God could not appear to man except by pouring down on their heads His superabundance, while at the same time remaining in His place. So an equilibrium was maintained, and the relationship between these two irreconcilables reinforced. He visualized a fantastic rainfall that came streaming down from heaven's confines directly onto the earth, and these raindrops were so many slender flames, bright and transparent as pearls of glass that shattered upon the brows and shoulders of men who stood bareheaded beneath them. The language the men, thus smitten, began to speak was none other than the sound of the wind, a mighty wind blasting wildly through heaven and earth. Night-of-gold-Wolf-face loved nothing so much as the wind: he never tired of listening to its whistling or howling as it blew. And he never thought of death as anything but a last gust of wind wrenching your heart right out of your body and rushing away with it, carrying it up there, way up there, through a gap in the sky.

Augustin and Mathurin were so alike that their parents could not distinguish between them. While they owed to their father their brown-red mops of perpetually disheveled hair, as well as those gold flecks in their left eye, they had inherited from their mother the roundness of her high-cheekboned face. There was not one gesture or expression that the two boys did not share. However, they did not always share them in equal measure, and it was in minute variances that the difference between them was detectable. So, while their voices and their laughter were identical in timbre, they were not always modulated in the same way; given the same tone, they revealed a certain range of color. There was always more playfulness and clarity in Mathurin's voice, and especially his laughter, whereas an indefinable hesitancy subdued Augustin's. And the same was true even of their breathing.

This imperceptible nuance in their breathing was precisely what Victor-Flandrin was most sensitive to. Every evening he came and sat at the foot of his sons' bed and told the same stories Vitalie once used to murmur to him to send him to sleep. And the two boys would not be long in drifting off, entranced by marvelous images and adventures that they pursued yet a while in their dreams. And he would stay there for a moment, watching his sons sleep, listening to them breathe, trying to detect in their faces, full of calm and freedom from care, a little of his own childhood, which he had had to leave behind so early and so abruptly. Then he in turn would go and dive into bed, where Melanie awaited him, nestling under the big eiderdown. In the warm darkness under the sheets, her curled-up body exuded a damp smell like the smell of brush after an autumn shower. He liked to creep into this closeness, to roll his head in her thick hair that lay to one side of her pillow, and brusquely slip his leg between his wife's tucked-up knees. He always began by interlocking with her body in this way, then they would embrace each other by a process of entanglement, both lithe and rapid, that kept binding and unbinding their limbs until they were completely knotted together.

Melanie was as passionate in love-making as she was silent, as though her deeply ardent sensuality had to vie with a shy modesty, which gave to their coupling an aspect of ritual combat. But everything about Melanie was similarly tacit and contained. Indeed, she spoke very little, expressing herself primarily with her body and her gaze. She seemed to have a great fire hidden within her belly that consumed words and yet shot tall flames into her movements and her eyes.

The century was drawing to a close; as it turned, as though to salute this renewal of the world, Melanie again gave birth. This time she had two little girls — twins, like their brothers, and also bearing the mark of gold in their left eyes. Unlike their brothers, they had their mother's thick black hair and their father's more angular features.

Once again Victor-Flandrin had that strange impression of being confronted with a single person duplicated as in a mirror. But in this mirror, too, he learned to distinguish the discrepancies that had imperceptibly stolen into the play of reflections. In one child, Mathilde, everything seemed to have been carved out of hard rock, while the other, Margot, appeared to have been modeled out of soft clay. And it was upon such imponderable differences that the closeness between these sets of twins, and the affection one had for the other, were most strongly forged, each of them seeking and loving in their double this next-to-nothing that was precisely what they lacked.

The people of Blackland saw in this quartet of Peniel children a new sign of the peculiarity of Night-of-gold-Wolf-face, who was decidedly persistent in always doing everything to excess and in defiance of convention. These children at least, on whom some of their mistrust was immediately reflected, each had only one gold fleck in the eye, and above all they were not tricked out with that terrifying, wandering light-shadow of their father's.

Melanie for her part felt neither perturbed nor surprised. She felt equal to all the other double births that it might be given to her to accomplish. Besides, she was never so beautiful and healthy as during her pregnancies. She liked to feel maturing inside her this fantastic burden that made her ever more firmly and deeply rooted to her land, to life, to Victor-Flandrin. For her, all that was good and beautiful in the world derived from plenitude and roundness — the fecund roundness of grass, wheat, light, happiness, of desire and strength. And her love for her own was in the image of this roundness of life and of all things in the world — full, calm, and voluptuous. The roundness of the days, in which she saw her children grow and her fields bear fruit, was followed by that of the nights, still more ample and magnificent.

Meanwhile, Victor-Flandrin remained in the sight of God, that distant if not absent God, toward whom it was imperative to keep straining across the void so as not to upset the world's equilibrium. And his children were for him so many balances grafted onto his own body to enable him to make all the more secure his footing on earth.

6

The nearest village to Blackland was three miles from Upper Farm by road. But this road that hugged the side of the hill on which the farm stood seemed to go on forever, skirting around peat bogs, rocky outcrops, small ravines filled with thorny scrub. Then it went through the little village nestling below; wound around the edge of Love-in-the-open Wood, followed the meandering Quinteux River for a while, and headed off across the fields and meadows again, before finally reaching the village of Montleroy.

Consequently, when his sons were old enough to go to school, Victor-Flandrin decided to make a footpath that cut across his fields, straight to another, shorter, and less tortuous route to Montleroy, so his children would only have a mile and a half to walk every morning and evening.

Augustin took to school right from the start and applied himself eagerly to learning to read and write. He felt immense curiosity toward books and liked them just as much for their weight in his hands, for their cloying smell and the grain of the paper, for the lettering printed in black on white, as for the illustrations that reinforced the words. And he very quickly took to founding his dreams on books and pictures: one book in particular, and two pictures, fired his imagination. These were *Two Children's Tour of France,* by Bruno, and the two big maps on either side of the blackboard.

To the right of the board was France, in all its majesty, ensconced in the stability of its age-old hexagonal boundaries — eaten away on one side, however, by the purple canker of the new frontiers marking off the lost provinces of Alsace and Lorraine. This vast expanse lay spread like the skin of a beast stretched out to dry; on it, the rivers traced their turquoise blue winding course through green areas of forest and agricultural land, studded with black stars of different sizes representing prefectures and subprefectures. He knew by heart the course of the Meuse and could recite like a litany the names of all the towns built near its waters.

Paired with this map, on the left of the board, was a map of the globe, on which the various continents extended like light-colored inkstains on the indigo background of the seas. The names of some of these waters, with strong currents running through them indicated by numerous arrows of dark blue, enchanted him: Pacific Ocean, Arctic Ocean, Red Sea and Black Sea, Baltic Sea, Sea of Okhotsk, Gulfs of Oman, Panama, Campeche, and Bengal. None of these names meant anything to him; they were words, magical words, free as the air and vital as bird cries. He recited them solely for the pleasure of their sounds in his mouth.

Land masses were shaded ocher, the areas not yet explored were a gaping white; as for those territories conquered by France, they were a lovely bright pink. The schoolteacher never pointed to the pink of these colonies with the end of his ruler without some pride. "This is French Africa!" he would say, describing a vague circle in the center of the map. "And this here, is French Indochina!" he would go on, flinging his ruler out eastward. These far-flung bits of France utterly bewildered the little country boy Augustin, but he nonetheless made them the territory of his dreams and imaginary adventures.

Mathurin did not at all share his brother's infatuation with school. He himself liked nothing so much as running in the meadows, climbing trees to find birds' nests, and making all sorts of things that he carved out of wood. Books bored him, and he liked only the pictures. He would have sooner learned to read elsewhere, from the very land around him. And this land was all he needed; he had no use for those distant French territories, pink like sweets, with unpronounceable names, inhabited by people of a different color.

He loved animals, especially oxen. On market days, he always went into town with his father. The cattle were penned on the main square. There you could see the finest oxen in the region. He loved these animals for their quiet and deliberate strength, for the beauty of their enormous bodies with that warm and tender breath, and above all for the utter gentleness of their eyes. At the farm it was he who looked after the oxen.

Mathurin, with the help of his father, had built a little cart. When the weather was fine, he would harness one of the oxen from the farm and take his brother and sisters for a ride along the narrow path their father had made for them on the western side of the hill. But he even went out on his own for a drive some days when it was raining. The cart bumped along the muddy path and, seated behind the ox's streaming-wet rump as it squelched through the mire, he held the reins of his cart like a captain at the wheel of his ship, caught in a tempest. At such times the world around him opened up like liberated territory, a fulgurating infinity of solitude.

On return from his outings, he always found his mother standing at the farmhouse door waiting for him, and as soon as he arrived, soaked through and covered with mud, she would lay hold of him and, chiding, rush him over to the hearth, to rub him down and dry him. But Melanie's scolding was more an expression of her love for the child, alarmed by his foolhardiness, than of anger. Of all her children, Mathurin was the one closest to her, for he had a sense and love of the land similar to her own. Augustin, too, would be waiting for him, but he said nothing. With a sorrowful look that seemed to reproach Mathurin for having left him on his own, he watched in silence as his brother came in from the rain. It was not that he particularly liked oxen or rides in the rain, but he could not do without his brother. Indeed, when Mathurin left school, Augustin did likewise, despite his desire to continue studying.

Victor-Flandrin, on the other hand, retained a love for horses. They had been the only companions of his solitary childhood. So one market day he came home with a cart horse, bay coated and plumed with a magnificent brown tail with russet glints, as thick and bushy as Melanie's hair. He called the horse Scheldt, in memory of his earlier life, when he did not yet belong entirely to the land, a life of which he alone held any memory. All his children were born on this soil that he had come to at the age of nearly twenty, and already their memories were different.

But he also brought something else back from town, something more fantastic still, which reconciled the memories of all of them, by awakening them to images absolved of time and space — other than the time and space of pure dream.

It was a box, a big, black box of linen-faced cardboard. It contained another box of a more complicated form, made of sheet metal painted with plum-colored varnish, decorated with a frieze of little pink and yellow flowers around the base. It looked like a miniature stove equipped with two pipes, one horizontal and the other vertical. The former was short and wide, with a little round window at the end of it, the latter much longer and crenellated around the top.

When Victor-Flandrin brought this mysterious box back to the farm, he would not say anything about it, and locked it away in the attic, where he spent several evenings working alone in the greatest of secrecy. At last one evening he summoned the entire family and Jean-François-Iron-rod to the attic and invited them to sit on the benches he had set up in front of a translucent white cotton sheet, with the famous box, standing on a table, silhouetted behind it. He slipped behind this screen and bustled for a moment around the box, whose window suddenly projected a bright light that illuminated the cloth, while a shadowy smoke escaped from the crenellated chimney. Then fantastic animals came into view in the darkness of the attic. First of all, an orange-colored giraffe, busy nibbling a little cloud in the sky; then a rhinoceros with its blue-black coat of armor; a laughing monkey suspended in the air, hanging by one arm from the branch of a banana tree; a peacock fanning its tail; a whale leaping out of turquoise blue waves and sending a great spout of water up into the sky; a polar bear balancing on a wheel, held on a leash by a gypsy in brightly colored dress; a camel sleeping beneath a starry sky beside a green-and-yellow-striped tent; a sea horse throwing out its chest like a coat of bronze armor; a pink and red parrot perched on an elephant's uplifted trunk; and many more creatures besides that filled the children with wonder. Then came trains wreathed in black smoke, snow-covered landscapes, comic scenes featuring misshapen little characters, and more terrifying scenes showing little devils armed with pitchforks, ghosts flying beneath the moon, and all kinds of monsters, with wings, horns, talons, claws, with lolling tongues and rolling eyes. The show went on for a long time and was often repeated throughout the winter.

When he shut himself up with his family like this, in the darkness of the attic, and worked his magic lantern for them, Victor-Flandrin experienced his greatest joy. It seemed to him then that these were his own dreams he was projecting, images inscribed within his very body, and that he thus set off with all those he loved on a journey through inner landscapes known only to them. And these locations consisting solely of splashes of color and light led them on still further, down the corridors of time and night, there where the dead abide. And he never lit the oil lamp, before sliding it into the lantern's dark chamber, without thinking of his grandmother. Each time it was as if the slender flame that brought to life all these images was none other than Vitalie's smile. He even ended up making his own images himself, by painting on plates of glass naive sketches of barges towed by horses illustrating the stories he had so often told his children.

7

With spring came a return to work, and the magic-lantern sessions became less frequent. But nature was setting her own magic in operation. Only just emerging from the snow, she started flowering, fruiting, and growing again. The birds returned from their long exile, their cries rending the air, and found their old nests, hidden away in the trees, thickets, or banks of streams and marshes. The animals issued from the torpor of their sheds, their bodies swollen with a new hunger and clamorous with desire. Scheldt, with no mare to cover, brayed louder and more fiercely than any of them.

The magic of spring worked even on him, and so powerfully that he seemed uncontrollably skittish. One morning he broke loose from Victor-Flandrin and Jean-François-Iron-rod, who were trying to harness him to the cart. It was market day and Victor-Flandrin was preparing to leave for town with his sons.

Scheldt knocked both men to the ground, as well as overturning the cart, which tipped onto its side, and he went charging through the yard, sending squawking poultry scattering in all directions. Then he came and stood restively in front of the steps to the house, stamping the cobbles with a great hammering of hoofs and swinging his head as though in the throes of some incantatory dance. The whinnies he gave were so raucous they seemed to come from a body other than his own — some ancient body buried deep within his distended flanks.

Alarmed by all this racket, Melanie came rushing out of the kitchen, wiping her flour-covered hands on an apron tucked around her waist. She did not have time to retreat. With a single kick the horse dashed her against the steps she had just descended, and she tumbled backward, her arms outspread, like a disjointed puppet, while her apron fell over her face. Scheldt lashed out once more into space, and went bolting off toward the barns, whinnying more than ever.

Night-of-gold then bounded toward the steps, followed by Jean-François-Iron-rod, who came hobbling after, holding his back. Melanie had not stirred. She lay sprawled across the steps, the top of her body covered by her apron, which was gray with little mauve flowers, her floury hands dangling in space and her feet pointing up in the air in a peculiar way, with her clogs all awry.

The four children had also come running and stood huddled together at the foot of the steps, staring at their mother, open mouthed, their eyes widened in amazement and fright. Night-of-gold drew back the apron from Melanie's face. She, too, was open mouthed, but the look cast from those narrow black eyes was keener and sharper than ever. "Hu . . . rts," she moaned, without moving her head.

Margot began to cry, but her sister at once shook her roughly. "Quiet, silly! There's nothing the matter with Mama! She'll be fine," Mathilde told her.

"For sure, she'll be fine," Iron-rod echoed, "she's tough, your mother is, you know . . ." But his voice was mournful and his eyes already misting with tears.

Night-of-gold very gently took Melanie by the shoulders and Iron-rod took hold of her legs, then together they lifted her. She gave a very sharp cry, which almost made the two men let go. Margot fled to the other side of the yard, no longer holding back her tears. Augustin stood stiff as a post beside his brother, who was squeezing his hand fit to break his fingers. The two men managed with difficulty to carry Melanie up to the bedroom and lay her on the bed. Her face was so white it looked as if it, too, was covered with flour.

Melanie did not take her eyes off Victor-Flandrin, fixing him with a gaze at once imploring and ardent. But he would not have been able to say what it was that gaze burned with — anger, desire, fear, despair, or pain. Indeed, maybe all of those things at the same time. She tried to speak, but open her mouth wide as she might, no sound came out, except a dreadful rattle that wrung her lips. Night-of-gold brought her face right up close to his, wiping her sweat-drenched forehead. Strands of hair stuck to her temples, her cheeks, her neck. For the first time he noticed a few white threads streaked his wife's dark heavy tresses, and for the first time the passing of all the years that had gone by since his arrival in Blackland suddenly came home to him. He also realized how close he had grown to this woman, to the extent of no longer distinguishing his own life from hers, and it was something of himself that he held, lying there, moaning, a surprising part of himself. She tried to lift her head toward him, but at once fell back.

She had the strange sensation of falling back not onto the pillows but of sinking into some bottomless well, marrowy with mud, mellow with silence. For all that Night-of-gold held her firmly by the shoulders, she nonetheless continued to sink slowly into this dark soft mud. He slid his arm under her torso and gently raised her once more, pressing her close to him. She clutched at his shoulders, her head buried in the hollow of his neck, seeking in her husband's strength and in the smell of his body a refuge against being swallowed up by the mud. But the mud was so viscous it seemed impossible to break free of it.

77

A sparrow that had ventured onto the inside windowsill merrily hopped about, piping shrilly. Morning bathed the bedroom in its blue light and freshness. Melanie suddenly had the impression that the sparrow had entered inside her, that it was her heart. "Peep, peep, peep," it went, hopping about ever more brightly. Splashes of a very soft and luminous green, like a swarm of mayflies, clouded her eyes. "Peep, peep, peep . . ." It was hopping around in her stomach now, as though her heart had rolled deep down into her entrails.

With all this jumping about, everything actually came adrift in the end, carried away in a tremendous rush of blood that splattered her thighs and abdomen. She clung yet more tenaciously to Victor-Flandrin, not to hold herself back any longer — she felt inexorably drawn into that swirl of slimy mud — but to take him with her in her fall, as she was sucked down.

She would not let him go, for he was more to her than her own life, and to die without him was to lose her salvation. She loved him with a love too fierce, too carnal, not to feel jealousy's dread at that moment of loss and death. She forgot everything else, did not even think of her children, her land, and especially not of the terrifying mystery already opening up to her, inside her. "Don't leave me! Don't leave me!" she wanted to shout at him. But the taste of blood was poisoning her mouth, and already death was choking her with silence. She clutched at him so tightly that she tore his shirt and scratched his neck. What her body was experiencing was no less than the unbearable laceration of her love, and this pain was soon raging, all at once toppling that jealously fraught love into the throes of hatred. "Peep, peep, peep . . ." went the sparrow, hopping about in the sun.

At the very instant when she felt her heart fail her, she tightened her grip even more violently, digging her nails into Victor-Flandrin's neck and biting into his shoulder. But more than these scratches and this bite that had just rent his skin, he felt the sudden petrifaction of Melanie's nails and teeth embedded in his flesh. He tried to free himself from her grasp but she put up insuperable resistance. Death gave her greater strength than she ever had in her life.

Night-of-gold was suddenly seized with fear. The image of the wolf whose pelt he wore flashed through his memory. He could see it prowling the clearing, its fangs bared, ready to bite, its slanted, honey-colored eyes fluorescent in the dark, and he had the impression the fight that had not taken place then was being fought now. He had never really known fear until this moment, not even that night with the wolf. The day when his father had cut off his two fingers, he had at one stroke razed that obscure feeling of fear. Another feeling had grown in its place — revolt. And even during his time at the bottom of the mines, where death organized regular raids, he had never felt fear. Faced with the bodies of his workmates reduced to smithereens by fire-damp explosions, or crushed beneath roof falls, he had never felt anything but anger and rebellion, not fear. He had never been in terror of his life. Yet, lo and behold, fear suddenly showed itself, surprising him in his own bedroom, on a fine spring morning full of bird song, through the body of the woman who had been his companion, his wife, his love.

So his father's craziness may well have razed his fear, but it had not rooted it out. And now all of a sudden fear was germinating, unruly as a tuft of couch grass. It even began to flower and proliferate so much that it smothered any other feeling, robbing him of memory, grief, thought. Melanie had ceased to have a name or a past, now she did not even have a face. She was just a she-wolf, pregnant with death, whose fangs and claws held him prisoner. He tried again to free himself, but she did not relax her grasp at all.

The gashes in his neck began to throb and his bitten shoulder became increasingly painful. Exasperated by the predatory corpse's stubborn resistance, he ended up by grabbing one of the heavy wooden clogs he was wearing and using it to bludgeon the hands and jaw locked onto him. The fingers cracked with the dry sound of a bundle of sticks thrown onto the fire; the jaw responded to the blow with more of a thud. These sounds resonated within his own body as though some organ made of plaster was being shattered inside him.

The grip on him slackened at last, and he immediately stood up, roughly thrusting aside the defeated corpse. He put his shoe back on and moved away from the bed, going to the window as though to get some fresh air. The bird, still whistling, engaged in its antics on the sill, did not have time to fly away. Night-of-gold grabbed it and closed it in his hand. He felt consumed with incredible rage. The sparrow instantly stopped its twittering and cowered, trembling, in the vice that had fixed upon it. Night-of-gold felt the terror-stricken animal's tiny heart beating in his cupped palm and he was seized with the desire then and there to crush it in his fist, and likewise put an end to his fear. Every kind of fear all at once disgusted him. The sparrow, half-suffocated, tried to keep its head in the air and held its beak half open.

Night-of-gold raised his hand and looked closely at the wretched bird. He was about to smash its little round head against the window frame when his attention was caught by his victim's eye, although no bigger than a pinhead and almost lusterless. But in that minute eye was so much gentleness and frailty, such entreaty, that he could not find the strength to do it. Fear and anger were both eclipsed, suddenly dispelled by another feeling, one not in any way violent, but on the contrary completely disarming. It was shame that, even before he was aware of it, had touched his conscience in his body, brushing against the hollow of his hand, warmed by the all but impalpable throbbing of the sparrow's racing heart. His hand opened up, freeing the bird, which flew off, its flight erratic and uncertain at first before it swooped toward the vegetable garden, where it disappeared. Night-of-gold turned back to the bed.

Melanie was lying curled up on the blood-stained eiderdown.

Her skin was extremely pale; she was completely drained of blood. He bent over her once more and tried to lay her in a more digni- fied position, the position in which the dead are always laid. Her body had become amazingly tractable again, allowing itself to be handled like a rag doll. Her broken fingers were completely limp and could be twisted this way and that. As for her jaw, it was so dislocated that it kept dropping pitiably onto her chest, giving that livid face a grotesque appearance. Night-of-gold tore a strip of material from the bed curtain and tied it around Melanie's head. It then occurred to him to clothe her entirely in the chintz drap- ery patterned with large red, pink, and orange flowers. It was she who had bought this material the year before; but instead of mak- ing a dress and aprons out of it, for herself and her daughters, she had chosen to make curtains for the bed. Come the very first days of fine weather, she had taken down the heavy wool drapes that kept them warm in winter to replace them with these new flow- ery hangings. They did not actually serve any purpose, except to play with the light. Melanie loved to see morning break through this flamboyant airy fabric, splashing their bed with pools of vivid color as it grew brighter. He himself loved to watch that aqueous morning light creeping over Melanie's naked skin, watering it with deliciously delicate rosy reflections.

He set about undressing her, then washing her clean of all that already dried blood caking her body with blackish crusts. He went down to the kitchen to fetch some water. He did not even notice his children, seated around the table, locked in silence, waiting.

"Father," Mathilde suddenly asked in an oddly muffled voice, "what's all that blood?" But he did not answer and hurried out of the kitchen with his jugs of water.

As soon as he had finished washing Melanie, he tore down the bed curtain and wrapped the body in it, from shoulders to feet. With her skin now white as alabaster, her face wimpled, and her body swathed in the floral fabric, Melanie did not look herself any more. He gazed at her without recognizing her, appalled to see her so white and still, and so small, too. Indeed, Melanie suddenly seemed to have lost her robustness and her curves; she lay, all contracted and shrunken, in the middle of the bed that was now too big for her. He did not hear the discreet taps on the door and the footsteps of his children slipping into the room. They stole up to the bed and for a long time stared uncomprehendingly at the strange scene that presented itself to them: sheets, eiderdown, their mother's clothes, all stained with blood, thrown in a heap in the corner; their father standing with his back to them, facing the bed. His shoulders seemed to them fantastically broad. And then beyond, in the hollow of the unmade bed, there was that tiny little woman, half-naked, ridiculously wound up in the drapes.

"Where's Mama?" Mathurin asked abruptly, unable to recognize his mother in that poor mannequin lying in front of them.

Night-of-gold started and turned to the children. He did not know what to reply.

Margot went up closer to the bed and exclaimed, as though in a trance, "Oh! She looks like a doll! Mama's turned into a doll! How pretty she is!"

"Mama's dead," said Mathilde bluntly.

"She's pretty . . ." Margot repeated, and paid no further attention at all to the others.

"Mama's dead?" asked Augustin, uncertain of the exact meaning of these words.

"Pretty . . . pretty . . . pretty," Margot tirelessly kept murmuring, bending over her mother.

"She's dead," Mathilde snapped again.

Night-of-gold saw his children grow distorted before his eyes, as though consumed by flames. He suddenly burst into tears and collapsed at the foot of the bed. Their father's tears and collapse terrified the boys even more than their mother's death. Augustin flattened himself against the wall and began to recite, very fast, in a mechanical voice, the list of *départements* and their chief towns, in alphabetical order: "Ain, chief town Bourg-en-Bresse; Aisne, chief town Laon; Allier, chief town Moulins . . ."

Mathilde went to her father, and trying to force his head up, she said, "Father, don't cry. I'm here. I'll never leave you. Never, truly. And I'll never die."

Night-of-gold caught the child in his arms and hugged her tight. He had understood nothing of what she had just been saying — but she knew what she had said. It was a promise, and she was binding herself absolutely to fulfill it. Mathilde was indeed to spend her life keeping a promise she alone had heard, and by which she was to exact of herself an inveterate attendance upon her father. An attendance, moreover, fraught with constant loneliness, for her promise of care and loyalty was accompanied by a fierce jealousy, as though all that she had inherited from her mother was her total and possessive love for Victor-Flandrin.

"Pretty . . . pretty . . ." Margot whispered over and over again, timidly stroking Melanie's cold cheeks.

". . . Somme, chief town Amiens; Tarn, chief town Albi . . ." Augustin went on in an obstinate manner, like a child made to stand in the corner and recite a lesson a hundred times as a punishment.

Night-of-gold suddenly pushed Mathilde aside and got up as though nothing had happened. In stifling his tears, he seemed to have stifled everything — fear, shame, grief. He left the bedroom without a backward glance, hurried down the stairs, and went out onto the doorstep. Scheldt had calmed down. There he was in the middle of the yard, swinging his heavy head from side to side, as if trying to roll it in the sun, which was already high, whitening a sky dappled with little round clouds. Night-of-gold made his way to the barn, came out armed with the big wooden-handled ax, walked back across the yard, and went straight up to the horse.

As soon as he sensed his master approaching, Scheldt began to paw the ground; then the horse looked around toward him, slowly swaying its head in the air, as though already preparing to rub it against his shoulder. But Night-of-gold evaded the horse's nuzzling, went slightly around to the side, and grasping the handle of the ax firmly in his hands, at once steadying himself and gathering momentum, he raised the ax up high and brought it down heavily on the animal's neck. A peculiar shudder ran right through Scheldt's body, throwing him off balance, as though he were skidding on a sheet of ice. The cry he gave was more a ghastly raucous braying than a whinny. Night-of-gold raised his ax once more and delivered another blow. The horse's cry rose without any transition to a high pitch, then turned croaky again. Its legs began to give way. For the third time Night-of-gold brought down his ax, invariably aiming for the enormous gash he had opened up in its neck. This time Scheldt fell. Blood was spurting out spasmodically, already forming a sticky brown pool on the ground. Night-of-gold went at the downed horse unrelentingly, until he had completely severed its head. The decapitated body continued moving for a while, convulsively shaking its legs in the air. The eyes in the head were still bulging with fright, staring at their master incredulously.

Just as the peasants used to hang the carcasses of the wolves they had succeeded in killing from the branches of trees at the entrance to their villages, as a warning to their fellows and to keep them away from their farms, so Night-of-gold hung the horse's head on the outside wall of the gateway into the yard. But this defiance was not addressed to any other animal or even to mankind — it was intended only for Him in whose sight death was always striking, without rhyme or reason, venturing to destroy with a mere kick the slow and laborious building up of men's happiness.

For days, reveling harriers, goshawks, and kites circled around the gateway to Night-of-gold-Wolf-face's farm.

Melanie left Upper Farm via the children's bypath, so she did not have to pass under Scheldt's head, left to feed the birds of prey, whose skull was for a long time to emblazon the Peniels' farm.

Victor-Flandrin would not have his wife's body taken to the cemetery in the cart drawn by oxen. He loaded the coffin onto an ordinary wheelbarrow, which he himself pushed all the way along the footpath he had opened through his fields, and so brought her, escorted by his children and Jean-François-Iron-rod, to the church at Montleroy, with its cemetery spread around it, in which Old Valcourt and all Melanie's forebears already lay.

Immediately on their return from the burial, Mathilde took her mother's place, assuming responsibility for the running of the household and looking after them all. No one, Night-of-gold included, challenged the authority of this seven-year-old child, who proved capable, right from the start, of rigorously and skillfully setting the pace of family life. Augustin, who had left school more than a year ago, went back again to accompany Margot, who continued to attend, as was actually Mathilde's wish, who dreamed of seeing her sister become a schoolteacher later on. Margot, moreover, was already breaking herself into this role, by sharing with Mathilde and Mathurin what she had learned in class, every evening when she came home. Thus did relations between the children change with no adults around.

For, after Melanie's death, Night-of-gold turned in on his grief, like a savage, hardly speaking to his family any more, and staying later and later laboring in his fields. It was as though everyone's childhood had been buried along with Melanie. And then, something of the look in Scheldt's eye, struck with astonishment and fear by Victor-Flandrin's crazed gesture, was reflected in the eyes of the children and in their hearts. From now on, even for them he had become Night-of-gold-Wolf-face, a man endowed with a rare strength, terrible even, trailing everywhere that unnaturally light shadow, and wearing around his neck, along with the string of his father's seven tears, the traces of Melanie's fingers, like a second necklace inlaid into his very flesh.

As for Jean-Francois-Iron-rod, also left disconsolate by the death of his mistress, he was always hovering around the children, ineptly seeking from them a few crumbs of affection, of which his heart — the only one of them all to have remained so artless and vulnerable — was starved to tears.

⌒ III ⌒

Night of Roses

". . . WELL, I AM THE CHILD . . ." she had written. "It is not wealth and Glory (not even the Glory of Heaven) the little child's heart craves . . . What it wants is Love . . .

"But how will it show its Love, since Love proves itself by deeds? Well, the little child will scatter flowers.

". . . I have no other way of proving my love to you, except to scatter flowers, in other words to let slip no small sacrifice, no look, no word, to turn to account all the smallest things and to do them for love . . . I want to suffer for love's sake and even to be joyful for love, so shall I scatter flowers before your throne; not one will come my way without strewing its petals for you . . . and as I scatter my flowers, I shall sing . . . I shall sing, even when I have to pick my flowers amid thorns, and the longer and sharper the thorns, the more sweet-sounding will be my song . . ." ★

But the thorns became so long and lacerating, she had to close the little black notebook in which she cast the petals of her love. And she entered her death throes. She, the rose-child. "Mother, is this the agony?" she had asked. ". . . How am I to die? I shall never know how to die!" And she had cried out again, "But this is sheer agony, with no touch of consolation . . ." Yet she died, absolved of any regret for having surrendered herself so absolutely to her love.

★ Theresa of Lisieux, *Notebooks*

Flowers grew all over the world, even at Upper Farm, on that little out-of-the-way patch of austere land, forgotten by everybody. There were wild flowers that grew in the forests and clearings, in the meadows, fields, and peat bogs, by streams and marshes, and even amid the rubble of buildings. There were others, too, growing in gardens and greenhouses, that were cultivated to be beautiful.

But beauty is thorny, unpredictable, and irascible, as love can be. And both left Victor-Flandrin, called Night-of-gold-Wolf-face, with a bitter taste that did violence to him, for it was always combined with the acrid smell of blood.

Yet beauty, like love, will always recur and scale the heights. It has childhood's blithe and insolent charm, its instinct for play, its art of pleasing and lack of remorse.

Indeed, there were masses of flowers at Upper Farm; there were some even on the bed curtains and in the children's memories, and all of them crying out to have their petals strewn. But the Peniels, at that time, did not yet know of a song such as the one sung by that rose-child consumed with passion. Beauty and love blazed so violently in their hands that all they knew of desire was its power of urgency, its shooting flame, and crying fall.

But the simplest words jotted down in a notebook need to remain for a long time cloistered in silence, lying idle in oblivion, for their voice to be scattered like petals. And maybe such a song only becomes audible to those who in their turn live wonderingly through sheer agony, deprived of all consolation.

I

Mathilde's reign lasted less than five years. Another woman came along, who ousted her. In fact, this was only an illusion that caused just a brief disruption. Mathilde had pride and willpower in abundance, while the other woman was alarmingly lacking in self-confidence.

It was Margot who brought about the advent of this newcomer. Then age eleven, she still continued to attend school, but for some time she had been going on her own, Augustin having finally joined his father and brother at work in the fields and on the farm. Often on her way there she wandered off elsewhere — always in the same direction, to the church at Montleroy. It was a very old church, dedicated to St. Pierre, which was its name, and whose feast day it celebrated once a year with much ringing of its cracked-tone bell. But Margot did not go in. She used to stay outside, in the cemetery surrounding the church, where she always strolled for a while before going and sitting by the Valcourt tomb.

There, she would root out from the bottom of her bag a little bundle containing the doll she had made for herself. It was a crudely sewn rag doll, stuffed with straw, and with hair made of black wool. She would lay it on her lap and then swathe it in a piece of calico, printed with red, pink, and orange flowers. Afterward, she would devote herself to lavishing her loving care on the doll, combing its hair, cradling it, telling it stories, and above all feeding it. It did not much matter what kind of a meal — it could just as well consist of earth, or moss, or twigs — what counted was that the doll should eat. But one day this suddenly seemed insufficient to Margot, who began to fear the cold and dampness of the earth, for her mother's sake.

She set about covering the grave with whatever lay around, even collecting up the crosses and flowers from the other graves. It only made her feel an even sadder coldness to see all the half-naked Christs exposed to the wind and rain, and she decided to bury them in the earth as well. But this failed to calm her anxiety; the cold had penetrated her deep enough to chill her heart.

Another idea occurred to her. She entered the church, went up to the chancel, climbed onto the altar, and pulled off the gilded wooden Christ from the cross in front of the tabernacle. In his

stead she hung her doll, in the flower-patterned dress, and returned the crucifix to its position. Then she collected all the little vigil lights that bathed the feet of the saints' statues in their
weak ruddy glow, and grouped them around the cross. This
formed a kind of bed of roses, blossoming over their glass hold-
ers, with their lighted stamens. Amid these dim red glimmerings,
the doll on the cross cast a wavering shadow on the tabernacle's
embroidered curtain.

This transformation of her doll into a flux of shadow and light,
tinted red, pink, and orange, delighted Margot, who found in it
the long-sought-for image of her departed mother — an image
that glorified death and at last calmed her own fear. Standing on
tiptoe, with her elbows on the altar, she admired her gaudy doll
suspended on the cross, like a ballerina.

She was roused from her contemplation by the sound of a raucous
and spasmodic cough by which she immediately recognized
Father Davranches.

The parish priest of Montleroy, whose house adjoined the
cemetery wall, was a man prematurely aged by illness and, as the
years went by, he increasingly immured himself in a morose silence
from which he emerged only for his sermons and services, and in
order to cough. His explosive cough always came in rapid bursts
of hollow sounds that violently shook his shoulders and was constantly interrupting him in the least of his activities. For this reason he had ended up by hardly speaking at all anymore, for he could
not finish a sentence without being cut off by one of these bouts;
by the time he had recovered, he had often lost his train of thought.
This perpetual distraction provoked by his incurable cough sometimes put him in a tremendous rage, and it was not unusual for his
sermons, thus stricken with incoherence, to end with his ranting
and raving and stamping his feet up in the pulpit. His impatience
and anger were particularly excited by children, who nicknamed
him Father Rat-a-tat and made fun of him at every opportunity.

So Margot was seized with terror the moment she heard him coming, and she hurriedly crept into the confessional box next to the little side chapel.

Father Davranches bumped into a pew, which worsened his cough and at the same time his bad mood. Margot, huddled in the humid darkness of the confessional box, felt her heart pounding so hard she was afraid Father Rat-a-tat would hear it. But all his attention had just been arrested by the sight of the altar, with its desecrated crucifix draped with a hideous rag doll. Margot made no sense of the exclamations he uttered as he rushed toward the altar; she thought he was just bellowing. This bellowing was of course soon stifled by a fit of coughing more violent than ever.

This fit went on and on, indeed it lasted so long it turned into a convulsive seizure of the poor man's entire body, as he spun around like a top on the steps of the altar, hopping with anger and frustration.

Margot, who remained crouched in her corner, blocked her ears so as not to hear Father Rat-a-tat stamp and rage anymore. She prayed confusedly to the Virgin, the saints, and all the dead souls in the cemetery, to come to her rescue, to open a trap door under her feet, and to save her from this unbearable fear. Which of them answered her prayer, she did not know, but the fact was, when she took her hands away from her ears she heard nothing more, as though it was Father Rat-a-tat who had just disappeared through a trap door.

She waited a good while longer before risking a look outside, gingerly raising a corner of the heavy purple curtain that screened the confessional. She saw just the priest's feet and a bit of his legs. His feet, shod in big mud-encrusted boots, lay on the top step of the altar, with their soles in the air. His rumpled cassock exposed his gray-wool-stockinged legs up to his calves. All the rest of his body was masked by a pillar. She stole out of the confessional box and ventured forward on tiptoe, behind the pillars. When she came to the altar, she took another quick glance, as much curious as anxious, at Father Rat-a-tat. He was lying full length across the steps, with his head down and arms outstretched as though he had tried to dive and had come to grief on the way. His coughing fit had so shaken him that he had lost his balance and slipped on the steps while stamping his feet, and banged his forehead on the ground. The impact had simultaneously put an end to Father Rat-a-tat's cough, his anger, and his life.

Margot went closer, holding her breath. She saw a thin trickle of blood flowing from the priest's mouth, gradually forming a pool of thick, shining red on the flagstones. She raised her eyes to the doll hanging on the cross and thought that this splash of red was just another reflection cast by the vigil lights around it. She climbed up to the altar and took down her doll, then blew on all the wicks of the little lamps, which released a tallowy acrid smoke. She tried to put the Christ figure back in its place, but she only succeeded in attaching it all askew to the cross. Then she stuffed her doll under her dress and descended the steps again.

But she was afraid to leave the church, suddenly imagining another Father Rat-a-tat storming into the churchyard, a whole crowd of other Father Rat-a-tats even, gathered there to fulminate against her as they coughed and to spit blood in her face. So she sat down in the first pew and waited. Since there was nothing to wait for, she slowly fell into a kind of doze. This time she was roused not by the sound of coughing but by peculiar little plaintive cries, soon interspersed with sobs. Her eyes opened, rounded with amazement and misted with sleep; a young woman was weeping, crouched before Father Davranche's body. "Mama?" said Margot, standing up.

It was Blanche, Father Davranche's niece. He had taken her in when his sister died, and she served as housekeeper at the presbytery. She had come in from the garden, with her arms full of greenery, peonies, and roses for the altar. But her uncle's body was lying implacably between her and the vases standing at the top of the steps, and she had dropped her flowers all over the floor.

Blanche was already over twenty, but she had never been seen going out and taking part in village life. She spent her whole time secluded within the precincts of the church and the presbytery, looking after the house and garden, and attending to the upkeep of the church. She liked being behind all these walls that protected her from the rest of the world. For the world, of which she knew nothing, never having ventured into it, inspired her only with fear. Yet how could she have dared to present herself to this world she had entered illegally, fraudulently? The fact of the matter was that Father Davranche's sister had given birth to her without even taking care to give her a father as well, which meant that she was born guilty of inadequacy and wrongdoing. This unforgivable sin, as her uncle deemed it, committed by her mother, had inevitably redounded upon her, and this was why she bore on her face the mark of that congenital shame. Her mother's sinful desire was engrained upon her skin, covering the left half of her face with a huge birthmark the color of wine dregs.

When his sister died, Father Davranches had nevertheless agreed to take in this misbegotten child, then just entering adolescence. As soon as she came to her uncle's house, the poor girl was confirmed in her misfortune and in the disgrace of having been born, of which he was constantly reminding her.

"That mark," he was in the habit of telling her, his stabbing finger intended to convey an attitude of disgust mingled with opprobrium, "is the very proof of your mother's sin. You see what vice, lechery, and lust lead to! You were conceived in filth and now you are sullied forever. To be sure, it's unjust that you should expiate the sins of your mother, but it's even more unjust that you should have been born, so all things considered justice does not come down on your side!"

Blanche understood nothing of what her uncle was saying, not even knowing the precise meaning of some of the words he used, such as lechery and lust or indeed expiation, and she could make no sense of his reasoning, but she understood this at least: she was not wanted and she felt irredeemably guilty of every evil in the world.

Anyway, when she came upon her uncle lying stone dead, sprawled across the altar steps, she felt this death to be another consequence of her baneful presence in the world, and this was why she sobbed, overwhelmed by this crime she had just unwittingly committed.

It was with some dread that Margot noticed the blemish covering the left half of the young woman's face, for that birthmark was of the same size and color as the pool of blood that had trickled from Father Rat-a-tat's mouth. She even imagined for a moment this blood stain was contagious, and that she herself perhaps had just been affected, raising her hands sharply to her face as though to check it was all right.

"But why?" Blanche asked the child.

"Why what?" said Margot.

"Why did he die?" said the girl in tears, trying desperately to understand what was happening.

"Don't know," replied Margot, "he must have fallen." Then she added, uncertainly, "I want to go home. I'm scared."

Blanche, too, was scared, but she no longer had a home to go to. She had nothing any more. She gazed at the child and felt an immediate closeness to her, forged by their common fear. "Yes, yes," she said hurriedly, rising to her feet. "We'll go back to your house." She came up to Margot and gave her a tentative awkward smile.

"You'll come with me, won't you?" asked Margot, taking her hand.

So, without looking back, the two of them left the church, keeping close together as they scurried down the central aisle, brushing past the pews, like two thieves being chased by dogs.

Blanche asked no questions, allowing herself to be led by the child, who did not let go of her hand. They were silent all the way, walking swiftly, never turning around, both terrified at the idea that Father Rat-a-tat might be coming after them to punish them. When they reached Upper Farm, they met Night-of-gold-Wolf-face leaving the fields. He was surprised to see his daughter coming home in the middle of the day, when she should have been at school, and he wondered who this woman accompanying her was. At the sight of him, the two fugitives came to a standstill.

"Well now, Margot," he said, "what are you doing here at this hour?"

"The priest is dead!" was the little girl's only reply.

"So?" he said, not understanding how the priest's death concerned his daughter.

"He really is dead," added Blanche in a little voice.

Victor-Flandrin then looked at the stranger, the side of whose face was covered with an enormous mark the color of wine dregs, as though she had just got a terrible dose of sunburn. "So?" he repeated, addressing himself this time to the young woman.

"He's my uncle," she said. Thereupon she clammed up, succumbing to her fear, and stood with her head bowed in the middle of the path.

Victor-Flandrin was touched by the woman's plight and distress, and on this occasion tempered his usual unsociability. "Come," he said, inviting his daughter and the stranger to enter the farm.

2

Blanche Davranches was never to leave Upper Farm again. Night-of-gold-Wolf-face's simple invitation to come into the kitchen for a moment to rest after her long walk became an entitlement to stay and even concluded in marriage. All this happened very quickly in fact, to the greatest surprise of everybody, and in the first place of those most directly concerned, who continued to be amazed by this unexpected turn of events. Mathilde apart, the Peniel children accepted without any fuss their father's strange and sudden marriage. The two sons took hardly any interest in it, for they had reached the age when all attention is concentrated on oneself, to the point of becoming an obsession with one's own body, which is suddenly assailed by new impulses and desires — lechery and lust, Father Rat-a-tat would have said. Margot joyfully welcomed the fact of Blanche's coming to live with them, for she felt secure with the young woman whose frailty and fear were familiar to her. Each of them felt for the other that obscure sympathy the sick, the infirm, or strangers have for one another.

Mathilde, on the other hand, reacted with hostility and openly declared her enmity. She could not accept that another woman should come and usurp her mother's place, and this was all it took to provoke her resentment and anger. By daring to take another wife, her father had failed and betrayed Melanie — and this betrayal of her mother reflected upon Mathilde, who had declared herself the keeper of her mother's memory. She felt hurt, humiliated even, whereas she was simply discovering the pernicious sickness of jealousy, which was to eat away at her heart all her life. From that day forward she adopted a new formality toward her father.

And besides, Mathilde could not understand her father's unseemly choice, for she was of the opinion that the terrible disfigurement marring Blanche's face should have sufficed to disqualify this woman from marriage, or even from love in general. That huge purple mark was nothing but a tremendous slap across the face which destiny had given to this woman spurned by life. So thought Mathilde, who shared this attitude toward her. The fact is that Blanche herself shared this view, but she nevertheless undertook for the first time to defy her shame, drawing from the interest Victor-Flandrin was kind enough to take in her, enough strength to dismiss that clinging disgrace always brought to bear against her until now by her illegitimate birth, her stigma, and her uncle — and also by her own self, out of habit and fatalism.

It was precisely that stigma, which so disgusted Mathilde and so depressed Blanche, that had in the end captivated Victor-

Flandrin. He himself had a strange enough mark in his eye, and he trailed around a still more peculiar shadow, which had always attracted more or less malevolent curiosity. This was sufficient cause for him to regard the young woman's preposterous blemish with some tenderness.

Besides, Blanche was quite pretty if one took the trouble to examine the rest of her face. She had curly chestnut hair coruscating with countless glints the color of straw, honey, or corn, depending on the light, and very fine eyebrows whose perfect curve gently emphasized the oval shape of her eyes. Her eyes were green, sometimes bronze green, sometimes more pallid, also depending on the light, but above all on her mood. When she was pensive or tired, her eyes grew lighter, tending toward pale green, even taking on the faded hue of dried lime blossom whenever she was overcome with one of her spells of shame and guilt. On the other hand, the moment she brightened up and recovered her taste for life the greenness of her eyes became more intense, watered with brown, gold, and blue. So it was not long before Victor-Flandrin learned to recognize Blanche's moods simply from the color of her eyes, for otherwise she never complained and had very little to say for herself. Yet she was sometimes apt to start talking; it would come over her all of a sudden, without apparent reason, and then she would release a flood of words in a high-pitched vivacious voice. This way she had of prattling on, out of the blue, with much waving of her little hands and tossing of her curly head had the art of charming Night-of-gold-Wolf-face, who found Blanche particularly desirable at such moments, and since her chirping bouts generally came upon her in bed in the evening, he never failed to make love to her, again and again, until sleep finally got the better of Blanche's twittering, and by consequence, of his own desire.

Throughout her pregnancy Blanche was in excellent health, as though the burden growing in her belly fully ballasted her with life at last and gave her more secure anchorage in the world. The green of her now almost laughing eyes had a lovely bluish brown gleam all the time, and she chirped away incessantly. But as soon as she had given birth, she lapsed again into fear and doubt. She suddenly felt that by giving birth herself, she had just perpetrated her mother's crime. And her own crime was all the more serious for being double.

For she brought into the world two little girls no bigger than puppies and as wrinkled as apples. However, the little girls were not long in gaining strength and charm, and when they opened their eyes they in turn attested to the power of the Peniel heritage: gold flecks glistened in their left eyes. But they had a dual heritage, not only because their eyes were the same color as their mother's and they had her beautiful curly hair, but most of all because on their left temples they had birthmarks the color of wine dregs. These marks, however, were much smaller and more discreet than their mother's; they were the size of a sou and shaped like a rose. Thus equipped with a dual legacy, the babies were each given as a bonus a double first name. One was called Rose-Eloise, the other Violette-Honorine. These first names they were later to exchange for other names, endowed with a heritage infinitely weightier and more exacting.

But it was not only this double birth that so defeated Blanche. She had a presentiment of something terrible, insane. She did not rise from her childbed, so greatly did this fearful thing that had revealed itself to her torment and exhaust her.

She saw the earth put to fire and bloodshed, she heard screaming, screaming all around her, fit to drive a person mad. She described outrageous things — men in the thousands, horses and strange machines reminiscent of the rhinoceros seen in the magic lantern, exploding, torn to pieces in the mud. And enormous iron birds swooping down upon the earth, on towns and roads, in bursts of fire. And her eyes, bleached by her terror and her tears, grew paler day by day, so that in the end they were completely drained of color and left absolutely transparent. She told herself that if it was given to her to see all this, to hear and to suffer all this misery, violence, and death, it was in order to punish her. To punish her for having dared presume to exist, for having dared contaminate the world with her sin by giving birth. And all that blood she saw flowing from men's sides, enough to muddy the earth, the roads, and towns, surely the source of it was that deeply malignant slick spread across her face.

She closeted herself in her bedroom. Margot brought meals to her, while Mathilde looked after the babies. But Blanche soon refused to eat; food tasted to her of decay and blood, and any drink had an acrid smell of sweat and tears. She became so thin that her skin, drawn across her protruding bones, like broken stones, began to look like transparent paper. Transparency worked upon her like gangrene, gradually effacing her from the visible world. And this was what finally happened to her — she disappeared. All that remained of her was a great sheet of skin tanned to the weft, of a texture that seemed to be made of glass fibers. When it came to putting her in the coffin, she shattered like a windowpane, with a pretty sound, identical to the laughter of a very small child.

Margot slipped the doll that she had always kept a secret into the coffin, to keep Blanche company and save her from that much too great a loneliness in which she was now enclosed.

This time the wheelbarrow to which Night-of-gold-Wolf-face harnessed himself to take his second wife to the cemetery was so light in weight that he had the impression of walking with empty hands. So once again he took the children's bypath, the very same one on which Blanche had appeared three years before. His sons and Margot, as well as Jean-François-Iron-rod, accompanied him. Mathilde stayed at the farm, pleading the need to look after Rose-Eloise and Violette-Honorine, by then a few months old. With the two sleeping babies held firmly in her arms, from the top of the garden overlooking the path, she watched the cortege of death move away across the rippling ripe corn that had pilfering birds dipping into it despite the fierce and derisory presence of two scarecrows planted there by her brothers. Though she felt no sorrow, nor did she experience any pleasure; it was a long while since her aversion toward Blanche had turned to indifference. As for the two little ones that had now fallen to her, she would be well able to cope with them. Her own strength was intact. Sometimes it even struck her, not without a sense of unease, that she had taken everyone else's share.

What remained of poor Blanche's body was buried in the cemetery at Montleroy, in the tomb where her uncle lay. Father Rat-a-tat thus found himself once more obliged to take in his niece, who had strayed into the world of the living, and whom terror had now driven to the world of the dead. She returned to the peace and quiet of the churchyard enclosure, with its thick walls covered with ivy and bindweed, far from the sound and the fury.

That day the church bells tolled out across the countryside for a long time; from village to village the churches sent back to one another their solemn echo. But this echo came from far away; it was in Paris that the bells had started to ring, the chimes ricocheting around all the bell towers in France in one endless majestic alarum.

It was not for Blanche that the bells tolled so solemnly, for even among the inhabitants of Blackland and Montleroy her disappearance passed almost unnoticed, as had her life. It was in order to announce another, much grander, more fantastic death — a very dignified death, with its head held high — and featureless, not yet having had time to assume bodies, faces, and names. And to honor it, neither shrouds nor winding sheets were produced; flags were hung from windows — blue, white, and red, like fine festive kerchiefs. But all these big striped kerchiefs were soon to prove inadequate to wipe up all the tears and bloodshed.

So it was as they came out of the cemetery that the Peniels heard the bell of St. Pierre ring out. Try as it might, the cracked bell had little success in producing an imposing sound equal to the occasion; there remained something feeble, something faltering about it, as though Blanche's fear and pain, now that she was buried just there, were already making their plaintive voices heard.

People came out onto their doorsteps, and those who were in the fields, bent over the land, straightened up. Everyone stopped what they were doing, in midstride, in midsentence, and all turned with a look of consternation toward their church bell tower. The old men were the first to uncover their heads, and the old women the first to weep. Some men shouted, raising their fists and proudly holding up their heads, others remained with their heads bowed, ponderous, and silent, planted on the ground as though they had now taken root in it. War had just issued its great invitation to vengeance and honor, and already each individual was responding to it according to his heart.

But the drums and trumpets of the ball about to begin would not be long in making unisonous all these more or less discordant hearts by reducing nearly all of them to silence.

Victor-Flandrin, who was approaching forty and father of six children, was not called up. In any case, his father's provision had made him ineligible. His sons, on the other hand, soon to celebrate their seventeenth birthday, were fine boys with strong bodies and firm capable hands. And for the first time the thought came to Night-of-gold-Wolf-face that he would never have believed possible: he regretted not having passed onto his sons his own infirmity of hand, instead of the golden sparkle in his eye. He would have liked at least to have been able to give them a share of that light-shadow Vitalie had attached to his footsteps to protect him. But neither that mutilation nor that shadow were hereditary, and under no circumstances were they separable from his body. They belonged to his body alone, a body of whose terrifying solitude he all at once became aware, even more violently and more painfully so than after the deaths of Melanie and Blanche. For this was not the solitude of a body suddenly deprived of the tenderness and pleasure of its mate, but of a body threatened in its own vital impulse and posterity, a body threatened in something other and greater than itself, its sons. And for the first time, too, there stole into his heart a touch of pity for his father, or even forgiveness.

After so many years of oblivion, here was his father, beginning to make a return. The time of banishment had now elapsed, and Night-of-gold's memory was regaining its rights; it suddenly proved as prolific in images as his magic lantern. He recalled his father's face disfigured by the cut of the uhlan's saber and the wound on his head pulsating with madness. Eventually he could even imagine the young horseman's face with his fine blond mustache upturned toward the sun and his smile of sickeningly sweet indifference. Perhaps he was still alive, perhaps he too had fathered sons, who had in turn engendered other sons, all armed with the same saber, the same mustache, and the same smile, and ready to repeat their forebear's gesture. Against his own sons. The sons of Victor-Flandrin.

3

Surely the uhlan must have engendered a very great many sons and still more grandsons, for they soon came down in hordes, sweeping across the frontiers and threatening this time to crush the whole country in the vice of a gigantic Sedan. They had exchanged their ancestor's flamboyant costume for a stiffly tailored gray uniform, and they advanced carrying their heads high, chasing before them, to new pastures, droves of frightened humans, hastily fleeing their burning towns.

It was truly amazing to see such migrations surging across a flat landscape at the height of summer, man and beast together, with no distinction or discrimination between them. The ranks of all these fugitives kept swelling, so greatly did the tales they spread abroad in the course of their stampede terrify those who heard them, rallying them to the throng. For, from what they said, there was not a town that was not once more twinned with death once these gray horsemen entered it. Liège, Namur, Louvain, Brussels, Andennes — no longer did all these names at once conjure up stones, streets, squares, fountains, and markets, but only ashes and blood.

And the small village of Blackland found itself yet again wrested from its corner of oblivion and favored with a ringside view of history in flames. From Upper Farm at night, the great glow of fires could be seen reddening the sky on the horizon, like glimmerings of dawns that came too soon and too quickly.

But all of a sudden time ran riot, the days and nights no longer ruled by the regular chimes of the clock, but with highly freakish or capricious hours sounding stridently at any moment. It was in fact perpetually the same time, the same impossible last hour, that went on and on discharging from life hundreds of soldiers who had only just reached the age of manhood.

So naturally everything had to be speeded up to keep pace, starting with love. Mathurin thus learned the art of conquest — an art it would soon be his turn to exercise on the so-called fields of honor — tumbling more than one girl in much humbler fields of corn or alfalfa. One of these girls, however, a pretty brunette with dark blue eyes, was able to bridle his rampant desire by attaching it to her sole person. Her name was Hortense Rouvier, she lived in Montleroy, was sixteen, and had firm round breasts that left a lasting imprint in the hollow of a man's hand.

Whenever Mathurin left her, he seemed for a long time afterward still to feel the delicious warmth and weight of her breasts on his palms and the taste of her lips in his kiss-crazed mouth. There were even some evenings when he had no supper so as to preserve that one taste all night long, and he used to fall asleep, with his face buried in his hands, his body aching with both want and fulfillment.

As for Augustin, he fell in love right from the start with a girl as gentle and dreamy as himself and five years his senior; she was from the village of Blackland, from the house called the widows'. For in that house, situated on the edge of the village, lived five women who had each lost a husband to war, or sickness, or some accident. Juliette was the sixth, but she had never been married. It was not at all because she was not desirable that she remained single, but death had on each occasion so brutally struck down the men in her family that people had come to believe some obscure curse was attached to these women always dressed in black. Her grandfather had fallen at the battle of Fröschwiller as a very young man; then her father, at an even younger age, had quite simply fallen from the roof one day, having set out to remove the branch of an oak tree, brought down on it by a storm. Her uncle had died an older man, but had fallen from a much lesser height, his own height, in fact, when seized with a fit of apoplexy. Her brother had not fallen at all; it may even have been to save himself from ever falling that he had hanged himself one fine day, for no apparent reason, at the back of the barn. Juliette's elder sister had nevertheless taken the risk of getting married, but it was not long before she joined the clan of widows. Her husband was killed in a hunting accident. So Juliette lost the taste for marriage even before having thought of it, and just as her brother had hanged himself so as not to fall she had from the first shut herself up with her loneliness, so as not to have to suffer another kind of loneliness later, more painful for its grief. But Augustin came along and jeopardized this defense, and desire exorcised the fear of a curse.

Joffre had proclaimed: "Victory is now in the legs of the infantry!" But victory kept everyone waiting with such deadly coyness that the infantry actually ended up with legs missing. So it was decided to bring forward the call-up for young recruits, and boys not due to be drafted until 1917 were sent to join their elders on the front. But Augustin and Mathurin, to whom this early call to arms applied, were already unable to respond; without even having had time to fight, they had been taken prisoners of war. Surely the uhlan's grandsons had excellent legs, for they had already penetrated deep into the territory, pushing back and distorting the frontiers, now marked by a continuous fluctuating fire — a fire that thrived on towns and villages, forests, fields, and roads. Now the land around was nothing more than immense tracts of cleared ground burned too deeply and too long for the possibility of any kind of crop's being raised there again. The plows of war opened up big slimy furrows, like wounds, in which were thrown, as sole seeding, the fragments of bodies.

Blackland was now reduced to a zone cut off from the rest of the country, expelled from time and from the world, a zone taken by an army that Mathurin and Augustin could not even join the fight against. Moreover, the enemy that occupied this zone took the precaution of deporting deep into its own hinterland those men trapped within this encirclement of fire who were of an age to fight. So it was that just when Mathurin and Augustin heard they had been called up by one side of the front, they were summoned by the other. At that point the blatant happiness love brought them in the midst of the debacle, their insouciance in growing in strength and desire amid the ashes, suddenly balked. All at once the war rose up before them like an obstacle, simultaneously defying the dash of their youth, the ardor of their love, and the eternity of their land. Already they were from nowhere, and now they were being threatened with exile to some even more terrifying elsewhere. Then anger gripped them both and held fast. This was why they decided to respond to the call from the other side of the front.

"But you'll never be able to get through," Victor-Flandrin kept telling them, "the area's occupied, the fighting's raging all around, there are soldiers in every corner of the fields and forests." But neither their father's warnings nor Hortense and Juliette's entreaties succeeded in dissuading them.

"You'll write to me?" Hortense had asked Mathurin, unable to come to terms with his departure; but she no more knew how to read then he knew how to write, and in any case no letter would have been able to cross the lines. "Never mind," insisted Hortense, "write to me anyway. Augustin will write for you, you can dictate to him, and Juliette will read it to me. And then, if need be, I shall train the birds, the fishes, all the animals, and the rain and wind to carry our letters to each other." She gave him a long lock of her hair. Juliette would not give anything to Augustin, for fear that the curse rooted in the widows' house might revive and make fatal the talisman she would have bestowed on him.

They left at nightfall one autumn evening, stealing through the forests whose outskirts occasionally flickered and glowed red here and there in the distance. They floated down rivers, mingled with hordes of distraught people leaving their villages in ashes, and even with herds of animals driven from the devastated meadows. They cloaked themselves in shadow and silence, and often lay down to sleep among the dead strewn along their way. They passed through their father's homeland, but were unaware of it; besides, there was nothing to see. The landscape since they had set out was the same everywhere; the war had leveled everything, removing all distinguishing features. But the farther they traveled from home, the more their hearts went back to it.

Throughout their flight they did not talk to each other and never parted. All that counted for each of them was to hear and feel the other's breath at his side.

One day they reached land's end and came upon the sea. Being men of the fields and forests, they had never seen the sea. They stayed for a long while gazing at this enormous lead-gray mass that boomed a continuous husky lament, like some empty entreaty.

Mathurin liked the sea, which reminded him of the lowing of his oxen. Augustin did not like it; he thought it had a tang of death.

When it came bounding up to them, out of breath, they did not recognize it. It sank down at Mathurin's feet and collapsed onto its side. Its paws were bleeding and its black coat was singed, mud-stained, marked with sores in several places. Its eyes shone with the dull fixed gleam of stones under water. Around its neck it was wearing a little leather pouch that a bullet must have gone through. It was panting so hard the sound of the sea died away to a murmur.

"Folco!" Mathurin eventually cried, lifting the dog in his arms — his dog, the guardian of his oxen, here at the end of his trek, at the land's extremity. He hugged it close, rubbing its head against his neck. "Folco," he repeated over and over, cradling the exhausted animal.

Augustin, too, had come up and was stroking Folco with a smile. "He's carrying something around his neck," he said.

The dog was quietly whining now. Augustin removed the pouch and opened it. He took out a big bundle of rolled up pages, stuck together by dampness. "Juliette!" he said, running his fingers over the painstakingly neat handwriting that covered the paper.

"Juliette?" cried Mathurin. "But then Hortense has written as well. Read it, read it quickly!"

But with the paper being so damp and crumpled, the letters were illegible.

"We must leave the pages to dry. Then I'll be able to read them," said Augustin, slipping the bundle under his clothes.

The dog had fallen asleep in Mathurin's lap and the sea's long-drawn-out booming once again filled the deserted beach. The two brothers dozed off, too, sitting shoulder to shoulder, watching the purplish gray sea ponderously ebbing before them. Rain was falling on the horizon, bruising the sky, like a great dark gauzy curtain. They had crossed the impossible zone, crawled beneath bullets, and waded through the mud of unharvested fields, where black ears of grain twined around the wreckage of weapons and dead men's fingers. They had gone astray so often they had thought themselves hopelessly lost. They had fed on roots and drunk the water from puddles. They had slept huddled up at the bottom of holes, on ice-cold stones. And now here they were, safe together, seated facing the sea that retreated before them as though the better to open up to them once more some space and hope.

It even seemed to Mathurin that the sea had calmed and its lowing was of infinite gentleness. He dreamed of Hortense, of her warm and tender body, and felt in his hands the delicious weight of her breasts, and the wind from the sea brought him the moist freshness of her sex.

The sea rose and fell seven times more before they embarked. The detour they had had to make in order to be able to join their army became ever greater and more roundabout. They were two apprentice soldiers, without weapons or uniforms, perpetually on their way to war without ever getting there.

They took Folco on the boat with them. When the pages had finally dried and Augustin was able to unfold them, he saw that the dampness had so blurred the ink there was not much left to read. The words seemed to have dissolved into one another. The hole made by the bullet that had gone through the pouch carried its blank space through from page to page. Juliette's soft voice seemed at every line to be on the point of falling silent; it came only in snatches as though she were hesitating, losing the thread of her thoughts. But Augustin was able to hear in this confused murmur what Juliette wanted to tell him. She spoke to him of her love, her trust, her patience, and gave him news of Blackland.

Then the very restrained tone of the letter suddenly changed after a few pages. Juliette was now writing at the dictation of Hortense, who cried to Mathurin the passion of her love and the pain of their separation. Even Juliette's handwriting seemed slightly altered, as though the power and boldness of the words dictated by Hortense had frightened her, and Augustin in his turn felt a profound disquiet upon reading them. These words, moreover, seemed to have better resisted effacement than those of Juliette. Then suddenly the letter broke off and the following pages carried no further writing but were a riot of color. Having run out of words and at the same time no longer able to bear having to pass through two intermediaries in order to communicate with Mathurin, Hortense had had the idea of drawing. The vitality of her naive figures more accurately expressed her love and desire. The last drawing showed Folco leaving Upper Farm to go in search of his master — a black dog racing off down the deserted icy bypath.

The two brothers followed Juliette and Hortense's example. Augustin wrote a long letter in which he told of their shadowmen's journey through fire and ruin, of their sea passage to England, and their return from there to the Continent. "And when I come home again a free man," he wrote at the end of his letter, "I shall marry you, and you will leave your widows' house forever and come to live with me on my father's farm."

Then he wrote for Mathurin, who spoke of a love so violent, so carnal that Augustin was amazed. Hortense's body, stripped naked by his brother's words and images, revealed itself to him with fantastic shamelessness and he, too, began to dream of her even though he spent the whole day thinking of Juliette. But Mathurin soon abandoned words and in turn started to draw, making particularly intense use of contrasting splashes of color.

Exaggerated colors, bursting like overripe fruit. Colors that did not even exist in the meadows and fields of Blackland in summer, and perhaps nowhere else in nature. Colors that sprang solely from his desire. His drawing of Hortense's body then began to distort into crazy images, of intoxicatingly crude colors, in perpetual metamorphosis. Now he multiplied her arms and legs, now he set fire to her hair, or filled it with swarms of bees, now he covered her whole body with enormous gaping mouths. Sometimes this body flowered like a wild garden — poppies blossomed on the tips of her breasts, orange thistles stung her armpits, bellwort and brambles coiled around her limbs, bunches of red currants tumbled from her lips, periwinkle-blue-winged dragonflies flew out from beneath her eyelids, bright yellow buttercups and acid green lizards entwined her fingers. On her buttocks he crushed strawberries, her sex he tangled with bushes and covered with ivy, he spangled it with cornflowers, and always left showing through, in the midst of all this bushiness, a round fleshy bulb, like a rosebud about to bloom. He covered pages and pages with such drawings.

Folco set out again on his hazardous journey, the leather pouch bobbing around his neck. Augustin and Mathurin watched the black dog race off down the road, and they remained staring at that road for a long time after it was empty again, unable to tear their eyes away from that brown track cutting through the snow-covered trees, running flush with the sky toward home. Their gaze tore away from them rather, and went after the dog, traveling beyond their range of vision, becoming immanent in the dog's very body. "What if he doesn't get there, if he's killed on the way...?" was the thought that kept tormenting Augustin, but he dared not express his fear, the tensed presence of Mathurin at his side so forbade any doubt.

4

They were sent first to a training camp, where they were hastily initiated in the practice of war. But however intensive their training, it revealed to them nothing of the reality of war. And it was with the springlike name of greenhorns that they were sent with their companions, the imprint of childhood still upon them, to join their elders at the front. Mathurin and Augustin each slipped into the bottom of his kit bag, along with his linen and tin mess bowl, the notebook he kept, one of them to draw in, the other to write in.

"I don't know what scares me most," wrote Augustin the day before their departure, "whether it's killing or dying. At training camp, we always pretended to kill, but out there we'll be confronted with men. Real men, like Mathurin and me. And we'll have to shoot them. What becomes of you when you've killed other men?" This question obsessed Augustin; sometimes he even saw in his dreams the heads of those he was going to kill displayed on the front of the gateway at Upper Farm, as in the past Scheldt's skull had born witness to both the horse's own crime and Night-of-gold-Wolf-face's.

Mathurin was surprised at the name of the front where they were to go: Le Chemin des Dames — Ladies' Way. Such a pretty name, like an invitation to a Sunday stroll. He thought of Little-morning Wood, where he had so often made love with Hortense — the smell of their bodies heightened by the rough sweet smell of leaves and branches slowly decaying on the moss. He drew a sunken path bordered with flowering hedgerows, and women with loosened windblown hair picking the flowers and gathering them in fiery sprays. At the end of the path bloomed a huge rose, undaunted by the wind, fire, and death raging around it. Ladies' Way — a path of brambles and death, defied and exalted by the yet more violent beauty of a rose of flesh.

On the train taking them to the front, however, they forgot their dreams and imaginings, so greatly did the reality they saw exceed and overwhelm their imaginations. The land kept throwing in their faces the terrifying spectacle of its injuries, and the more disfigured and destroyed the countryside, the more painfully human it became, as though the earth were flesh.

And true enough, earth and flesh were indistinguishable, combined in a single substance — mud. They could tell from a distance where the line was. The sky was a dirty gray, rent at its lower edge by incessant bursts of flame, like a huge cloth catching on fire. This line of open fracture between sky and land was further thrown into relief by an uninterrupted din of cannonading, shell explosions, and heavy gunfire. The newcomers, fresh from their short spell in military training camp, were hurled into the fray. They were crammed, by the hundreds, in the bottom of muddy trenches that the snow, although persistent, never succeeded in turning white.

But there was not just snow falling in this place; there was everything: shells, rockets, planes occasionally, men all the time, enormous clods of earth, pieces of wood, stones, bits of barbed wire. In the end they expected to see fragments of sky falling down, the clouds, the sun, the moon, and the stars, such an extraordinary power of attraction did this patch of ground seem to have. A real scene of the fall. It was in this place, at the bottom of a trench, beneath the glimmerings of shell fire that they celebrated their twentieth birthdays.

Mathurin and Augustin were more inseparable than ever before, fighting shoulder to shoulder for fear of losing each other. It was not long before the others made fun of this unusually close couple, whom they nicknamed the Siamese twins. But nothing and no one managed to dissuade them from sticking together like this all the time. Though love had certainly brought them to a parting of the ways, leading them to two women who differed in every respect, this had not divided them. They actually found themselves even more deeply united in the very distance their different loves had opened up between them. But there could be no question of their dying separately, at least not yet, at the age of twenty, for they clearly sensed that for one to bear the absence of the other all the rest of his life would have been much too onerous and painful a burden.

This pathological attachment that assigned one perpetually to the presence of a twin did not prevent them, however, from fraternizing with their comrades. They became particularly close to seven of them. These were Roger Beaulieu and Pierre Fouchet, two Parisians who had just been mobilized; Frederic Adrian, from

Alsace, who had rushed to join up as soon as war was declared and had already been through Verdun; Deodatus Chapitel, a peasant, like them, but from the Morvan; François Houssaye, a landscape painter whose eyes, even in the trenches, reflected the gray luminosity of the Normandy skies; Michel Duchesne, from Orleans; and Angel Luggieri, who was completely disorientated, having had to leave his island of Corsica for the first time in his life. Their friendship had the fervor that danger and urgency kindle; a few days spent at the bottom of those hell holes of mud and blood, enduring the lack of water, food, and sleep, fearing death at every instant, had sufficed to knit closer and deeper ties than a long friendship sustained over the course of a quiet life could possibly have done. It was a friendship forged in haste, one that grew amid that desolation like a hothouse plant that each day produces unexpected new flowers and whose bright green leaves reach ever higher.

Their comrades used to talk about their respective homes, and Augustin soon began to dream about all those parts of the world from which they came, and the name of every place was a window on some fabulous landscape, which he described in his notebook. The Seine, the Loire, the Rhine set boundless waters flowing for him, marked by bridges, trees, and islands, passing through towns and stealing the reflections of stone angels and women's legs. The Morvan uplands and Normandy's vast beaches evoked for him infinite drifts of wind and water; and amid the chastely shadeless blue of sky and sea reared the vivid pink and austere ocher of Corsica's rocks — unfamiliar names, landscapes, and colors pictured through their friends' homesick accounts of them. And now the two brothers who had gone to war to defend their own little corner of land, perched up on the far edge of the country, extended their struggle to include the defense of those regions from which these comrades came. After the war, Augustin sometimes said to himself, once the world was back to normal, those roads would be open to them, and together with his brother he would set out to discover all these regions, sallying forth like those two young boys who had traveled across France and whose adventures he had so often read in the book by Bruno.

But accounts and legends, as well as desires and plans, were soon nipped in the bud, for each of their companions' stories ended right here. Pierre Fouchet was the first to go. Having just glimpsed, through the milky white fog that had clung to the earth for days, a row of skirmishers down on the ground, he tried to jump for cover into a trench behind him. But he got tangled in the barbed wire coiled up in front of it and a burst of gunfire punished him for his clumsiness, riddling him like a sieve, from head to foot. It was not even the skirmishers, flattened on the ground, who shot him in the back, for they were all dead, which was why they were lying there on their stomachs, all in a straight line. And if the fog had been less dense he would have been able to see that they were in French uniform. The shots had come from behind them.

François Houssaye died in small stages. Following a serious injury that was not long in turning gangrenous, first his foot was cut off, then his lower leg, then his thigh up to the groin. After which, they could not cut off any more. So the gangrene spread freely over the rest of his body and he was already completely rotted even before he breathed his last.

Another day, while Mathurin, Augustin, and Deodatus were standing shoulder to shoulder, looking out over the top of a trench from which they were trying to repel the attack of a group of German infantry, after interminable heavy fire, quiet suddenly descended.

"What silence!" whispered Mathurin, "it could be the beginning of the world!"

"The beginning, or the end?" said Deodatus, scanning the surface of that vast landscape of smoking craters stretching away on his line of vision.

But it was neither the beginning of the world, nor the end, just a brief pause, time to reload and realign weapons, and Deodatus had no sooner asked his question than a sharp whistle of bullets settled the matter. Then silence fell again, as though to point up this response.

"There, you see," Augustin said to Deodatus, "it wasn't the end."

But Deodatus said nothing more; he simply dropped his helmet on Augustin's shoulder. A helmet filled to the brim with a steaming soft whitish substance that poured into his hands. With the top of his gaping skull sliced off, Deodatus was still scanning the horizon.

From that day on, Augustin's accounts spoke of nothing but mud, hunger, cold, thirst, and rats:

". . . We spent three days at the bottom of a shell crater, surrounded by continuous gunfire. We ended up drinking foul water from muddy puddles and even licking our clothes. It's freezing cold, our coats crackle with encrusted ice. There are some black fellows with us. They are even worse off than we are, if that's possible. They fall ill right away, and they cough, they cough all the time, and they cry. If people only knew how we suffer here, what hell it is here, well then, they, too, would fall ill, and cry, and never be able to stop. Blanche — she saw all this, she knew all about it, even before it began. That's why she died. Blanche was too gentle, too kind, so she died of grief. It's really too much pain. The other day, one of the black fellows went mad. Five of his companions, sent flying in the air by a shell, came raining down on him, in pieces. So he sat in the midst of those scraps of bodies and began to sing. To sing the way they do in their country. Then he undressed. He threw away his gun, his helmet, he tore off his clothes. He stripped completely naked. And there, in the middle of the circle marked out by his mangled comrades, he began to dance. I think the Bosch opposite were as astonished as we were. It went on for a long time. It was snowing. There were some in the trench who wept at the sight. Because with his song, it didn't matter that you couldn't understand any of it. It was beautiful. I wanted to scream and go and join him, but I felt paralyzed. And his body —

so long and thin, and so black — that was also beautiful. Maddeningly beautiful. The way Mathurin put it, was: 'It's just not possible, the earth's going to stop turning!' Well, no, the earth didn't stop turning, and there was some bastard who had it in him to kill the big black fellow, to shoot down a completely naked man. And I don't even know which side the shot came from, whether it was ours, or the other side. I wept. And there was Mathurin, wanting to go and fetch the body, to protect it, comfort it. Beaulieu and I had to hold him back, otherwise he would have been killed outright. Blanche was right to die, to die without delay. At least she was properly laid to rest in the ground, in the silence, beneath the flowers. Here, we're trampled in the mud, and our remains — they're eaten by rats . . ."

But it was not so certain that Blanche had been right to die, for even her peace had been violated. The occupier's demands knew no bounds any more, and wherever its law prevailed it grabbed everything, robbing those the war had confined to their homes, stealing their very door and window latches, their mattresses, and even the fur on their dogs and cats. Having stripped the living of the least of their possessions, the occupier then turned to the dead and fleeced them, ransacking the cemeteries to make sure that nothing escaped its rapacity in the darkness of the tombs. This happened to the cemetery at Montleroy, and both the Valcourt and the Davranches graves were opened and plundered. Long-live-the-Emperor was even forced to lay down his arms again — his old rusty rifle was stolen and the buttons torn from his uniform. As for Father Rat-a-tat, he was divested of the bronze cross he wore on his breast, and St. Pierre's bell tower was bereft of its old cracked bell. Only the doll Margot had slipped in with Blanche was not stolen: a little bundle of old rotten rags.

Augustin kept up his journal irregularly over the days and nights. He did not even know any more why he was still doing it, or for whom. At first, he had written for his own folk, for his family and for Juliette, so as to maintain some link with them; while being a soldier, to remain in the first place a son, a brother, a fiancé — a man alive, safeguarded by love. But life was constantly ebbing away, hope dimmed, anger stole into his heart. Already, he no longer wrote for his folk, he wrote for nobody, for nothing; he wrote in rebellion. Against fear, hatred, madness, and death.

Angel Luggieri got himself killed for a ray of sunshine. The winter had been so long, so hard, that when spring made a feeble breakthrough, Angel could not resist poking his nose out, venturing his head over the barrier of sandbags he was sheltering behind with the look of a rapturous child.

"Just smell that, boys, it's spring!" he exclaimed raising his face to the bluing sky. But a grenade swiftly overtook the timid ray of sunshine and carried off Soldier Luggieri's head, whose cheerful smile exploded into pulp.

For all that, spring did not lose heart, stubbornly making the churned-up earth flower with pink daisies, clumps of periwinkle and golden cress, primroses, and violets whose fragrance drifted in the air that was rank with the stink of gunpowder and decay. And as though to highlight even more the absurd prettiness of this flowering, unseen birds began to sing. They were returning to nest on their land, heedless of the war that yet fiercely disputed it with them, and it was possible to hear, in counterpoint to the gunfire, the dainty twittering of warblers and the fluty whistling of thrushes and blackbirds. But other animals, more numerous and visible, were also scattered over the field of battle. These did not migrate with the seasons, but only with the comings and goings of the war. They were rats, which did not even wait any more until the soldiers were dead, just as readily attacking the wounded on their stretchers.

"Actually, we're rats ourselves," wrote Augustin. "We live like rats, crawling day and night through slime, rubble, and corpses.

We're turning into rats, except that our stomachs are empty, whereas their bellies are so full they weigh them down. And then even our mess tins are infested with vermin."

The vermin ended up infesting the soldiers' imaginations, for they amused themselves by catching lice and bugs and setting fire to them, having first named them Hindenburg, Falkenhayn, Berlin, Munich, or Hamburg, and ceremoniously awarded them the Iron Cross. The others opposite did just the same. There were a few more cold spells that returned to defy the spring, then summer set in. The war dragged on.

". . . Everything quakes. The earth is like some great animal vomiting. I don't even know what day, what time it is. Columns of suffocating black smoke go swirling past. The sky is black, like an enormous chimney that hasn't been cleaned for centuries. We can't even see the sun, and yet it's as hot as a furnace. We're ordered to fire. So we fire. But we don't even know at what, at whom. We can't see anything. The smoke stings our eyes, which are all swollen with grit, so we fire with our eyes shut. Sometimes I say to myself, 'Fancy that, I'm dead, and I'm still firing. I'm going to be firing like this for all eternity. Firing, firing, without ever stopping, for there will be no Last Judgment to put an end to this horror. This is death, and here I am, firing.' That's what I say to myself. Well, no, the smoke cleared, the firing stopped. It wasn't eternity. I rubbed my eyes, and when I opened them again I saw Adrian, who had come tumbling down right beside me. I thought he had fallen and that he was laughing, with his head thrown back. But when I went over to him, I saw. His jaw was smashed and he had no nose. He had also lost an ear and an eye. Nevertheless, I recognized him. He still had one eye, an eye that was a very bright blue, like a chicory flower. So, yet another comrade killed. When my turn comes, I won't be able to describe what happened. But it doesn't matter, for already there's nothing more to tell. It's always the same thing. So you people will be perfectly well able to make up some story of what happened to Mathurin or me when we're killed. Because now you know it all. But even so you can't possibly know anything. And anyway, you may never receive this notebook . . ."

But the next in line was neither him, nor Mathurin. Fate preferred Michel Duchesne and Pierre Beaulieu.

The lookouts had actually given the alarm and the soldiers had hastily put on their masks, but Beaulieu was too slow in adjusting his and he was seized with such a violent coughing fit that he was incapable of recovering his delay. He fell on his knees, bent double, and rolled in the mud until his cough became a rattle. Then a pink foam rose to his lips. He writhed for a while longer, with his hands clutched to his chest, his bulging eyes rolling, while the little pink bubbles that filled his mouth burst around his lips one by one with a faint sound. His comrades, powerless to do anything, bent their heads toward him, aghast, but all he saw at the moment of dying were gruesome eyeless and featureless faces, buried behind gas masks that made them all look the same.

As for Duchesne, he disappeared entirely. A shell fell right on top of him and within a second there was nothing left of him, not even a fingernail or a hair.

There was no account of these deaths either, for Augustin had grown weary of writing. Through constantly recounting death, the words themselves had grown exhausted, drained of meaning and of the desire to bear witness. Anyway, he had got rid of his notebook, which he had even tried to destroy, but Mathurin had rescued it and kept it at the bottom of his kit bag. Since he could neither read nor write, the writing with which his brother had covered all those pages seemed to him amazing, almost magical. Sometimes he would half open the notebook, gently running his fingers over the pages, touching the words otherwise denied to him. He thought of Hortense; he hoped that she, too, would run her fingers over these uncanny words that told why they had been parted and even how they were in danger of never being able to touch each other again. His desire for Hortense tormented him much more than the fear of dying.

At last they were granted leave. Since they could not go home, they went with one of their comrades, whose village was situated on the edge of the occupied zone, not far from the Blackland region, on the banks of the Meuse.

It was seeing the river again that gave him the idea: Mathurin decided to cast the notebook upon the water, having covered the last pages with drawings. He wrapped it in tar-lined paper, then closed it in an iron box to which he attached floats, and afterward committed the box to the current. Farther downstream, maybe, where the Meuse flowed past Blackland, someone might find the box drifting near the bank and deliver it to his folk — maybe. But Mathurin put more faith and hope in that slender and absurd "maybe" than he ever had in any god.

And already they were back at the bottom of their trenches, where the smell of corpses was all-pervasive, with the intense heat of summer hastening their decomposition. Storms occasionally broke toward evening, adding their fantastic thunderings and flashes to the blasts and flares of salvos that exploded on all sides. The torrential rains that came pouring down transformed the trenches into bogs. The sky, stricken with this dual convulsion of storm and war, then resembled the stomach of a monstrous reptile in the process of sloughing off its skin. This dead slimy slough was, Augustin felt, quite as much God's as the sky's.

And yet Juliette still invoked this desquamated God.

They did not understand how the women had contrived to send the envelope that was delivered to them right in the heart of the battle. The iron box cast upon the Meuse had been found, below Blackland, caught in the reeds by the riverbank, and the notebook handed over to Night-of-gold-Wolf-face.

Juliette wrote on behalf of him, their sisters, and herself. But it was not in her own name and words that she wrote, for reading Augustin's unfinished account she had sensed the curse of the widows' house rising again, to menace not just her destiny now but that of all the women in the land. So she spoke in the name of that universal fear and grief that she knew herself to be incapable of conquering on her own, and which she therefore laid in the hands of God.

"In God's torn hands," she wrote, "evil cannot but fail and all suffering disappear in his gaping wounds. I cried so much, for days and nights, when I read all that you wrote about. And then I stopped. Because in the end I realized that this affliction was too great, too heavy for us, and that it was sinful and arrogant to want to bear it alone. I went to church and I knelt before the wooden statue of Christ on the cross, which is on the altar, and there I cast my fear, my despair, everything. And I felt all that causes us so much pain fall away from me and drop into the wound in His side. Drop down to His heart and burn there. Now I'm not afraid any more. You will be saved, I know it, I feel it, and I await your return."

But these words had no meaning any more for Augustin; this faith had been taken away from him, and in his heart he began to curse Juliette for having let herself be duped by this lie. All that he shared now was his father's revolt.

Hortense had neither wept nor prayed. She had wanted only to cry. To cry louder than all the soldiers going over the top, falling under the bullets. To cry louder than the war. Yes, she was a garden, a big garden run wild, all vibrant with insects, heat, and bird calls, full of flowering undergrowth and animals' nests, tumid with damp shadows. But a garden has smells not just colors. And the strongest, most penetrating smell is always the smell of roses. So she had drawn for Mathurin the most exuberant picture she had ever done. It was a body abounding with colors, which had multiple arms and legs that were all in movement, like the twisted spokes of a wheel whose nave was a full-blown rose.

Before slipping her folded drawing into the envelope, she had slept a whole night with the sheet of paper pressed against her sex.

Day was about to break. Three of them crawled across terrain pounded by shells and bristling with shattered trees and barbed wire, silvered with dew, that glistened like thorn bushes in the rosy light of dawn. Long milky white streaks lined the eastern horizon. A lark soared, giving voice to its first call of the day. This break across the sky gave the signal for other flights, but on the other horizon, due west. There was an initial thud, then a long whistle rising to a pitch. The three men looked around toward this cloud of strange birds, with red shining beaks, advancing in arrow formation.

"Get down! Mines!" one of the group shouted as he rolled into a ditch full of water. The birds suddenly came plummeting down on them. There was a fantastic explosion, and the blast that accompanied it flattened one of them on the ground, while the other found himself flying very high up into the reddening air, as though he in turn were trying to respond to the lark's call and take the day by storm.

What came down again was a shower of stones, smashed weapons, pulverized earth, and an arm. A single arm, still attached to its hand, and wearing an identity tag tied with a bootlace around its wrist. The arm landed in front of the one who had been flattened on the ground. But he did not take any notice of the name written on the tag, nor of the lock of black hair entwined around the bootlace. All he saw was that it was his brother's arm and he forgot which of the two he was, still safe and absurdly alone. He picked up the arm, for a long time gazed vacantly at the hand, just like his own, then stuffed it under his coat. Another explosion bowled him over again, and this time he rolled into the ditch full of water, which came up to his knees. It was nearly autumn and the cold was already beginning to creep into the water and mud, but it was not because of this that his teeth started chattering. It was love that made his teeth chatter so, a crazy love that devastated his heart, his memory, and made him tremble in every limb.

A love that misted his eyes with unshed tears and forced him to smile steadily. A strange smile, as frozen as his tears, gentle to the point of idiocy. He remained like that, half squatting in the water, with his teeth chattering, and smiling into space, without taking any notice of what was going on around. The other fellow who had jumped into the ditch before him was still lying there; a piece of shrapnel had gone through his temple. He would have stayed there a long time, until the end of the war, or at least until he in turn was hit by some projectile or other, had his companions not found him on the third day and carried him away by force. Since he did not stop shivering and his teeth kept on chattering, and he seemed to have completely lost his mind, he was sent back behind the lines. His feet, for so long immersed in water and mud, had swollen so much they had cracked the seams of his boots, and he had to be put to bed in the infirmary. The arm he had kept, all that time, stubbornly held tight under his coat, had become strangely mummified. The skin had turned white and cold as polished stone, like the pearls on his father's necklace. In the hollow of its palm a pink rose shaped mark had formed.

During the night when one of the brothers had met with his death, Night-of-gold-Wolf-face was startled awake by a sharp pain that shot through his left eye. He felt a distinct burning sensation at first, immediately followed by an intense cold beneath his eyelid. But it was not until several days later that Margot noticed the disappearance of one of the seventeen flecks of gold in her father's eye. Hortense was not wakened. On the contrary, she was sunk in such a deep slumber, tormented by so many dreams of fire and blood, that in the morning she felt terribly sore, as though she had been given a thrashing during the night. Moreover, her body retained traces of that unseen nocturnal combat, for her skin was covered from her throat to her feet with countless little pink bruises. She looked as though she had been painted all over by some rose tattooist. Juliette experienced nothing unusual that night, but in the morning when she opened the shutters she thought for a moment that instead of the sun she saw a huge chalky white horse's skull rise vertically in the sky.

From that day forward, all of them, even Mathilde and Margot and old Jean-François-Iron-rod, felt that something must have happened, that one of the brothers had surely been killed. But no one dared voice their dread for fear of tempting fate. And their apprehension increased, poised more than ever before between fear and hope. This sense of misgiving they dared not mention lasted more than a year; during that time they received no news at all.

5

He reappeared on a winter's afternoon so clear and cold the view from Upper Farm seemed limitless, such was the remarkable distinctness with which the surrounding countryside was drawn.

He came along the children's bypath, the frozen ground echoing from afar the sound of his footsteps. Night-of-gold-Wolf-face, who was chopping wood in the yard, was suddenly arrested by that tramping of feet coming up the path. Who could possibly be venturing out to his farm in such cold weather? It was so rare that anyone came to see them. The isolation of his farm had become similar to that which had once prevailed over his father's barge. Yet he went on chopping wood, and his ax blows soon fell into rhythm with the footsteps climbing the hill. But the visitor climbed so slowly and ponderously that he seemed to be endlessly approaching without ever arriving.

There was a noise from the cow sheds: a long-drawn-out lowing punctuated with dull thuds, as though the animals were banging their heads against the feeding troughs. Victor-Flandrin planted his ax in the log and headed over to the path. Down below, he saw the huge bowed silhouette of a man holding a stick in his hand. He had never seen such a tall fellow in these parts. Yet there was something in the stranger's silhouette — he would not have been able to define it — that was familiar to him. What he noticed first of all were the man's feet. They were enormous, shod with neither boots nor clogs, but wrapped in rags tied with string and leather thongs, which gave the giant's gait the staggering heaviness of a bear walking on its hind legs. He had a thick bushy beard, glazed with frost. A big bag swung from his shoulder.

Victor-Flandrin waited. When the other man was several yards away, he looked up and stopped. The two men stared at each other. Their gaze was hard and fixed, like the looks exchanged by two strangers used to solitude and meeting for the first time, and it also had the painful intensity of those that know the innermost depths of each other's heart. The eyes of the man who had come glistened with the feverish brilliance that quivers in the eyes of hunted animals. Victor-Flandrin thought he even discerned something of that terrifying gentleness that widens and petrifies the eyes of storm-crazed cattle. He also noticed that the man's two eyes were dissimilar. The pupil in his right eye was contracted into a small black dot; that of his left eye was fully dilated into a large spot of gold, as though this eye had been so stricken by night that it could not adjust to daylight any more.

So fascinated was he by this peculiarity of the eyes, Victor-Flandrin did not even notice the sudden fit of trembling that overcame the man, whose jaws began to chatter.

"Is it you . . . ?" he said at last, hesitantly, then he added in a strangled voice, ". . . my son . . ." But he could not have said which one.

The other was staring at him with those hallucinating eyes that seemed simultaneously to see with the greatest acuity of vision and to see nothing at all. His teeth continued to chatter, and he grimaced a smile.

Night-of-gold-Wolf-face went up to him and gently raised his hand toward him. "My son . . ." he repeated, as in a dream, lightly stroking the trembling chilly face of this son he could not even name.

The other suddenly raised his head with a wild amazed look. "No, not your son," he cried. "Your sons!"

This time Victor-Flandrin grasped his son's face in his hands and held it firmly. He wanted to know, he wanted to understand. But the other's dual gaze — half diurnal, half nocturnal, half alive, half dead — silenced his questions.

Their two faces were so close to each other they were almost touching. The snow all around them reflected the luminosity of the sky almost blindingly. The wind briskly chased a bank of bluish gray clouds, whose shadow crept across the dazzling fields and across the almost still-flowing Meuse over in the valley beyond. However, Victor-Flandrin saw nothing but the face he held in his hands, a face yet vaster and emptier than the deserted countryside around them. And there, too, a shadow drifted. In the left eye, whose golden pupil remained fixed and dilated, there was a dark patch showing. Night-of-gold-Wolf-face stifled a cry. This gaping pupil was a burning mirror in which blazed not what was just now reflected in it but the images already chiseled into it. Images that rose like drunken birds soaring vertically up into the sky from the gullies of a demented memory. And these images were faces; Victor-Flandrin distinguished his sons' and those of other young men besides, whom he did not know. All had the same terror-stricken look, and no sooner did they appear than they caught fire, burning up immediately, endlessly vanishing and reappearing. He even saw his own reflection take shape for the first time in twenty years. And in all these overlapping faces he suddenly thought he recognized yet another, a face that he truly believed he had forgotten: it was his father Theodore Faustin's face, with his mouth twisted by the saber wound and by a fit of evil laughter. Never again did he want to hear that insane laughter, that laughter of pain, never again, and he abruptly let go of his son's head, almost pushing him away, but he did not have time to turn and run. He felt sliced at the knees by an indomitable weakness, and he collapsed in a heap at his son's feet. He wanted to cry out, "No!" to chase away the image, all the images, to repudiate his father's demented face, but he could only repeat imploringly, "Forgive me ... forgive me ... forgive ..." He did not even know whose forgiveness he was asking, or for what reason.

"But now," said Mathilde when they were gathered around the kitchen table, "you must tell us. Which of the two are you?"

"I don't know, I don't want to know," replied the brother who felt sure he could not name himself, thus separating the living and the dead, without at the same time ceasing to exist. He survived only by virtue of this inward duality.

"So what are we supposed to call you?" Mathilde pressed him.

The other simply shrugged his shoulders; it was a matter of total indifference to him.

"But the other one ..." Margot dared to ask, "is he really dead?"

This question, although they were all expecting it, made them jump and plunged them into silence.

"Here he is," said the brother at last, taking from his bag a long iron box that he put on the table in front of him.

The others stared at that incongruous object, not saying a word.

"A doll! A doll!" suddenly thought Margot, appalled, "my brother's turned into a doll as well!"

"Poor child!" murmured Jean-François-Iron-rod, who sat so hunched up at the far end of the table that no one heard him. Only one of the little girls, Violette-Honorine, sitting on his knee, gazed up at him with a look of amazement. Her sister, Rose-Eloise, had fallen asleep on the bench beside them.

The brother opened the box. He took out a long bundle wrapped in a piece of canvas, which he unrolled; he then placed a curious object in the middle of the table, along with two bootlaces attached to identity tags, each with the name of a Peniel brother.

"What's that?" asked Rose-Eloise, who had just woken up.

No one answered her. Everyone's eyes were riveted to the mummified arm. It was at that moment that the phenomenon so often to be repeated in the life of Violette-Honorine occurred for the first time. The pink mark she bore on her left temple became covered with a fine sweat of blood, and a thin red trickle ran down her cheek. The child rubbed her temple and simply remarked, "There's blood," but she was not hurting. She already sensed in some obscure way that this blood was not her own. That day Jean-François-Iron-rod was the only one to notice the phenomenon, but he did not say anything. He took the little girl in his arms and left the kitchen.

The survivor was not the only person who wanted to suppress the name of the brother who had died. His refusal was echoed by Hortense and Juliette. Both of them came to see him but neither recognized the man she had so loved and awaited. This fellow was inordinately tall, thin, and stooping, with a bushy beard and deformed feet. But this made no difference, and each claimed to recognize her lover. He made no claim. He responded in equal measure to the love of both women. One of them called him Mathurin, the other Augustin. Only by them would he allow himself to be named, for their voices were always made flesh, flesh that merged with his, until the pain of all separation was forgotten.

In Juliette's arms he became Augustin again and found the sweetness of rest. Lying with Hortense, he became Mathurin and sank with fantastic cries into the closeness and violence of a dazzling void. But from the rest of them he would not accept one single name, so they ended up calling him Two-brothers.

Though he began working in the fields of Blackland again, he always worked alone, and he moved into a derelict part of the farm buildings. Victor-Flandrin sometimes came at dusk to sit at his son's table. Then they would both sit face to face in silence for a long time before starting to speak. And even so, they only came to words by an infinitely circuitous route, as though frightened of coming up against some forbidden word that would at once have made any discussion impossible. They spoke of the weather, of the fields, of the animals. The box containing the dead man's arm and the two identity tags stood on a shelf above the wooden flap that served as a bed. Two-brothers refused to allow these last remains of his twin to be buried in the earth; nor would they be, until death consumed the departed's surviving half which continued to exist in him.

And sometimes the two little girls came to play in silence at his door. Two-brothers loved them, because they reminded him of their mother, the gentle Blanche, whose grave at Montleroy cemetery he visited every week. One of the little girls in particular had a strange effect on him; her gaze was clear to the point of transparency, and when she looked up at him he felt suddenly relieved of his suffering, momentarily reconciled with himself, and with his other self. Violette-Honorine's gaze was, in its extreme tenderness, like a breeze capable of overturning and lifting any weight whatsoever, of holding everything, every sorrow, suspended in amazement — indeed, wonderment. Violette-Honorine's gaze "was not of this world," avowed Jean-François-Ironrod, who bore the child a love that knew no bounds.

6

An ash gray rain, fine as mist, flitted over the countryside. Hortense threw a shawl over her shoulders and went out bareheaded; she took the path to the widows' house and walked steadily, with a strange determined smile on her lips. When she came into the yard she noticed the curtains at every window twitch and felt the five widows' chilly gaze upon her. "Six widows!" Hortense was forever correcting everyone, stubbornly persisting in now counting Juliette among their number.

It was the first time she had been back to this house since

Two-brothers's return, which had immediately made Juliette her rival. When she knocked at the door, her knocks seemed to reverberate in the emptiness of the house as in a big damp vat, and she shrank back from the threshold. It was Juliette who came and opened the door to her. She had bluish rings around her eyes and her hair hung loose. The two young women stared at each for a moment in silence.

"Come in," Juliette invited her at last.

"No," Hortense replied abruptly. "I just came to tell you that ..." But she could not find the words to finish her sentence.

The other woman waited. She had bowed her head. She had understood.

"It moved," Hortense resumed, continuing then in a jerky voice. "It moved this morning, in my womb. Now I'm sure. That's what I wanted to tell you. It's Mathurin's child. Mathurin's and mine."

Juliette looked up. "Ah?" she said, clinging to the door. Then she added, in a voice so low that Hortense barely heard her, "I'm expecting a child, too. By Augustin."

Hortense grabbed her violently by the shoulder, then immediately pushed her away. "You're lying!" she yelled. "It's not possible! Augustin's dead. He's dead, do you hear? He died there, like all the men who come near the women in this blasted house! It's my Mathurin who came back, and it's his child I'm carrying!"

Juliette gently shook her head. "No," she said. "You know very well, they both of them partly died there. And yet they still came back, but only half. So the two of us as well will just have to come to terms with sharing."

"Never!" cried Hortense. Then she turned on her heels and strode off through the drizzle.

When Two-brothers heard the double tidings he felt at once dejected and happy; now life gathered strength and hope inside him, now death came piercingly to the fore.

Night-of-gold-Wolf-face took in the two young women on his farm. It was Juliette who came first. She did not want to stay down below in that widows' house, where terrible fears haunted her. She was afraid her child might fall as soon as it was born and die on the spot. Margot shared her bedroom with her, and Mathilde moved in with the two little ones she was raising. Hortense came hard on the heels of her rival and also took up residence at the farm. A bed was made up for her in the corner of the kitchen, but she would often slip out at night to go and join Two-brothers.

As her pregnancy advanced, Juliette increasingly fell victim to an inexplicable desire to eat insects. She was constantly catching crickets and grasshoppers, or stealing from spiders little flies trapped in their webs, in order to crunch them. As for Hortense, she developed such an obsessive hunger for earth and roots that she spent the whole day running across fields and woods in order to devour the damp earth from the foot of trees or the trough of furrows.

It was during that spring that Margot became engaged to Guillaume Delvaux. He came from town and had not been very long in Montleroy, where he had taken the job of village schoolmaster.

The children did not like him and immediately nicknamed him the Switch, for he was never without a long pliant cane that he liked to swish as he passed by their benches. The people from the village and from Blackland were no more fond of him, because of his rather peculiar ways and somewhat haughty manner. He did not mix with anyone, never went out, either to go to church or to the café. Eventually people associated him with some occult activity, and there were even those who made their children wear amulets to protect them from the Switch's evil eye.

Margot met him when she took the two little girls to school. She certainly had not armed herself with any amulet and she was utterly defenseless when she fell for this newcomer's charm. He seemed to pay no attention to her at all and never spoke to her. Yet one day he stopped her outside the school gates and said to her,

"Mademoiselle Peniel, I'd like to talk to you. Come this evening, after school. I'll be waiting for you in the classroom."

Since she just stood there, completely bemused, he asked her, "Will you come?"

She simply nodded and went off without asking any questions. She did not return to Upper Farm that day, but walked along the road straight ahead of her, without stopping, her head filled with emptiness. A cataclysmic emptiness. But the time was engraved within her, and all of a sudden she turned back, like an hourglass reversed. When she crossed the playground, the hourglass had emptied, the school was deserted, and it was exactly the right time for her appointment.

She entered the classroom, which was steeped in shadow, and saw nobody. Filling the big blackboard, which still had on either side of it the map of France and the map of the globe with the borders of its pink areas redrawn to history's liking, was a portrait of her, done in chalk. It was a portrait in three-quarters profile, eyes closed. She went up to her likeness and felt the sleep depicted in the portrait slowly steal over her. She sat on the edge of the platform, laid her hands in her lap, and began to sing under her breath, gently swaying her shoulders so as not to fall asleep. In her drowsiness she saw herself as a child again, sitting quietly on her bench next to Mathilde; she was listening to the teacher describing the wonders of the three French territories on the wall maps — Metropolitan France, French Africa, and French Indochina. But yet more fantastic was this fourth territory revealed today, French-Margot, French-Guillaume.

It was then that he emerged from the shadows of one of the corners of the room and came toward her.

He stepped up onto the platform and went over to the blackboard, as if he had not seen her. She stopped singing, but did not stir.

"A face in three-quarters profile is unsettling," he said, gazing at the portrait, "you can't tell whether it's going to turn the other way and go off, or turn right around to face you. What do you think?"

"But that face has its eyes shut," replied Margot. "Whichever way it turns, it won't see anything anyway."

"And what will it see if I open its eyes?" asked Guillaume, seizing the duster.

"It will see you," said Margot.

"Then what will it do, will it turn away or face me?" he pressed her, as he redrew the eyes.

"It will face you," she said.

"In that case I'll have to wipe it all out and start again. But I need a model for this new portrait. Will you sit for me?"

This time she did not reply. She rose, went up to him, took the duster from his hands and began slowly to wipe the board. When there was nothing but a whitish blur left on the black wood she returned the duster and stood facing him.

"There," she said, standing very straight with her back to the board. "You can start again now. I won't move."

Then he gripped her by the hair, tipped her head back slightly, and gently ran the duster all over her face and neck, smearing her skin with chalk.

Margot had closed her eyes, and meekly allowed herself to be covered with chalk. Nor did she offer any resistance when he began to slowly unfasten her blouse. When she opened her eyes again, darkness filled the classroom and all that could be discerned were shadows. She was still standing in the middle of the platform, completely naked, her skin covered from head to foot with white powder.

"Now that I've dressed you in the loveliest wedding gown," Guillaume then said, without relinquishing his schoolmasterly tone, "I have to put the ring on your finger." He took her by the hand, drew her over to the desk and dipped the index finger of her left hand into the inkwell.

"But the wedding-ring doesn't go on that finger," said Margot.

"No, but that's the finger for pointing at what you want. So it's the finger of desire. The only one that counts," replied Guillaume.

Then Margot pointed at him, and placed her index finger, dripping with purple ink, on his lips. He in turn dipped his finger in the ink and, using it as a brush, painted her nipples, earlobes and eyelids, as well as her pubic hair, purple.

When she got back to Upper Farm, day was already breaking. She found Mathilde sitting on the steps outside. She took off her shoes and soundlessly approached her sleeping sister. In the very weak light of incipient dawn Mathilde's face seemed to her even more like her own, tiredness and sleep having toned down the severity that over the years had hardened her sister's features. It was like seeing the portrait Guillaume had drawn on the blackboard, but this time it was upon her — her folly and her sin — that the image was going to open its eyes.

She wanted to call out to Mathilde, but it was her own name that she murmured: "Margot! Margot! What are you doing here?"

Mathilde started and got up at once. She stared at her sister with amazement but could not say anything. She chewed her lips as though to check her cries, or tears. Margot, still daubed with chalk and ink, stared at her vacantly. But Mathilde recovered herself, and taking her sister firmly by the hand, she led her into the farmhouse and said to her, "Come along. You must wash and go to sleep." Then she repeated in a hollow voice, "Wash and go to sleep."

Mathilde did not question Margot at all, but the next day she announced, "I'm taking Rose and Violette to school today. You stay at the farm and get lunch ready." Margot made no reply and let her sister go in her stead.

Mathilde went into the classroom with the children and took a seat on the bench at the back. She remained there the whole morning, without moving, without taking her eyes off the school teacher. For his part, he did not question her and dared not even speak to her. He did not understand who this woman was, in whom he saw Margot, yet without recognizing her. As soon as the bell rang in the yard and the pupils went out to play, Mathilde rose, crossed the room, and came and stood in front of Guillaume.

He looked at her for a while and finally said to her, "I don't recognize you. You're so different today!"

"I'm not Margot," she said dryly. "I'm Mathilde, her twin sister."

Guillaume stared at her at first in astonishment, then he began to circle around her, tapping his cane into his hand. "What a strange family you are!" he exclaimed ironically. "So you always come in pairs, do you? One, two, one, two, one, two . . . You ought to go around goose-stepping!" He gave a little mocking laugh, but Mathilde instantly cut him short. She turned on him, grabbed the cane from his hands, and snapped it in half on the edge of the desk.

"I don't like your laugh or your manners," she said, tossing the bits of cane onto the platform. "In my family we know how to behave, and we hold our heads up high. Very high. And you'll have to learn to hold yours very high if you're to go and speak to my father and ask him for Margot's hand in marriage. But mind you practice well beforehand, because you're still very small and you run a great risk of cricking your neck when you speak to old Peniel!"

She did not give him time to reply. She turned her back on him and went straight out of the school.

Some time later Guillaume Delvaux came to make his request to Night-of-gold-Wolf-face. He did not crick his neck, looking at him, but he felt profoundly uneasy. He could not forget the humiliation Mathilde had inflicted upon him, and he did not know whether his marriage proposal was motivated by his love for Margot or a fierce desire to defy her sister.

As for Margot, she had absolutely no doubts. She loved Guillaume blindly, to the point of total self-extinction. Since that day when he had whitened her with chalk, her body had been nothing but a dazzling blank page, all keyed in expectation of the new writing that would make her and her life a thrillingly festive and crazy book. The wedding was fixed for the beginning of the new year, on Margot's birthday.

7

They came in single file up the path leading to Upper Farm. The corn stood so high on either side of the way, the five widows trotting along in the sunshine looked like a few black ears of grain plucked from the fields and blown by the wind away from the crops. They crossed the yard in silence and, having wiped their feet at length on the threshold, they went in. Inside the house, the groans of the two young women, whose time of confinement was nearing, could already be heard. The widows went up to the bedroom where Juliette lay. Hortense was just next door; she had been moved to Victor-Flandrin's room.

"Go away!" yelled Juliette, on seeing the black figures approach her bed. But she had not the strength to fight any more, so acute was her pain, and she submitted without further resistance to the care of the women under the grandmother's direction.

There was a tremendous cry uttered in unison by Hortense and Juliette, but one voice dropped to a low pitch and the other rose to shrillness. When this dual cry fell silent, there was but one single echo. Only from Hortense's bedroom came the squall of a newborn infant. In Juliette's room, there was no other cry at all — just a fantastic sound of rustling wings and chirring. It was like the roaring of the wind or sea. Thousands of tiny insects of a bright phosphorescent green burst from Juliette's gaping body. They flew out of the open window in a whirl and descended on the corn fields, of which there was almost immediately nothing left but completely empty dried husks.

Hortense, on the other hand, had just given birth to a little boy.

He was a fine, strong, kicking child, but with a curious swelling on his back. He was named Benoît-Quentin.

When the widows returned down the path, between the ravaged ears of corn, there were six of them. They took Juliette with them. As soon as she had been delivered of the lost fruit of her loins, she had sat up where she lay, jumped out of bed, and rushed to the window. She had seen the cloud of green insects descend upon the corn and destroy the harvest. She had seen the sun directly overhead, yawning like the mouth of a white-hot oven. She had stared at the sun until blinded and seen every single thing, every form, dissolve in that excess of light as in a bath of quicklime. Then, her eyes scalded with tears, she had turned back to the women, who were still standing there holding the needless linen, bowl, and jug of water.

"Put down all that," she had instructed them. "It's time to go now."

The women had folded the linen in silence, straightened the spotless bedclothes, tidied the room.

"I'm coming back with you," she had declared. Then she had added, "I'm cold!"

Her sister had given her shawl to her, but she was still cold. Then the other four also wrapped her in their black shawls, but she felt just as cold as before. This coldness did not leave her until they brought the newborn baby to her and she took it in her arms and suckled it.

For as it turned out, Hortense could not feed her child. There was no milk in her breasts; they were engorged with mud. Only Juliette had any milk, and it was she who nursed Benoît-Quentin. So Hortense, too, had to leave Upper Farm and move into the widows' house, so as not to be separated from her son. She agreed to live there until the child was old enough to be weaned. And during all that time Two-brothers was to be seen going down to the widows' house after work. He would share a meal, in silence, with the seven women, sitting between Juliette and Hortense; then after dinner he would go up to the bedroom where his son slept. And it was he who rocked the baby to sleep every evening, after which, he made his way back to Upper Farm, where Hortense sometimes came to join him in the middle of the night.

Benoît-Quentin had a double fleck of gold in his left eye, and a hump on his back.

Margot made her own wedding dress. She went off to town to buy fabrics, pearls, and trimmings. But she showed her purchases to no one but Mathilde, who helped her with the sewing. And it was a real oeuvre that she produced: her dress owed not so much to the art of needlework as that of sculpture and illumination. And this work went on for months. It was all her love, her body maddened with desire and anticipation, that Margot crafted in this way. Her wedding outfit became a poem of whiteness, of brilliance, of the sparkling play of light. Actually, it was not really a dress but an extravagant assemblage of petticoats. She made thirteen that were layered depending on their different shapes and sizes. The longest was made of satin damask and its hem trimmed with little silk tassels, then came petticoats of linen, velvet, moiré, percale, and wool mesh, each one point-laced and trimmed with a mass of braids, bows, and ribbons. Gathered around the waist was a broad taffeta belt embroidered with the initials G and M. The two letters were worked in glass beads, and intertwined in an amazing arabesque. Then she made a silk bodice; a high-collared lace blouse fastened at the wrists and at the nape of the neck with clusters of mother-of-pearl buttons, and a velvet jacket that she tricked out with feathers and tulle roses. She then fashioned a veil out of a piece of batiste three yards long and covered it with hundreds of finely embroidered stars, flowers, and birds. She also bought some white fur with which she made a muff as well as a wide headband to keep the veil on, and she used it, too, to trim her ankle boots. This outfit cost so much that all the dowry money

was spent on it even before the marriage, but Night-of-gold-
Wolf-face thought both joy and beauty such rare and fleeting
things on this earth that they should be duly celebrated when they
occurred, were it only for a day; so he considered his daughter's
amorous caprice well worth the expense.

The marriage was to take place on the first day of the new year.
And indeed on that day, when Margot left the farmyard, newly invested with her twenty years and her fabulous dress, and sat beside
her father in the cart harnessed to two oxen whose horns were
trimmed with white ribbons, and drove through the scintillatingly
snowy countryside, it was possible really to believe that beauty had
descended on earth and the world was visited with joy.

Margot carried a big bouquet of mistletoe, and when she entered the precincts of the church at Montleroy, she laid a sprig of
mistletoe on her mother's tomb and another on Blanche's. She
cherished the memory of the two women who had turned into
dolls: the one all stiff, like a little wooden doll, quaintly wrapped in
pieces of floral-printed calico; the other, like a poor shattered glass
doll. And she invited them to join in her wedding, her happiness,
her transformation. For she herself was still but a doll — a chalk
doll all swathed in lovely fabrics, trimmings, and fur. But soon she
was going to become flesh, before God and before eternity, and
consummate this new flesh in nakedness and abandonment.

St. Pierre's new bell started swinging and sent its chimes gaily
ringing out across the village, while the Peniel family gathered in
front of the church. Margot, on her father's arm, stared smilingly
at the square where Guillaume was to appear. Everyone else had
eyes only for her, so extravagantly pretty was she. The square was
soon filled with people; all the inhabitants of the village, of Blackland, and the surrounding hamlets had come to admire Night-of-
gold-Wolf-face's daughter, and all of them discovered whiteness
as they had never seen it before. Margot was so splendidly dressed
in white that every other white, even the brilliance of the sun or

the snow, seemed to derive from her petticoats and veil. She stood in regal glory, before the church's open door, like those snow queens children encounter in fairy tales. And Night-of-gold-Wolf-face held her firmly by the arm, a peasant king dazzled by the beauty of his daughter and proud to show her off to the people, and to the land.

But it was getting late and still Guillaume had not come. Margot began to stamp her feet a little on the freezing cold stone to warm them. But this discreet tapping took on a fantastic resonance that soon drowned the crowd's clamor of admiration and the church bell's joyful pealing. Everyone fell silent and gazed in astonishment at those neat white ankle boots frantically marking time and making more of a din than a thousand drums. Wherever Guillaume might have been at that moment, he must have heard that call.

And a response came. A little boy elbowed his way through the crowd packed into the square and came running up to the porch. There, all out of breath, he handed a note to the bride and ran off just as quickly as he had arrived. Margot unfolded the sheet of paper. Guillaume had written three short lines. His handwriting was neat to the point of preciosity, a real little masterpiece of calligraphy. She read: "Margot, don't expect me. I won't come. I shall never see you again. Forget me. Guillaume."

The Switch was true to his word; he was never seen again and no one ever knew what had become of him.

Margot slowly refolded the letter, slipped it under her belt, then threw her head back slightly and began to laugh. A pretty little laugh, like the tinkling of glass bells. Then tearing away from her father's arm, she started to spin around, gently swaying her shoulders and head and beating the ground with her heels. Her veil billowed and floated in slow motion, while her petticoats rose and opened up like whorls of flowers. She had raised her arms and was turning faster and faster, like a top. And twirling around in this manner, she went flying into the nave, dispelling the church's darkness with a great flurry of petticoats. Her laughter and the sound of her quickened footsteps reverberated oddly beneath the vault. It was then that, catching sight of the confessional box behind the pillars, she sped over to it, still spinning around, and tore down the old purple curtain, all moldy with dampness, and threw it over her shoulders like a sheet of tarpaulin. She danced for a few minutes more across the church, upsetting chairs and pews, and suddenly collapsed with a shrill cry like a puppet that has just had all its strings cut.

"Margot! Margot! What's the matter with you?" cried Mathilde from the church door, rooted to the spot with terror. In her fists held clenched against her hips, she squeezed the hands of Rose-Heloise and Violette-Honorine, who stared, openmouthed, at the great froufrou of white fabrics now lying still, down there, at the far end of the nave.

Night-of-gold-Wolf-face came into the church and went up to Margot. When he lifted his daughter's senseless body in his arms, he found it weighed so little he almost lost his balance as he stood up. And walking unsteadily, he carried this body that had shed all its weight up to the altar, on which he laid it. He knocked over the vases, candlesticks, and religious objects, then seized the gilded wooden crucifix and broke it in two against the tabernacle, shouting, "You God of woe, so this is how you like to see your children, struck down by death and madness? Well, take a good look, take another good look at this daughter of mine, this child, for in the end there won't be anything more to see. When you've ruined us all and there's nobody left on earth!"

Outside the crowd had gathered in front of the church in a sea of heads and shoulders, and a great murmur surged from it, but no one dared step through the portal, where Mathilde still stood with the two little girls.

For the second time, Violette-Honorine felt blood seeping from her left temple and slowly running down her cheek. This time she said nothing. She knew now that this blood was not her own, that it flowed from the wound of another body, from the sorrow of another heart. And this time, too, Jean-François-Iron-rod was the only one to notice the child's bewildered pity, the derangement in her eyes. He went up to her and timorously placed his hand on her shoulder. He wanted to speak to her but could not find the words, he only managed to stammer out some indistinct mumblings and he tightened his hold on her shoulder until he was positively grappling it and bearing on it with all his weight. So he remained, bowed over the child's strained profile, as though blinded by that thin trickle of blood oozing from her temple. He felt himself caught up in that tide of tenderness, all alarm and suffering, and he had the impression of suddenly becoming a very small child again, much smaller than Violette-Honorine.

But there was a stir in the crowd around them, and he was separated from the little girl. Victor-Flandrin came out of the church, carrying his daughter in his arms, and everyone made way for him, then the crowd immediately closed in again like black water, murmuring a name that was to stay with Margot forever more.

"The Jilted Bride, here comes the Jilted Bride!" they all said, following Night-of-gold-Wolf-face with curious eyes as he carried away his big frilly white doll wrapped up in the old purple curtain from the confessional box.

Night of Blood

GOD CREATED THE WORLD and all things in the world, but he did not give anything a name. He maintained a discreet silence and let his entire Creation shine in the perfectly pure naked light of its mere presence. Then he entrusted this unnamed multitude of things to man's discretion, and man, scarcely awakened from his clay torpor, began to name everything around him. Each word he invented then gave things a new aspect and a new dimension; names overlaid things with a facing of clay in which similarities and vague differences already came into play.

Consequently, there is not one word that does not carry in its recesses eddies of light and volleys of echoes, and which does not quiver at the urgent plying of other words. Thus, the name of the rose opens and closes, and then sheds its petals, like the flower itself. A single petal sometimes contrives to catch every reflection of light and to consummate the beauty of the whole flower. Likewise, just one letter can take the whole word by storm and completely overturn it.

When the name of the rose burns with too much desire and begins to take flesh, it blossoms open until it turns into Eros. Then the name goes crazy under the pressure of other words, and all of a sudden it steadies, fixing as the verb *oser* — to dare.

Eros. *Oser la rose* — dare for the rose, the gift of the rose.

But now the verb, too, becomes active, and revolves. When the name of the rose runs away with itself like this and goes into a spin, it becomes *roue* — wheel. Then the name of the rose scratches itself on its own thorns and starts to bleed. Sometimes the rose's blood takes the color of day and glistens like the clear saliva of laughter. On other occasions the rose's blood brews in the night, and then a dark and bitter sweat mingles with it.

To dare. The rose-wound. Violent rose, and violated.

Bright burst of rose-blood, red-blood, no sooner bled than it darkens, then blackens.

At Blackland, the names of things, animals and flowers, the names of people, kept going through endless declensions, forever evolving in a maze of assonances and echoes.

Assonances sometimes so unexpected, so incongruous even, that they splintered into dissonances.

Rose-blood, rose-night. Night-blood and fire-wind-blood.

Rose-red-raw.

I

Margot never progressed beyond the hour of her awakening, forever remaining on the threshold of that bright morning that had greeted her twentieth birthday and the preparations for her wedding. She opened her eyes slowly, very slowly, then sat up in bed yet more slowly. Both her body and her voice thus took to breaking down words and gestures into slow motion — a slowness verging on stillness and silence, in which time slumbered. It was by virtue of this, time's deep and lengthy sleep, that she was able to endure the thirteen years of life left to her, by reducing them to a single day.

Forever age twenty, Margot never relinquished that January-morning gaze, nor her wedding dress. She was constantly looking forward to the sacred hour of her marriage when she would set out for church. She never uttered any other words but those she had spoken that morning, and perpetually repeated every move, every step she had made then.

However, as evening approached, it seemed that some misgiving abruptly intruded upon her, and for a moment her body and voice broke out of their torpor and resumed a faster pace.

"Where are they?" she would then ask.

"But who?" Mathilde had inquired the first time.

"Guillaume and Margot, of course," Margot replied. "They must be far away by now. They've taken the train, but they didn't tell anybody where they were going." She later added, "They're right. A honeymoon should remain secret. Otherwise . . ."

"Otherwise what?" asked Mathilde.

But Margot never knew the answer, and ended her sentence waveringly. "Otherwise . . . otherwise . . . I don't know . . . Love is a secret, that's all. You mustn't ask too many questions."

Then she would look away and dream of Guillaume and Margot's never-ending honeymoon.

Mathilde, though, did not dream, and did not at all consider love a secret. It was a betrayal, it was the most deceitful lie, it had been men's privilege to invent. And she made up her mind to eradicate from her heart even the tiniest rootlets of love and to quell all desire in her body. During the night following Margot's uncelebrated marriage, she was woken by violent pains in her stomach and her back. She was quite familiar with this pain, having suffered it every month for years, but this time it seemed to her terrible, excessive. All of a sudden her menstrual blood filled her with horror; she felt sullied in her flesh, abused in her being. This bad blood had to be stopped, at once, and forever, otherwise it would never cease to flow, to spill over the earth its unclean redness, its sickening warmth — the very redness and warmth of desire. So she had risen and run out of the house, barefoot, in her nightgown, and rolled in the snow until the full coldness of the night penetrated and chilled her. She had rubbed her skin, her breasts, stomach, the nape of her neck, and her back, with lumps of frozen snow. Then, when she felt that all the blood in her body had receded deep inside her, stilled in its flux, she cut herself with the sharp edge of a stone. And no blood flowed from this wound. Her menses never returned and all her life her body remained fiercely contracted around the coldness that had petrified her entrails and her sex.

Yet, despite this unyielding coldness lodged inside Mathilde, the seasons continued their cycle, unperceived by Margot's constant gaze, succeeding one another regardless of human desires, hurts, and eccentricities. Victor-Flandrin followed this dogged and unremitting course that time plotted in the earth, and he kept equal pace with it. He never said anything about Margot's madness, but for a long time he thought that if he ever encountered the man who had turned his daughter into this incurable Jilted Bride, he would not hesitate to cut off his head, as he had cut off the horse Scheldt's head. And he would have hung that head on the front of his farm, as a defiance to faithless, heartless men, and especially that even more heartless God.

On Sundays, when all the inhabitants of Blackland set out for mass, he would make for the forest. He had learned to use a gun with his left hand and had very quickly become expert. He never missed his quarry, which he always killed with the first shot. He was better than any dog at running game to earth and waiting for exactly the right fraction of a second when the beast he was aiming at could not escape his bullet. It was this extreme precision of movement and of the eye, and their lightning fusion in the finger of death, that excited his taste for hunting. He liked to hear the very dry smack of each shot fired reverberate among the trees, he liked to feel the very brief kick of the firearm thump against his shoulder, he liked the smell and the red flare of that bright tongue of flame that flashed from the mouth of his gun.

More than anything else he liked to see the entire mass of the beast's tremendously vigorous body suddenly felled. He went after every kind of animal — ducks and birds, hares, squirrels and badgers, as well as foxes, red deer, and roe deer — stopping the beast dead in its tracks, or in midflight, shooting it down, to drop there at his feet. But the game he prized above all else were boars. He never saw any wolves again; in fact, had he encountered any, he would certainly not have shot them — as if a perverse belief in the werewolf had finally insinuated itself in him. He had no fear whatsoever of this animal, which had escorted him through the forest and brought him to land, light, and love. And it might well have been that these werewolves could escort him to other places, and to other unexpected bodies.

He was no more afraid of boars, but these beasts with their incredible torsos, their close-set tallow-colored bristles, and their triangular heads armed with enormous everted tusks, were a challenge to him, a kind of violent attraction. He always aimed at their brows, firing off as they came charging toward him. He liked their courage, their obstinacy. The stricken animal would then suddenly swerve oddly, deviating slightly from its path and all at once collapsing, at an oblique angle to his lethal gaze. Night-of-gold-Wolf-face felt the thud of those brutally dispatched bodies in the innermost depths of his own body. And he experienced a feeling of insane happiness that brought him close to crying out loud. It was a happiness full of fury and darkness, a great rush of raw happiness that whiplashed his heart, overstrained with death and rebellion. A dark and heavy happiness, like that rich earth the boars foraged for roots. That earth in which so many of his family had already decomposed to become mud in their turn. And it was precisely all this mud, all this accumulated darkness the dead had deposited inside him, that he exorcised by killing boar. Yet he never touched sows or young boar, he shot only the males whose prodigiously massive snouts, surrounded by a short spiky mane of stiff bristles, seemed to bulge with mud, black blood, and contained wind.

One day he came upon a boar's lair beside a marsh. A boar of extraordinary size immediately broke away from the flushed-out herd of swine; it must have stood more than a yard high and had the weight of an enormous rock. Indeed, the animal looked as though it had been carved out of a block of granite, and when, realizing it had been cornered, it charged at him, it came hurtling toward him with the blind force of a boulder hurled down a steep slope. Night-of-gold-Wolf-face almost felt the beast's burning breath on his hands by the time he fired. Struck right between the eyes, the boar gave a harsh grunt and was lifted a few inches into the air for a moment, then its entire bulk dropped to the ground and rolled over onto its side.

Night-of-gold-Wolf-face had then gone up to the boar, where it lay, had crouched down beside it, and, lifting its heavy head, still hot and streaming with greasy sweat, he had started to drink the blood spurting from the wound. And he had drunk all that blood not as someone seeking to draw strength from the blood of a vanquished animal but as a man swallows his own tears, fear, and anger. He had drunk it until he forgot himself, his sorrows, and his loneliness, until he forgot his own forgetting. He had drunk it until he discovered in his mouth that violently mawkish taste the flesh of the dead acquires in the earth. And he had risen again, delirious at having found that taste.

Night-of-gold-Wolf-face never knew the identity of the woman he encountered that day as he emerged from Love-in-the-open Wood. Moreover, the gaze he rested on her was as defective and surprised as the gaze animals rest on humans. He had a sudden fuzzy image of her, but he was so forcibly struck by it he could not turn aside and pass by. He was stopped in his tracks by that big splash of dark colors moving against the verdant background of the forest outskirts. She was bent over, gathering in a basket mushrooms or plants that she was picking among the roots of the trees. He saw that she slowly straightened up when she heard him approach. With one hand supporting her back, she wiped her brow with the other. She must have noticed the very strange expression on his face just then, that animal look in his eye, at once scared and terrifying, for she dropped the hand she was passing across her brow, down over her mouth, wide open for a cry she never actually uttered. And she slid her other hand around from her back to her stomach, and held it there, over her belly, like an enormous belt buckle. He came straight toward her, very calmly, and she began to take little stumbling steps backward. This walking backward went on for a long time, for neither of them quickened their step, and the distance between them remained always the same. But the woman finally tripped over a big root and fell heavily on her back without even having the reflex to break her fall with her hands.

It was Night-of-gold-Wolf-face who removed her hands from her mouth and her belly. So, too, did he lift her skirts and force her knees apart. She seemed to be dazed and terror stricken to such a degree that she offered no resistance to this intractable violence upon her. And he rolled on top of her with stubborn brutality, clutching her to him as if he would have entered his entire body inside her, immersed himself in her, or crushed her. He felt he was penetrating the woman right down to her deepest entrails, to the blood in her flesh and her heart — right down to the earth beneath their bodies. And he experienced a sensual pleasure he had never known before. A pleasure so overwhelming it immediately plunged him into a profound state of torpor, in which the woman, too, was engulfed. Indeed, their two bodies were so fiercely entangled their sensations could not but be shared. Yet when he woke, after dark, Victor-Flandrin was lying all alone, flat on his stomach on the damp earth, and for a long time he thought he had been dreaming. He could not remember exactly what he had dreamed, and he got to his feet reeling from the sluggish sleep that without his being aware of it had cast him face down upon the earth, his belly upon humus and roots, a sleep that had left him with a sticky taste, like the taste of blood, in his mouth.

2

Hortense never appeared at Upper Farm again, nor at the widows' house. She vanished, just like that, without warning, without even taking the son she so jealously loved, abandoning him to Juliette's breast.

But Juliette's milk eventually dried up. Benoît-Quentin was nearly two when he decided to shun her breast. It was at precisely that time that Hortense went away. No one knew where she had gone or what became of her. Some said they had seen her in other towns, but the names of the places were never the same: she must have become a real wanderer. During the months following her disappearance, there were even those who claimed to have seen her big with child. But from what they said, Hortense was so terribly big and her gaze so painfully blue, such accounts were not to be trusted. Then people stopped talking about her.

As for Juliette, the moment the child was weaned, she lost her reason for existence and vitality, and drifted into a state of total indolence. She turned away from Benoît-Quentin with the same indifference with which he had turned away from her breast. Soon she refused to get up and for the rest of her life dragged out an endless series of empty days confined to her bed. The five widows living with her then decided to take the child to Upper Farm. They felt their house could no longer be a home to the little boy, since its walls inevitably brought misfortune on any man who lived there. And in any case, they did not much like this child with a misshapen back. After all, he did not even belong to them. He was the offspring of that crazy woman who was always loitering in the woods and had so often humiliated them, and now, to cap it all, had run off, God or the Devil knew where. As for the father, no one was even sure who he was exactly. Besides, they suspected the child of harboring some monstrosity inside that frightful hump, perhaps even some power capable of directing against them, the womenfolk, the persistent curse that had so far oppressed their men. Had not this curse already begun to turn against them, by thus afflicting Juliette with lethargy and melancholy? So they wrapped the infant in a big shawl and took him over to the Peniels'. After having rejoiced in two mothers, Benoît-Quentin suddenly found himself without a mother at all. But the Peniel farm was a huge place, and he was joyfully welcomed by Rose-Eloise and Violette-Honorine. Mathilde did not have to bother much with this new child, for Two-brothers took his son to live with him and looked after him. For Benoît-Quentin's sake, he even discovered new vigor and joy and started to take part in life more fully again.

The child often worried about his deformity and questioned his father about the load on his back, which attracted so much derision from the other children in the village. Two-brothers would then take the little boy on his knees and rock him very gently in his arms and stroke his hair so tenderly the child forgot all his pain. And his father used to tell him such lovely stories that Benoît-Quentin sometimes began almost to grow fond of his deformity. For Two-brothers told him that his hump contained a very great and very wonderful secret, that inside it slept another little boy. A tiny little brother of remarkable beauty and gifted with great talents, and if Benoît-Quentin could learn to love this little brother and carry him boldly all his life, well, his little brother would look after him and protect him against all misfortune. And deep down, Two-brothers was even gladdened by his son's deformity, for, thus misshapen, he would never be drafted and sent off to another war. Little hunchbacks are not made for uniforms and glory, but for dreams, memories, and grace aplenty.

Before long, more brothers for Benoît-Quentin arrived. They were only a few days old when found. Someone, who had immediately vanished, came one night and left them on the doorstep of the Peniels' house. It was Jean-François-Iron-rod who discovered them in the morning. There were three of them and they were at the same time totally alike and totally different from one another. Absolutely identical in terms of the shape of their bodies and their facial features, they looked like three copies of one child, but they were radically different in skin coloring, in the color of their eyes and hair. One had an olive complexion with very black hair and translucent blue eyes; the second had pale skin, extremely fair hair, and translucent black eyes. As for the third, he was simply an albino.

These children did not resemble anybody. They were of startling beauty, almost inhuman in its perfection, almost animal in its barbarity. Yet there was a sign of their family identity — each of them had the same gold fleck in his left eye. This was enough to establish their parentage, though it failed to explain it. It was Mathilde, alerted by Jean-François-Iron-rod, who went to tell her father. This time she entered his room without knocking, and came and stood at the end of his bed, shouting, "Get up! Come and see what new misfortune you've brought upon us now! And this time there are three of them! Three, do you hear? Three bastards from heaven knows where! But I'm telling you now, I won't look after these ones. No fear! They can die for all I care! In any case they will die since their whore of a mother has abandoned them and they won't have anything to eat. There's no wet nurse for them here!"

At first Victor-Flandrin understood nothing of his daughter's shouts and threats, but when he came downstairs and saw the three children, the dream he thought he had dreamed some months earlier suddenly came back to him. Yet he could not remember the woman he had raped in Love-in-the-open Wood; he still saw her only as a vague patch of shadow. Could a dream possibly produce real children?

"What archangels of woe are these?" exclaimed Night-of-gold-Wolf-face upon seeing this extraordinary progeny blessed with terrifying beauty. Then he recovered himself and declared, "Well, we've got three more Peniels. It doesn't much matter where they come from, they're here. And whether they live or die, in any event they'll need names."

The three children were given the names Michael, Gabriel, and Raphael, and they survived. They were reared on cow's milk and thrived on it. It turned out they were equally happy to drink the milk of goats, sows, and ewes, whose teats they would go and suck by themselves as soon as they were old enough to crawl. The three children's taste and tolerance for animal milk confirmed Mathilde in her aversion to these bastards, who, moreover, never mixed with the other Peniel children; they always kept to themselves and invented between them a language incomprehensible to anyone else. But very quickly a special bond developed within this clan between the fair-haired Michael and dark-haired Gabriel, who were never apart. Even at night they slept clasped in each other's arms. As for Raphael, the albino child, he went his own way and talked to himself in a voice so clear, so melodious, it was entirely self-sufficient. And he had no shadow, for his body was so transparent it never cast any. And all three children understood the language of beasts, whose company they seemed to prefer to that of humans, and they were able to make themselves understood by them. Sometimes Raphael came up to his brothers and, gently swaying his head and shoulders, he would start to sing. His very pure voice had extraordinary tones and sounds that immediately inspired Gabriel and Michael to start dancing. This song and these dances could carry on for so long the three children would go into a deep state of trance.

For his three sons by an unknown mother, Night-of-gold-Wolf-face felt a very special love that was a mixture of admiration, fear, and doubt. He felt them to be born not so much of his flesh as of some dark corner of his heart, one of those corners where thought does not penetrate and cannot bring to order the chaos of mad desires and enduring visions that spring up there. Were they not born of a dream, a dream fraught with the taste of blood and mud?

Night-of-gold-Wolf-face regarded his grandson more as his son than these three, for Benoît-Quentin was truly the child of love and sorrow, molded of the Peniels' flesh and Blackland's history. And besides, Benoît-Quentin had such a sweet smile, which seemed always to be wistfully apologizing for not being quite like everyone else, with this hump on his back — a smile that went straight to your heart. But the other three were sons of pure desire, not love. Blind uncanny desire — he could still feel the blood, and the cry, of that desire throbbing inside him.

Some attempt had to be made to take all these various children in hand, since Mathilde, the only woman at Upper Farm capable of it, would have nothing to do with them. All her care and solicitude were for her sister Margot. Every morning she came to waken her, to get her ready for her wedding, helping her to put on her thirteen petticoats, to dress her hair, and to lace her boots. And every morning Margot would open her eyes to greet her with that everlasting gaze of January 1920, and she would smile at Mathilde like a radiant child. Then began the Jilted Bride's ultra-slow day, her every lingering move undermining all haste to set off for church, carefully delaying the moment of that illusory departure. Mathilde never lost her temper with her sister and never tried to put a stop to this desperate game, the only thing that kept her beloved Margot alive. But every day she, too, was filled anew with the pride she had felt in January 1920, a pride in which she had been humiliated, as her heart had been mortified, to see her other self betrayed and in a sense dealt a death blow — that other self to whom all her own self-love was directed; a self so elevated that day in beauty and joy, only to be dashed down into madness, tossed aside like an old castoff. And every morning her hatred and desire for vengeance were restored to her intact.

As for the three bastards her father had promiscuously sired, she suspected them of harboring some evil spirit ready to hurt and betray, as the Switch had done, and she transferred to them all her impotent hatred.

So Victor-Flandrin made up his mind to hire a servant whose task would be to look after the children and help out on the farm. But neither in Blackland, nor Montleroy, nor in any of the villages around could he find a young girl who would agree to come and work at Upper Farm. Night-of-gold-Wolf-face and his brood of yellow-eyed twins and triplets aroused more distrust and fear than ever. And people had come to believe that the Switch had actually been very wise to make his escape before falling into the jaws of those Peniel wolves.

Victor-Flandrin heard about the Château du Carmin, over on the other side of the province. In this château, so it was said, was a home for young girls of all ages who had been born of illicit liaisons and were brought up there until they were old enough to go and work in local factories, farms, and businesses.

It was the old marquis, Archibald Merveilleux du Carmin, who had founded this charitable institution nearly twenty years ago. It was called the Little Sisters of Blessed Adolphine, for it had been set up in accordance with the wishes of the marquis's youngest daughter, Adolphine, who had died at the age of fifteen.

A few months before young Adolphine's death, a wing of the Château du Carmin had been destroyed by a fire, which started during a ball held in honor of Amélie, the marquis's eldest daughter, who was that day celebrating her eighteenth birthday.

It was at the end of the ball that the fire broke out. As she danced with her partner, Amélie twirled around and knocked over a candlestick. The flames caught the folds of her gown, immediately turning it into a blazing torch. Her partner just had time to let go of this human firebrand, but the Marchioness Adelaide rushed to her daughter to try to save her. Amélie then concluded her interrupted dance in the arms of her mother, whose gown also caught fire, and the two women thus closed the ball with a dazzling waltz, fastened to each other by thousands of little talons of flame.

The fire then swept through the whole room, swooping upon tablecloths, furniture, and curtains, chasing the guests out through the blown-out windowpanes.

Adolphine was not at the ball; she was lying in her room, to which she was already confined by the illness that was to carry her to the grave. All she saw was a great red glow that filled her window, and in her fever she thought the night had been contaminated by her own illness and had started spitting blood, as well. But Archibald Merveilleux du Carmin saw what happened. He saw his wife and eldest daughter writhe and go up in flames; he saw the windows shatter and the roof collapse; he saw people run off screaming through the illuminated park. He saw his horses rear violently in their stalls and flail the air with their hoofs, making loud cries, as though to ward off the assault of those maddening glares — some even broke their legs and had to be put down afterward. Then he saw the fire die out and sink, sated, into its huge bed of embers and ashes. He saw his château partially destroyed, and saw amid the debris the completely charred bodies of his wife and eldest daughter, still wearing their diamond pendants around their carbonized necks and where their ears had been.

Then he saw the earth open up beneath his feet and all his happiness, love, and faith fall into this abyss before it immediately closed again. But Adolphine wanted to exorcise the hold that evil and anger had taken on her father's heart and she extracted from him the promise that he would rebuild the destroyed wing of the château as a home for all the abandoned or orphaned little girls in the region, for in this way, she told him, he would have more daughters than ever he had lost. And she also asked that after her death, her body should be laid to rest in the chapel of this orphanage, among all those little posthumous sisters.

3

Archibald Merveilleux du Carmin faithfully kept the promise he had made to his daughter, but he exercised total freedom in his interpretation and realization of the dead girl's wishes.

Adolphine had begun to jot down in a notebook the broad outlines of her project that was intended both to aid little girls in distress and to save her father's recalcitrant heart from despair, but she had to give up working on her mission of salvation, for in the end her hand kept falling onto the open page, no longer tracing anything but illegible words blotted by spittles of blood and splashes of tears. One day she even thrust aside her notebook and cried, "I don't want to die! I don't want to, no, I don't want to . . ." But she was already close to death, with no time left to fight any more, or to continue drafting her plans.

These last words that the frightened young girl had cried out were certainly the only ones her father heard and remembered, and it was by the dark light of these cries that he read his daughter's incomplete notebook. In fact all he read were scattered words and phrases: "Our Lady of Kindness," ". . . all the little girls will be placed under the protection of Mary Mother of God," ". . . Amélie Dormitory," ". . . saints' days should be feast days for the girls," "Adelaide Hall," ". . . and I shall always be among them in the chapel," " . . . so everyone will console everyone else." But most of all he read the tear stains and spittles of blood, and it was upon these word blots that he fed his imagination in order to accomplish the wishes of his younger, and now his only, daughter.

He duly had the burned-down wing rebuilt, and even enlarged, and Adolphine's heart was lodged in the chapel dedicated to Our Lady of Kindness. Only, he ordered this chapel to be built at the very far end of the building, underground. This subterranean sanctum was entirely covered in black marble and lit by the sole light of candles. In the center stood the altar with a magnificent reliquary, containing the deceased girl's heart, occupying pride of place. The way into the chapel was down an endless stone staircase that led into a small room with such a low ceiling it was necessary to stoop to cross it. In this entrance room stood the tombs of his wife the marchioness and his daughter Amélie, as well as a huge glass shrine containing Adolphine's embalmed body.

The marquis's lugubrious inspiration was evident in every last nook and cranny of the building. There was not one wall, either in the dormitories or the refectory, that was not painted dark gray; not a bedstead that was not of iron; nor a single dress not made of anything but dark cloth. In the central aisle of the dormitories he had wooden tubs, like watering troughs, installed, into which were poured jugs of nothing but ice cold water for the inmates to wash in. The discipline and rules of silence he imposed were stricter than in any monastery.

When his vast funereal monument was complete, the marquis threw open the Institution of the Little Sisters of Blessed Adolphine, and soon all the little local-born girls who were unwelcome love children were brought there. These children arrived so unprovided for, they did not even have any identity. The marquis then instituted a system for naming these poor little waifs who ended up in his home. He decided that each year would have a corresponding letter of the alphabet, but since the letter A was the sole prerogative of his family, he began the series with the letter B. This alphabetically determined first name was to be followed by the name of whichever Christian feast day happened to fall on the day the child came to the château, and rounded off with the name of Mary, under whose divine protection the whole flock of orphans was placed. This trinity of given names was rounded off with a patronym shared by all; that patronym was none other than Holy Cross. These discarded infants, tares that sprang from faithless and illicit loves — he hated them with all his grieving heart, with all his fallen pride, with all his lost faith, and he contrived to make their absurd illegitimate lives a very discreet and decorous hell, rank with the black odor of sanctity.

Victor-Flandrin was received by the marquis, who did him the honor of showing him around his garden, his greenhouses, his vast aviary stocked with barn owls, and his stables. These were in fact what the marquis was most proud of: his ancient trees whose night blue or purple shade triumphed over the grayish and derisory shadows of passing visitors; his exotic flowers with fleshy petals like sugared tongues; his barn owls whose plumage was as bright as their cries were somber; and above all, his horses, which enjoyed the privilege of sharing the initial letter of their master's first name. The marquis introduced them to his guest one by one: there was Acrostic-Amour, Atlas-Ambassador, Apostolic-Abyss, Arabesque-Alarm, and Absinthe-Abelia. And they were so delicate, so graceful, that Victor-Flandrin was amazed. Such delicacy in an animal was a surprise to him, who had only ever known dray horses and plow oxen.

However, Archibald Merveilleux du Carmin never showed anyone around the premises of his institution, which were kept more secret than the cloister of a monastery. Visitors were taken to a room adjacent to the orphanage buildings and it was there that they were presented with the young Holy Cross girls old enough to be employed.

It was an attractive high-ceilinged room, with whitewashed walls, and a big west-facing stained glass window that cast a bright reddish light in the afternoon.

The marquis invited Night-of-gold-Wolf-face to sit beside him on a bench with a high sculpted back. On a table in front of them was a stack of large logbooks. Each logbook was a different color and had a different letter written in black on the spine. The marquis slowly ran his index finger down the pile, stopping near the bottom. He pulled out three books, one bright green, one ocher, and one brown, corresponding to the letters G, H, and I.

"Let's see," he said, placing an eccentrically old-fashioned pince-nez on his nose. "These girls are between fourteen and sixteen. You will certainly find among them the servant you're looking for. I'll have them presented to you."

But Victor-Flandrin specified that he would prefer an older girl, capable above all of looking after his children.

"Hmm," said the marquis, "there are few girls of that age left. They've already been placed."

He then drew from the pile another logbook, with a red cover, bearing the letter E.

"There are still five from year E," he said, after studying the book. "They are eighteen years old. There aren't any more older ones, the girls from previous years have all gone. I shall have these five brought in for you."

Then, adjusting his pince-nez, he added: "But you know, you're wrong not to choose a younger girl. The remaining five are only here still because nobody wanted them. They truly are the ones who've been left on the shelf, the rejects. Anyway, you'll see for yourself. You can always change your mind."

A warden organized the procession of these five unwanted girls. With his head buried in the red logbook, the marquis called the roll and each girl answered to her name by taking three steps forward and giving an awkward curtsy.

"Emilienne-Corpus-Christi-Mary!"

A little fair-haired girl, all breathless and covered with eczema, presented herself.

"Ernestine-Pentecost-Mary!"

This girl was so squint-eyed it was visually disturbing to look at her.

"Edwige-Annunciation-Mary!"

A tall redhead, affected with rickets, limped forward.

"Elminthe-Presentation-of-the-Lord-Mary!"

A girl with absolutely no hair at all stepped up.

"Eugenie-Rogation-Mary!"

This one began to gurgle in a triumphantly imbecilic manner that emphasized the vacancy of her face.

The marquis turned to Victor-Flandrin and asked him, "Do you still insist on hiring one of these? I did warn you — rejects!"

Night-of-gold-Wolf-face did not answer right away. He considered the five orphans a moment longer, then made up his mind. "Yes," he said finally, pointing to the girl with eel-like skin, whose impossible name he had forgotten.

The marquis started slightly at this choice and began to twitch oddly around the eyes, but Victor-Flandrin paid no attention to his reaction. His choice was made, and he was eager to leave this unsettling and oppressive place.

Night-of-gold-Wolf-face and the girl did not exchange a single word all the way home. Neither did they smile, nor look at each other. Indeed, Elminthe-Presentation-of-the-Lord-Mary had a strangely fixed hard look in her eyes, and this fixity was further heightened by her lack of eyebrows and eyelashes. She clutched a big gray canvas bundle on her lap. He noticed her hands: they were not the hands of a farm girl. They were extraordinarily long and thin, very finely nerved with tendons and veins, and knotted at the joints. As for her fingernails, they were so delicate they looked like pink insects' wing sheaths. Night-of-gold-Wolf-face continued to examine the girl furtively. In the end he could not have said whether he found her ugly or pretty, with her denuded skin, her smooth skull, and lashless eyelids. He merely found her strange; but the blue vein that snaked at her temple struck him as remarkable. Even in young children he had never seen anything like it. And because of this vein, he found her attractive, and since he just could not remember her name, he called her Blue-blood.

Mathilde had not a moment's hesitation about the physical appearance of the servant girl her father brought back with him — she thought her quite simply hideous and cruelly called her Baldy, as if the poor girl were not lumbered with enough ridiculous names already.

Raphael, Gabriel, and Michael were still far too small at the time to be surprised by their nursemaid's oddity. In any case, as they grew up they awarded her the same indifference, neither more nor less, that they felt for everyone. But Elminthe-Presentation-of-the-Lord-Mary took very little notice of what others thought and felt about her; she carried out her daily duties with equal diligence and detachment. Detachment was in fact her most striking characteristic. She was never seen to rebel, to lose her patience or composure, and she never betrayed the least boredom, tiredness, joy, or sadness. Whether she was called Holy Cross, Blue-blood, Baldy, the Eel, or the Fish, she would answer, "Here I am," in the same unchanging tone of voice, just as she used to respond to the various names and sobriquets with which she was dubbed by her custodians and sisters-in-adversity at Château du Carmin. For people in the outside world, she was simply "the daughter of a whore," and therefore, "a whore-in-the-making." She took it all with an even temper, and gazed on each of her detractors with the same cold and distant look that, with no eyelashes, was just like a statue's.

She all the more readily displayed this apparent imperturbable meekness, knowing her mind was elsewhere.

For she was totally removed from this world, having escaped from it at the age of fifteen. She made this escape after a dream. The dream, which had come in the midst of her sleep, had only one image: the eclipse of the sun.

She had seen a black disk creep up on the molten star, gradually covering it until in the end all that was left of it was a wavering band around the edge. Then a song had started. A truly fantastic song, inside her. Her entire body, now a huge empty drum, was transformed into pure resonant space in which this song, risen from the soles of her feet, swelled and traveled right through her. And as it traveled up through her body, various voices rose above the choir's very muted continuous canto. At her ankles, the voices of women singing alone soared to a crescendo; these gave way at knee level to very deep bass male voices.

When the song reached her stomach it was drowned by a peal of bells, in whose wake triumphed a solo female voice, very low pitched and gravelly. Then the choir reasserted itself, gathering up the solitary song in its swell, and then again quieted, allowing a male voice to pierce through at the level of her heart.

This voice was light, with plaintive accents like those of a beggar, or an idiot. The song then flowed up her throat and flooded into her head, where it swirled for a long time before settling down, like a pack of quivering dogs, behind her eyelids and in her mouth. But scattered voices rose again from every corner of her body, each returning the other's echo, now mounting to a cry, now dying away to silence: the beggar's voice inside her heels, like a gentle weeping; the woman's gravelly voice in the hollows of her elbows; the very dear voice of children in her hands, and also at the nape of her neck and behind her forehead — and then that most strange voice, neither a man's nor a woman's, half one and half the other, deep inside in her sex.

In the morning when she woke, the world had ebbed away, far away, from her body, mind, and heart. And she had found her bed strewn with all her molted hair, as if her body, which had only just reached maturity, had undergone some new metamorphosis. And she had also lost all memory. Nothing had occurred before this dream. She awoke washed clean of any past, purified of all history.

The next day she waited for her dream to return, but nothing happened, nor on the following days. The dream did not return until a week later, and since then it had recurred every Friday. She had not imparted the secret of this dream to anybody, and no one suspected that she had become the arena of such a song.

It was wash day. Elminthe-Presentation-of-the-Lord-Mary was stirring the laundry in a big steaming tub, in a corner of the yard by the cow sheds. Night-of-gold-Wolf-face, on his way to the fields, stopped for a moment. The girl had supple movements, with a sinuousness about them due to the reptilian look of her arms. But she suddenly made an even more snake-like gesture, when she threw against the cow shed wall the knotted handkerchief filled with blue powder that she had just been soaking in the water in order to bring out the whiteness of the linen. There was a splatter of bright blue against the wall. This splash dazzlingly rebounded in Night-of-gold-Wolf-face's eyes. He walked straight over to the servant girl, and came and planted himself in front of her, on the other side of the tub.

"Blue-blood!" he said.

The girl straightened up, taking her reddened arms out of the tub, and wiped her brow, which was dripping with sweat, with the backs of her hands.

"Yes?" she said.

Night-of-gold-Wolf-face tried to hold her gaze, but the steam rising from the tub completely misted her face.

"Blue-blood," he said again, "will you marry me?"

The girl raised her hands to her temples, threw back her head a little, then plunged her arms into the water again. The blue of her wet temple glistened fabulously.

"If you like," she replied, continuing with her task.

"But what about you," Night-of-gold-Wolf-face insisted, "do you want to marry me?"

"I don't know," she confessed simply, without interrupting her work. Then she repeated in a distant voice, staring peculiarly into space, "I don't know . . ."

4

Night-of-gold-Wolf-face did not seek to go any more deeply into his servant's feelings. She so blued his heart that he was determined to marry her — and marry her he did.

Appalled by this latest union, Mathilde warned him, "Be careful, with that frog face of hers she'll be spawning tadpoles!"

And Victor-Flandrin discovered Elminthe-Presentation-of-the-Lord-Mary's secret. He heard the song rise up inside his wife's body. He saw the breath of their voices swell her breasts and ripple weirdly through her limbs and up her sides. He saw the blue line at her temple fluctuate like algae under water and saw the pupils of her eyes open up, like eclipses. Holding her in his arms, he felt the extreme nakedness of her streamy-soft skin. He plunged deep into the dark trenches of her belly and mouth, and surrendered to the eddies of her song. And this song penetrated him, too, its echoes ringing inside him, sending the blood rushing lava-like through his veins. And when he yielded to the scourge of pleasure that flayed his back and lashed his belly, the harshest cry violently erupted from him.

Blue-blood loved this cry, she loved it even more than the fantastic song that inhabited her own body, so powerfully did it resound inside her, raising a great tremor within her flesh, like the tremor of the white barn owls' beating of wings, at night in the aviary at Château du Carmin. The world then resurfaced again, as archipelagos of reality amid the desert to which she had retreated, and she rediscovered things. She learned to love Night-of-gold-Wolf-face, and even to grow fond of the farm and some of those around her. But of all the children the one for whom she felt the greatest affection was Benoît-Quentin. To him she confided the secret of her song, and he in turn imparted his own secret; he told her about his mysterious little brother hidden inside his hump.

"The day will come," she told him, "when your little brother, too, will start to sing. Then you'll be the happiest of little boys! People will come from all over to listen to your song and they will weep to hear it, so sweet and beautiful will that song be, and they'll all be sorry not to have a hump like yours . . ."

Mathilde's batrachian predictions did not come true. Elminthe-Presentation-of-the-Lord-Mary gave birth not to tadpoles but to two sons whose only singularity was that inherited by all Peniel children. And life at Upper Farm began to return to the way it was before the war. The earth slowly recovered from the depletion and wounds the occupying army had inflicted upon it, the herds increased, the crops began to grow again, the houses rose up from their ruins, and Night-of-gold-Wolf-face even revived the magic lantern sessions in the attic.

Only the Jilted Bride continued to abide out of time, trailing her madness and her petticoats all day long through the countryside, to go and watch the train that came across the fields as it passed at about five in the afternoon on its way to that magical town where her wedding night awaited her. For her, the years were measured only by the wearing out of her petticoats; each year one of them fell to bits.

When the last of the Peniel sons, Baptiste and Thadée, were in turn old enough to go to school at Montleroy, Violette-Honorine decided the time had finally come for her to answer the call that had so violently afflicted her since childhood. Neither her father's anger, nor Jean-François-Iron-rod's tears could dissuade her from leaving and going to where she knew she was expected. At the age of seventeen, she entered the Carmelite order, accompanied by her sister, who preferred to follow her into exile rather than be separated from her.

"You were my little queen, my joy," Iron-rod told her, "what am I going to do now, without you? Who will have pity on me, where will I find happiness?"

Violette-Honorine gave the old man a pair of turtledoves that she had tamed, and he built them a cage so big it filled one corner of his hut.

Elminthe-Presentation-of-the-Lord-Mary awoke one morning feeling deeply disturbed. The image of the solar eclipse that began her great dream every Friday had suddenly ruptured. The black disk had gone and the star reappeared — not as the sun any more, but a purplish black rose; and the strident sound of horns and tubas had risen in the midst of her song.

This disruption of her dream sowed in her a fascination for roses, and she began to cultivate these flowers, with passion. She marked out a bit of garden behind the barns, which she screened off with a wooden fence, and she worked this patch of earth for months, planting every kind of rose she could lay hands on. Come the first flowering, the enclosure was submerged under a riot of rose blossoms. There were ramblers, bushes with large blooms, dwarf trees, and others with very tall stems. Then she started grafting and crossbreeding, continually seeking to improve the shape, size, and color of clusters and blooms. One of the loveliest rose trees was a weeping rose that she obtained by grafting a rambler with pliant branches on to the stem of a sweetbrier. But it was not so much shapes as colors that she strove to explore and perfect. And all these colors tended toward a single shade: purplish black, yet without ever quite achieving it. Only her dream knew how to make such a rose bloom.

The Jilted Bride sometimes used to slip into the rose garden. She would crouch down on her heels, in a corner, gathering up over her knees what remained of her old worn petticoats, and let her everlasting gaze of January 1920 wander over the mass of dark-colored roses.

"You'll give me some, won't you, you'll give me some for my wedding? But I'd like them to be white, like my dress," she always asked Elminthe-Presentation-of-the-Lord-Mary, who would then give her an armful of roses in response.

And the Jilted Bride would immediately start poking into the flowers, even tearing off a few petals, which she would then chew for a long time, with a dreamy look in her eyes.

All the children rushed into the yard when they heard the roar of the engine and the sound of the horn. They saw a black car rapidly getting bigger as it came up the road, and they only stood clear of the gateway just as the car came through it and swept into the farm-yard in a great cloud of dust. Gabriel and Michael ran after it, se-duced by what appeared to be a big stocky animal with a shiny black metal carapace, and by its strong smell of gasoline. They cir-cled around the machine for a long time, stroking its sides, with-out taking the slightest notice of the man who climbed out of it. He gave the youngsters hovering around his car a cold bleak look. He wore a light suit, a straw hat, and pale gray leather gloves that he tugged in a peculiar manner in order to get his hands out.

"This is Victor-Flandrin Peniel's farm?" he eventually asked, without addressing any child in particular.

"It is indeed, and here I am," replied Night-of-gold-Wolf-face himself, coming out to meet his visitor.

"A pleasure to see you again," said the other man, offering his hand. "I was passing by and I felt urged to pay you a visit."

Elminthe-Presentation-of-the-Lord-Mary, who was at that moment gardening inside her enclosure behind the barns, instantly recognized that voice and abruptly straightened up among the rosebushes she was pruning. In the suddenness of her movement she hurt her wrist, scratching it on a thorn. She not only recog-nized the voice, she recognized those words, some of those words. They were sickeningly familiar to her.

"A pleasure to see you," he had said on that occasion, coming up to her. "Wouldn't you like to take a walk?"

And without waiting for a reply, he had gently drawn her by the hand behind the barn owls' aviary. There, he had sat her down on the grass and had announced to her, while stroking her hair, "If you're good, very good, I'll show you her room. Would you like to see Adolphine's room?"

But she could not utter a word, not even a sound. She was ter-rified, aware only of the man running his hands through her hair, then slipping them under her blouse and touching her breasts.

"You know," he had said in a thick voice, "you look like

her... She had the same hair as you, with tawny glints, like yours
... yes, truly, you're very like her, I noticed it a long time ago... "

Relentlessly sounding at her back were the barn owls' raucous
and penetrating cries.

All of a sudden he had pounced on her, forcing her to the
ground and throwing himself on top of her, fumbling under her
skirt. Then everything inside her had completely seized up, her
body had stiffened, tensing so much it strained her muscles, and he
had not been able to force her lips apart or to penetrate her.

"Whore! Filthy little whore!" he had shouted right in her face,
brutally dragging her to her feet, and he had kept slapping her until
she dropped on the grass, unconscious. And all the time there were
the dismal cries of the barn owls flapping their white wings in the
aviary.

"Damn you!" he had continued to shout. "You look like her,
but you aren't her. You aren't her and you resist me! You aren't her
and you look like her and you torment me for nothing. Filthy little whore! You witch!"

His face bent over hers was as white as the barn owls, and his
crazed eyes, glistening with tears, were even yellower than the
birds'. The dream she had the following night had washed her
clean of all memory, and she had never since looked at the marquis
with anything but the same vacant and indifferent gaze that she
rested upon everybody.

But now all of a sudden her memory was fissuring, writhing in
the mustiness of reminiscences buried beneath more than ten
years' oblivion, and she felt sullied even in her love, her children,
and her roses.

"How's your servant?" asked Archibald Merveilleux du
Carmin. "Does she give you satisfaction? We've never had any
news of her. By the way, what was her name?"

Night-of-gold-Wolf-face confined himself to saying, "Her
name is Madame Peniel, I married her and am very happy."

The marquis gave an involuntary start. "What? Really?" he

said, looking askance at Night-of-gold-Wolf-face. "You are indeed a most strange person, Monsieur Peniel. People in the region say so, but now I'm inclined to believe it myself. For after all, to marry such a girl . . . a girl who . . . who . . ."

But he could not find the words to describe her, and suddenly, without any transition, he asked in a dry tone that sounded like an order, "I'd like to see her. Your wife."

But Elminthe-Presentation-of-the-Lord-Mary had already fled far from the farm; she had gone racing down the children's by-path and taken refuge in the fields, and there she had lain on the ground, in the hollow of the furrows.

The car was long gone when she finally decided to return to the farm. Night-of-gold-Wolf-face made no mention at all to his wife of the marquis's visit. Moreover, the marquis, with his final hand-shake, had left him with an impression of profound unease, almost repugnance, which he could not explain. Nor did he question Blue-blood on her incomprehensible flight into the fields, and he did not immediately notice the fine scratch on her wrist. With each new wife he observed silence, and each of his unions established itself in the sharing of this silence. It was more true of Blue-blood than of the other two that she never asked any questions and, still less, spoke of herself. She seemed to have been fashioned body and soul out of silence, right down to that very smooth skin of hers that imparted to her slightest movement the rippling impression of a fish darting in the watery depths. And it was the silence in them that he had most loved in each of his wives.

But inhabit silence too much, and in the end it rends with a cry. And this is what happened to Elminthe-Presentation-of-the-Lord-Mary. The following Friday her dream changed again: the eclipse shattered into pieces, giving way not to a rose this time but to the mummified face of Adolphine inside her shrine. She was grimacing a dreadful smile, and twisting her shoulders and hands, laughing. She actually laughed so loudly the usual song was completely drowned. Only the blasts of the horns and tubas could still make their piercing notes heard. Blue-blood's body was no longer an area of resonance, but a chaos of jarring dissonances. When she woke up, all streaming with sweat, she felt racked with painful contractions that wrenched her muscles. For the third time her body underwent a new metamorphosis — all her muscles tightened like bowstrings. And she recovered her memory, her entire memory. She saw with amazing precision every day of her life since the moment of her birth flash through her. She even saw her mother's face, the mother who had abandoned her as soon as she was born. She saw in the most minute detail the rooms, passageways, and staircases, the chapel and park at Château du Carmin. And all these spaces rang curiously hollow inside her. Her bones had become a network of empty corridors with an infinite number of doors leading off them, doors that kept slamming so hard they almost flew off their hinges. She saw her sisters-in-misery trooping along, dressed in black, gray, or brown. She saw her sons, Baptiste and Thadée, and young Benoît-Quentin, as she had never seen them before. She saw them to the innermost depths of their being, and her heart was overwhelmed with immense pity for them. She saw her husband from the moment of their first encounter, and the night-scourged face that was his in lovemaking. She saw each of the roses she had brought to bloom and the Jilted Bride's poor January gaze wandering among the rosebushes like a drunken bee.

All these images shot through her with violence, piercing her body like arrows. Her memory played the bowman and tightened her muscles with a vengeance, tearing them one by one, by overstretching them. In the end her whole body took the shape of a bow. And it let loose her dream, one last time, like some missile, sharp pointed in the extreme. The song swept through her like a tornado, gathering all the sounds into one single stridency that struck the eclipse's black disk. Then there was a fantastic clash of cymbals, sounded by the two unfixed stars, and out of this collision sprang the purple rose that then opened to reveal a rotating heart of fluorescent yellow. Her jaws slammed shut so forcefully that she smashed all her teeth against each other, and bit off her tongue. But this final shot was well aimed; it struck her right in the heart, which gave way like every other muscle in her body.

Elminthe-Presentation-of-the-Lord-Mary had to be soaked for several days in baths of hot water to relax her body, since Night-of-gold-Wolf-face refused to engage in any more bone breaking of the kind that old Valcourt and Melanie had had to undergo in the past. And so it was that Montleroy cemetery received a third Peniel wife, just as disjointed and just as much reduced to a doll — a doll of sound — as the previous two. As for the rose garden, it did not long survive the death of its creator. Night-of-gold-Wolf-face went at it with a scythe, and the last of the summer storms completed its destruction.

Raphael, Gabriel, and Michael, whom really nothing seemed able to affect, carried on totally regardless of the disappearance of the woman who for years had brought them up. They simply distanced themselves further from their other brothers and went further down the paths they marked out for themselves, on the margins of love. All they knew of love in fact were the most oblique cross trails that most deviated from tenderness and patience. Trails carved out on the precipice of desire, over a sheer drop into the void, riding on haste and madness, which they dashed along with reckless hearts. And these trails, like the magic paths that wind through the forests of legends, opened for them alone and immediately closed again after them. Gabriel and Michael, in particular, felt their bodies consumed by some unknown fire, speed-smitten to the point of dizziness, and they found no rest except at the limits of their passion, which they exhausted by dancing, fighting, running, and hunting in the woods.

As for Baptiste and Thadée, they were too young to appreciate the meaning and extent of the loss they had suffered by the death of their mother; they merely felt an obscure hurt to which they did not yet pay very much attention.

So Benoît-Quentin was left to face the mystery and anguish of her disappearance on his own, and he buried in a heap at the bottom of his strange hump-shaped memory all his recollections of Elminthe-Presentation-of-the-Lord-Mary. And later on, it was he who opened up to Baptiste and Thadée a shifting, twisting way back to their mother — a way of pure dreams that he unrolled before them like a bolt of rustling silk impregnated with a vague smell of roses.

He was also the one that looked after Jean-François-Iron-rod, who was gradually being caged in by old age, which created even greater fellowship between him and his turtledoves. Soon Jean-François-Iron-rod was confined to his hut, venturing no further than his threshold now, to take the air. Toward evening, he liked to bring a chair to his open door and sit there for a while watching the sky, inhaling the end-of-day smells, and listening to the sounds of the earth turning toward night. Benoît-Quentin often spent time with him. The old man and the child would then play at remembering, and the memory of one would flow into the memory of the other like bubbling spring water running through a standing pool, disturbing it and stirring up the mud.

5

And once again Night-of-gold-Wolf-face suffered the ordeal of loneliness. He took on a young farmhand to help him with those tasks he and Two-brothers could not manage between them, now that Jean-François-Iron-rod was too old to get about and Blue-blood was dead.

He saw his children, all his own motherless children, growing up around him — so far away from him. His ever-recurring, ever-increasing loneliness was constantly distancing everything all around him.

He no longer went hunting, no longer lit his magic lantern. He worked his land, tended his beasts, planted his fields and harvested them, and every night sank into an impervious sleep, bereft of dreams and memory. Sometimes he received a letter from his two Carmelite daughters, and Two-brothers would read it out loud to the whole family, but these words nurtured in the shadows and silence of a convent meant nothing to him. Besides, were they still his daughters, those far-removed enclosed nuns who had renounced everything — their family, their land, their youth, their bodies, and even their names?

Wherever were they now — Violette-Honorine, who had become Sister Violette-of-the-Holy-Shroud, and Rose-Eloise, renamed Rose-St. Pierre? His daughters were two strangers with untouchable bodies, invisible faces; two recluses, in exile for the senseless love of He who did not even exist — who had better not exist.

But were the elder girls any more his daughters than the younger two? Madness had alienated one of them from everything that was not her lost lover, and a hatred he could not explain had hopelessly distanced the other one. And what remained of his firstborn sons but this poor devil of a man with his twofold yet incomplete identity? As for those three wild young things from the forest, with their fugitive hearts and animal gaze, who were they? That left Baptiste and Thadée, and his grandson Benoît-Quentin — of all the children the one for whom he felt the greatest affection. For, truth to tell, while the terrible disgrace of a hump had been visited on him at birth, he had also been incomparably graced with the ability to win love, such was his gentleness, goodness, and infinite delicacy of heart and mind. Benoît-Quentin alone had the gift of consoling Night-of-gold-Wolf-face in his too burdensome and painful loneliness, as if the deformed child had loaded onto his own back the weight of all evils, all sorrow and griefs, the better to relieve others of them. Sometimes it even crossed Night-of-gold-Wolf-face's mind — an idea at once sweet and sad — that what his grandson carried inside his hump was none other than Vitalie's greatly comforting smile.

It was Mathilde who raised the alarm. It was already dusk and Margot had still not come home, although she had always previously returned from her wanderings across the countryside before the end of the day. For Margot was fearful of the evening shadows, which dimmed her January gaze and raised doubts in her; and what if Guillaume had left without her, if he had not waited for her and had taken the train on his own? Then she would lightly pick up her petticoats and walk quickly back to the farm, seeking refuge against her fear with Mathilde, who never failed to reassure her. As a matter of fact, she had only one petticoat left, the longest one, made of satin damask, trimmed with silk tassles. This last petticoat was actually no more than an old faded satin rag, all tattered around the edge. And she still wore the moldering purple curtain over her shoulders.

A search party was organized. All the Peniels, together with some people from the village, escorted by dogs, set out cross-country with torches and lanterns and cries of "Margot" and "Jilted Bride."

Night-of-gold-Wolf-face made for Dead-echoes Wood. He plunged deep into the wood without noticing which way he went. He roamed around for a long time, on the lookout for his daughter, hoping, at every sound in the night, to see her appear, but they were all unremarkable sounds, signaling only the presence of animals. His calls raised no echo, and Margot's name, which he shouted at every three steps, was instantly smothered in the dense silence of the close set trees. Eventually he sat down to rest on a rock that stood on the edge of a clearing. He was completely lost. A very pale glimmering began to lighten the sky far away. He slumped more heavily on the stone, suddenly overcome with tiredness after all those hours of walking and searching. He closed his eyes for a moment, but almost at once felt an acute pain in his left eye, as though pierced by an arrow point of fire; then followed a sensation of intense cold.

Night-of-gold-Wolf-face gave a start, and opened his eyes wide. This pain was familiar to him, familiar unto tears. And on the far side of the clearing, now bathed in the gray light of dawn, he saw two unfocused gleams pass by. Two very gentle and familiar gleams, like the January gaze that Margot had skimmed over people and things since she was wedded to madness. He tried to stand, to move toward that drifting light, to call out Margot's name, but he remained pinned to his rock, and could only weep, and weep, without even knowing why, until he was exhausted. He dreamed, wide awake; unless it was Margot dreaming through him.

He dreamed of a big four-poster bed, big as a room, with a canopy over it and purple velvet curtains. This bed pitched very gently as it floated down a river. He recognized the Meuse. But the river soon began to broaden, breaking its banks, and its waters becoming muddier and muddier. A woman in a white petticoat, sitting cross-legged in the middle of the bed, its curtains billowing like sails, was assiduously combing her hair. Her comb was a fish skeleton with very fine silvery bones. Tiny little fish, the color of chalk, fell from her hair as she combed it, and they darted off, just below the surface of the water, zigzagging in a funny way.

All vegetation had disappeared from the riverside. Looming over the river were high embankments built of stony earth and bristling with barbed wire. He glimpsed, but only very indistinctly, the silhouettes of men behind this barbed wire, and beyond them, the roofs of wooden huts with chimneys that continually belched out jets of black smoke. The silhouettes gesticulated in a very disjointed manner, twisting their limbs in every direction, as if these people were dancing or beseeching heaven.

The woman has stopped combing her hair; indeed, she has no hair at all now. She is kneeling on the edge of the bed, and with her body bent over the water, making ample motions, she is washing her tresses in the river, like a piece of childbed linen. The blood that flows from these tresses gradually dyes the river red.

But there are other washerwomen, all kneeling on little wooden boxes set side by side along the banks. They throw their laundry into the water and scrub it hard, beat it with round pestles, wring it, plunge it back into the water, and start all over again. Their laundry is neither cloth nor hair, but skin. Great sheets of human skin.

The bed is stranded in swamps of ash. The canopy is hanging all askew. The woman has disappeared, the washerwomen, too. Walking on the ashy water is a gypsy carrying a whip and leading a white bear on a leash; the bear is up on its hind legs and wears a bonnet that is sometimes square and sometimes round.

The bear is sitting in the middle of the bed, with its hat tilted over the corner of its eye. It is playing a tiny concertina, and swaying its head.

The gypsy, grotesquely dressed in Margot's wedding outfit, walks on the spot, pretending to advance. "Glassmaker! Glassmaker!" he shouts in an apathetic voice. His panes of glass, standing behind him, are engraved with pictures. These are portraits of women. Night-of-gold-Wolf-face recognizes them: they are of Melanie, Blanche, Blue-blood, Margot. "Glassmaker! Glassmaker!"

Another woman runs past, together with four young children. They are all naked and run with their hands above their heads; only the woman has her arms folded across her breasts.

"Ashes! Ashes!"

But this time it is not the gypsy shouting his wares; it is the bear. Or to be more precise, a man with a bear's head, wearing a little striped cap. He has the eyes of a haggard child.

The washerwomen have reappeared. They are walking by the river in single file, carrying their bundles of laundry on their hips. "Roses! Roses! Roses!" they mutter in incantatory tones. In the long line of them, Night-of-gold-Wolf-face thinks he catches sight of Hortense. "Roses! Roses! Roses!" The washerwomen's lament is like a light gentle breeze on a May evening.

Ash rain, of an extremely soft and silky gray, falls soundlessly from the sky.

The four-poster bed, the river, the banks, the washerwomen, the bear, and the gypsy have all vanished, leaving a doll with glass eyes sitting on a vertiginously high stool. Very bright searchlights fix upon the doll, their beams crossing each other at high speed. "Blood! Blood! Blood!" cries the doll in a breathless voice. "Blood . . . bloodshed . . . ashes . . ."

Night-of-gold-Wolf-face abruptly wakened. Throughout his dream his eyes had remained open. The sky was already rosy with dawn. He got to his feet and set off again.

Meanwhile, Nicaise, the farmhand, together with Benoît-Quentin, had scoured Little-morning Wood, and Two-brothers had searched Love-in-the-open Wood. They had no luck. Mathilde had made for the hill where her sister was in the habit of going to watch the train pass, as it came across the plain in the late afternoon on its way to her unconsummated honeymoon. But Margot was not on the hill either; there was no sign of her.

Mathilde tramped all over the hill until daybreak. It was on her way back that she found her sister. Margot must have slipped while running and had fallen into a ravine, striking her head against a stone as she fell. She was lying on her back, at the bottom of a swampy hole, in the dawn silence rippled only by the gentle croaking of frogs. One of these frogs, a tiny glistening creature, was hopping about on her shoulder. The Jilted Bride's last petticoat had been completely torn to shreds in her tumble through the brambles and rocks, and it gaped around her bare legs. She still had her eyes open — now more than ever with that lovely January gaze in them.

For a long time Mathilde leaned over the ravine, absentmindedly contemplating her sister's unmoving body and the lively little green frog. The whistle of a train crossing the valley abruptly roused her from her daze. She drew herself up and cried out, "Mathilde! Mathilde!" calling her own name instead of her sister's. But at that moment she could no longer distinguish between herself, who was nothing now, and the other, who had always been more than herself.

"Mathilde! Mathilde!" she said, calling across the silence of death, which had so peculiarly overtaken her by striking at this second body of hers. She called her own name to waken herself from this bad dream, to wrest herself from the silence, to bring herself back to life, to bring them both back to life. But vying with her was another voice calling her name. "Mathilde! Mathilde!" murmured this voice in the emptiness of her heart. And this voice was so white, so cold and sad, that it sent shivers running all over her skin and turned her hair completely white, as though her youth had suddenly been snatched from her.

Then, for the first time in her life, Mathilde began to weep. The tears she shed were tears of blood, for at last all that suppressed blood came flowing out of her body, all that denied forbidden blood, which for thirteen years had congested both her flesh and her heart.

It was in the months following Margot's death that Night-of-gold-Wolf-face decided to embark on a journey. Though he never ceased to extend his land holdings there, suddenly Blackland seemed to him too confined. Too many dead already crowded the soil he had been trying to make his own for close to forty years now. And he was the one who caught the train the Jilted Bride had so irretrievably missed. He entrusted the farm to Two-brothers, Mathilde, and Nicaise, and took Benoît-Quentin with him. They went to Paris. And there, in the big city, they lost themselves in the crowd, among the monuments, as at a fair. They stayed in a little hotel near the Quai aux Fleurs.

Benoît-Quentin loved the city, for there no one seemed to pay any attention to his deformity; people were always hurrying past. He was particularly struck by the women. He liked their brisk walk, their sometimes very startling clothes, their high heels, the way they had of talking with their noses in the air, with a shrill city accent. And then this river was so different from the one he knew back home. This was not a river with slow-moving waters, burdened with clouds and with the melancholy of vast landscapes traversed in silence, but a river with the same swift pace as the women, all twinkling with the lights of the city. You could keep crossing from one side to the other. Benoît-Quentin took pleasure in learning by heart the names of all the bridges over the Seine between Charenton and Issy-les-Moulineaux, as well as the names of all the quays.

The city was an endless surprise to him; it was like a huge magic lantern projecting new images all the time — but images that had body, weight and volume, movement, smell and sound. He found there, in broad daylight and in real life, everything he had so far only seen in the darkness of the attic during the magic lantern sessions. Night-of-gold-Wolf-face took him everywhere. They strolled around the railway stations, with huge halls, where trains, all frothing with white steam, kept arriving from every corner of Europe; they wandered through warehouses, and cemeteries that were bigger and more populated than his village; they went to the zoo, the cycle-racing track, the slaughterhouses, the covered markets; they went into stadiums, ice-rinks, museums, hospital quadrangles, and even the inner courtyards of apartment blocks. Night-of-gold-Wolf-face took him several times to the circus. Night-of-gold admired the horses, which were even more magnificent than those he had once seen at the Marquis du Carmin's. Benoît-Quentin watched the women. These women, all with wonderful headdresses and wonderfully bejeweled, had a way of drawing up their bodies and raising their pretty heads just as the horses came past, which enchanted him. They themselves looked like strange animals equally reminiscent of insects, exotic birds, wild cats, and griffins. He was in love with all of these women, who became confused in his dreams with the bridges, the river, the streets, and the quays.

But above all he loved the parks and gardens, with their fountains, their statues covered with chattering sparrows, and their big ponds surrounded by children playing with painted wooden sailing boats. And also their long avenues shaded by chestnut trees, where lady strollers made a delicious crunching sound on the gravel.

There was so much to see in these gardens, and so many things to smell, taste, touch, and hear, that he never tired of returning to them, mostly loitering about the green kiosks with pointed roofs, from which hung clusters of balloons of every color, windmills, skipping ropes, big wooden hoops, buckets, spades, tops, and shuttlecocks. Their narrow counters displayed an even more marvelous array — big jars of marbles, barley sugar, and sticks of licorice; bundles of lollipops; glass cylinders filled with pink and white aniseed balls; coconut tubs and boxes of toffee. And there were also traders selling chestnuts, waffles, gingerbread, and little pies, who touted around the puppet theaters, swings, and merry-go-rounds, their husky voices, full of languidness and enticement, mingling with those of the people hiring out goat-drawn carts, donkeys, and ponies.

But the loveliest sound of all was the shrill sound of the little barrel organs set in the middle of some of the carousels, to mark the tempo at which the children on their wooden mounts went slowly around and around.

Benoît-Quentin dared not ride the carousel; he felt already much too old, and besides, with his hump, he would soon have been the laughing stock of all the other children. So he sat on a chair, in the shade of a tree, and watched the little make-believe riders circle around on their brightly colored mounts — horses of gold, black, or brown, variously strutting and prancing; gray or white elephants; orange-colored camels and lions; giraffes; and very plump pink pigs. A big red pompom danced on the end of a pole held in the air by the keeper of this wooden herd, and its jigglings prompted shrill shrieks from the children, who stood in their stirrups attempting to catch it.

One day, on one of the merry-go-rounds in the Parc de Montsouris, Benoît-Quentin noticed a little girl riding a white elephant. She must have been about five years old. She had very fair hair that was a mass of unruly curls tied back with a big blue taffeta bow, and she wore a blue-and-white checkered cotton pinafore dress. Her face was amazingly small and pale, and full of a quaint seriousness. Her mouth was as tiny as her eyes were big — too big and dark for her face. She sat very straight and demurely on her mount, studiously holding the reins. The carousel attendant must have also noticed the little girl and been won over by her demure doll-like appearance for at every turn she jiggled the red pompom right in front of her, so that she might easily catch it. But the child never let go of the reins and seemed to pay no attention at all to the pompom that all the other little riders so eagerly coveted. When the carousel stopped she did not climb off her mount; she simply dug her hand into her pocket stuffed with tickets and held one out to the attendant for the next ride.

After the fifth ride, the woman eventually asked her, "Now, sweetheart, wouldn't you like to change to another animal, and ride a horse, or the lion?"

The little girl clutched the reins even more tightly and squeezed her knees against the elephant's sides.

"No," she replied, "I don't want to. I like the elephant." The woman burst out laughing and went on collecting tickets, repeating in a singsong voice, "Away you go then, elephant!"

Benoît-Quentin noticed that the little girl dropped the reins from time to time to stroke the elephant's ears and eyes very gently, and he even thought she said something to it under her breath. He never took his eyes off her, observing her every gesture, examining her features; and he was seized with passion for the child. He was dying to go up to her, quietly to ask her name, and to lift her in his arms and twirl her around. She was sure to be so light, so fragile to carry. He even ended up sharing the little girl's dream, that the elephant would come to life and climb down from the carousel, then go swaying off down the park avenues, swinging its trunk. He would lead the animal by the reins and accompany them, walking beside them in silence. And so they would go right across the city, then along the Seine, and they would continue like this all the way down to the sea. But he dared not get up and approach her; he was afraid of scaring her with his hump. And he thought sadly that it was a great pity the little girl had not preferred the brown camel ambling around three rows behind the elephant, next to a big rabbit with green eyes. It would have given him a little shred of confidence. He then began to search the crowd of women gathered around the carousel for the one that might be the little girl's mother. But he did not see anyone who looked like her.

An old woman came up to him and made him jump. She had a peculiar face, all furrowed with wrinkles, wrapped around with a flowery shawl so faded it was just a dirty gray now; and she kept one hand in the big baggy pocket of her apron that clinked with small change. It was the park chair attendant come to collect her fee. The calloused palm she held out in front of his face terrified him. It was as though she was showing him the lines of his own hand in the distorting and baneful mirror of hers. He clenched his fists in fear. So menacing was her hand, he almost expected it to slap him. The old woman grumbled and rattled her big money apron in annoyance. Benoît-Quentin hastily extracted a coin from the bottom of his pocket to send the old witch away. When he was finally able to turn his attention back to the carousel, the little girl had vanished. Another little girl with long hair had taken her place on the elephant. Anger and surprise almost took his breath away. He hastily jumped up and searched the crowd for the child's figure. He caught sight of her walking away down a side avenue, holding the hand of a woman wearing a green dress that showed her legs up to midcalf. The woman carried a big portfolio under her arm. He dashed after them and impetuously accosted the mother, without a good-day or excuse-me.

"Madame," he said, slightly out of breath after running, "your daughter . . ." But he did not complete his sentence, not knowing what else to say.

"What is it you want?" asked the woman, rather surprised. She was very dark, with bobbed hair, and her eyes were too big and too dark for her face. She spoke with a strong foreign accent that unnerved Benoît-Quentin.

"I . . . I . . . her name," he finally stammered. "I wanted to know her name."

He was standing now with his head bowed in front of the mother and her little girl, horribly embarrassed by his ridiculous audacity and by his so much more ridiculous hump.

"And why do you want to know her name?" the woman pressed him, looking at him with curiosity and amusement.

"Because she's so pretty . . ." whispered Benoît-Quentin, more hunchbacked than ever and almost on the verge of tears.

"*Liebchen*," said the woman, bending toward her daughter, "tell this young man what your name is."

The little girl looked at Benoît-Quentin with the same serious-ness she had displayed while riding the elephant.

"My name's Alma," she finally said after a moment.

"Alma!" cried Benoît-Quentin in total surprise. "Like the bridge?"

The mother laughed and said, "Like the bridge, yes. And my name's Ruth. It's your turn now to introduce yourself."

"I . . . I don't know . . ." confessed Benoît-Quentin, com-pletely nonplused. He wanted to run away as fast as his legs could carry him, but he remained paralyzed, with his arms dangling, and quite incapable of remembering his name. "It's the old woman," he kept saying to himself in his panic, "it's that witch of a chair attendant who stole my name!"

"His name is Benoît-Quentin. Benoît-Quentin Peniel," announced the calm voice of Night-of-gold-Wolf-face, who came walking toward them, returning from a stroll he had taken over to the group of bowls players gathered a little way off.

The arrival of his grandfather suddenly freed Benoît-Quentin from his fright and shame, and he turned to the little girl with a radiant smile. There now, he had a name as well, and a family. The little girl did not smile. She fixed her dark blue gaze on him, her eyes wide and her little mouth pursed, which further emphasized the disproportion of her features. But the child's gravity did not at all confound Benoît-Quentin's triumphant smile. He felt happy, infinitely happy, and he did not even pay any attention to what was said between Night-of-gold-Wolf-face and the woman called Ruth.

6

When Mathilde saw her father and young Benoît-Quentin come home with a woman and a little girl at their sides — the strangers' slate blue eyes too big for their faces — she bridled up and took an aggressive stance on the doorstep. She let them approach without going out to meet them, and her sole greeting was to shout from the top of the steps, with her hands clasped behind her back, "Well, father, you're back at last, and laden with baggage into the bargain! What are you going to do with these two?"

Night-of-gold-Wolf-face climbed the steps in silence, while the other three stood stock-still at the bottom, waiting. And when he came level with Mathilde, he replied, "Go and get us something to eat and drink. It was a long journey. We're tired." Then turning to the stranger and her child, he said, "This is Ruth and her little girl Alma. From now on they're part of the family. They'll be staying with us, here, at Upper Farm."

A peculiar shudder ran through Mathilde's body, and she threw back her head sharply as though she had just received, or rather delivered, some invisible slap. "Ah!" she cried in a crabbed voice. "So this is the fine present you've brought us back from Paris! Well, I don't like it, and I'll have none of it. Besides, this house has never wanted any of your women, it's always driven them out feet first! Not so, father?" Then, fixing her eyes on the newcomer, she added, "My father may not have told you, but he brings bad luck to women. All he can do is give them children, and what's more, two at a time! After which, he lets death carry them off, like bundles of dirty linen, and add to his flock of orphans. That's the way it is, my father has a widower's calling! So you had better leave at once before you join the other three Madame Peniels in the cemetery. Truly, you had better get back on the train and keep away from here."

Night-of-gold–Wolf-face was standing by his daughter, with his clenched fists dangling at his sides. He made no response.

It was Ruth who spoke. "Your father's told me everything," she said in a calm voice. "I'm not afraid, and I want to stay here with him."

Surprised by her accent, Mathilde turned to her father in a fury. "A foreigner, too!" she added. "That's all we needed! And, as if that weren't enough, a Bosch! You're taking your women from the enemy now? Bravo!"

"Mathilde!" Night-of-gold–Wolf-face burst out, in a voice thickened with anger. "I order you to be silent. I'm your father, remember."

Benoît-Quentin had his say. "For a start, they're not German! Ruth is Austrian," he explained, as if this distinction could mollify Mathilde. "And besides, if you don't like it, too bad. We're glad, and we want them to stay. And that's that."

"Well, let them stay, let them stay, these foreigners of yours!" Mathilde conceded. Then she added, "Let them stay — until death comes!" With that, she turned on her heels and went back into the house. As she turned, her dress gave a loud crack, as though its pleats were made of wood.

Alma, who had been listening to this discussion, looking grave and attentive, suddenly jumped at the sharp sound Mathilde's dress made and began to whimper softly.

"*Mayn Libinke,*" said her mother, taking her in her arms, "*vos vet der sof zayn?*"★

The little girl did not say anything, she merely pointed toward the door through which that terrifying woman, with her still youthful face and completely white hair, her nasty voice and wooden dress, had just disappeared.

Benoît-Quentin went up to Ruth and took the little girl's hand. "You mustn't be afraid," he said. "Look around you. All these fields, this land, these streams and woods are yours. They're yours to run and play in. And I'll be with you, always, to protect you. And I'll make you a fine wooden elephant, like the one on the carousel. Wouldn't you like that?"

Alma gave a little smile and nodded. Night-of-gold-Wolf-face came back down toward them, and taking Ruth by the shoulders, he invited her to enter his house with him.

When he crossed the threshold into his house, Night-of-gold-Wolf-face rediscovered in the darkness inside a coolness and gentleness of a kind he had forgotten, and that he had even thought lost for ever. He hugged Ruth in his arms and kissed her. He still could not believe in this new love and constantly marveled that such happiness should be his. He did not even know how it had all come about, everything had happened so quickly, and so simply. They had walked for a long time, very slowly, along the avenues of the Parc de Montsouris, and they had enjoyed being together so much they had continued their stroll into the evening, through the streets of Paris. The four of them, including the children, had even

---

★ Darling, what's the matter?

dined together at a brasserie in Auteuil, sitting outside on the terrace. Then, since they just could not tear themselves apart, they had met up again later, after the children had gone to bed, and walked arm in arm, like two old friends, through the deserted streets, talking about everything and nothing. Certainly Victor-Flandrin, who had always remained silent with each of his wives, had never talked so much in his life before. But there was in this foreigner's voice a kind of invitation to speak, to speak at length, free from all secrecy, and with great animation. Sometimes she would search for a word, and they would both stop for a moment and try to find it, and when at last he singled it out from the mass of possibilities, each of these words acquired a new resonance for him, a tone of playfulness.

In the end these words even acquired the maddening taste of kisses in his mouth, and when dawn came upon them unexpectedly, he caught himself feeling amorous desire. And without a moment's reflection, he had turned to her, seized hold of her head and kissed her. Then all words had become flesh and had put on a green dress.

That green dress dazzled his eyes and burned his hands still, he had not even waited for her to close the door of the bedroom to which she had taken him before tearing it off her. With that mad gesture which had so violently stripped Ruth's body naked, it was himself he had stripped to the heart, as though flayed. For the first time love was an anguish to him; with so many years and such differences between him and the young woman, he was afraid of losing her, no sooner having found her. This anguish had gripped him upon waking, while Ruth lay beside him, still asleep, with her head on his shoulder. He had run his hand very gently through her tousled hair and felt the warmth of her sleep — the warmth of her youth — beating under his fingertips. He had seen the green dress lying on the floor in the middle of the room, and suddenly he had dreaded seeing the dress go flying through the open window and disappear over the chimney covered rooftops, with his love being

carried away in its pockets to feed the early morning birds. Then
he got out of bed to fetch the dress and close the window.

"*Dortn, dortn, di Nacht . . . shtil un sheyn . . . dortn, dortn . . .*"★

Night-of-gold-Wolf-face turned around. Ruth was murmuring in her sleep. He came back to bed, with the dress rolled up in
his hands, and sat next to her.

"*Dortn,*" she repeated, "*der Vint blozt . . . in Blut . . . in Blut un
Nacht . . .*"† Her face then assumed a painful expression and she
cried out, tossing her head, "*Neyn! Neyn . . . neyn . . . ,*" and woke
with a start, staring at Victor-Flandrin with surprise and fright in
her eyes.

He held her in his arms and, rocking her gently, comforted her.
"There, there, it's nothing, a bad dream. Just a bad dream. Look
how fine it is! A wonderful day!"

"Yes, yes . . ." she murmured. Her voice seemed to come from
very far away, all fraught still with sleep and anxiety. Then she recovered and laughed when she saw her dress rolled up in Victor-
Flandrin's lap.

"What are you doing with my dress? It really is a rag now!"

And suddenly embarrassed, he had stammered, "Your dress? Ah
yes, here, take it. I had a bad dream myself just now . . . But it's
nothing. We're both awake now."

And the day got off to another start. A lovely bright clear day.
The light fell on the stone façades of the houses in patches of pale
yellow, like the reflections of water. They had taken the children
to another park and sat on a café terrace again. Night-of-gold-
Wolf-face recalled every detail of that day: the waiter and his tray
with clinking glasses, the small round marble table on which he
placed the blue glass soda water siphon, together with their drinks;
the little painted metal case in which Ruth kept her cigarettes, and
Alma's adorable laugh as she played with Benoît-Quentin; the

★ Yonder, yonder, night . . . quiet and beautiful . . . yonder, yonder.

† Yonder, the wind blows, in blood . . . in blood and night.

street trader pushing her cart loaded with vegetables across the road, and the cyclists riding along the pavement; the newspaper vendor, and then the woman selling balloons, who had come up to their table; the brief shower of rain that had started to fall without clouding the sun; the reddish brown dog that had come begging for a sugar lump.

"Where is it exactly, your village?" Ruth had suddenly asked completely out of the blue.

"Far away, very far from here. Very far from everywhere, in fact. It's right up in the north, a little bit to the east, near the border. There's the Meuse. And forests. Lots of forests. In the past there were even wolves prowling in them. And then there's the war, too, which always passes that way."

"And is it beautiful?"

"I don't know. It's my home. At least, it's become my home." He had not said anything else, because he wanted to ask her to come back with him, to see, but had not dared; he had been ashamed to. His poor little village, so dark, so remote, and his farm perched in the open, haunted with sorrows and with all those children running wild: it could not possibly be a place for a woman like Ruth.

"Suppose I came, to your home country full of forests, to see it?" she had asked. She had said this in such a lively, such a confident, tone of voice that she seemed already eager to leave.

He led Ruth into his bedroom.

"You know," she said when she was in the bedroom, "your home country's a beautiful place."

"But you haven't seen anything yet!" he exclaimed in amusement.

"It doesn't matter. I like it very much here. Your house, your bedroom. And the country, in fact, is you."

And she had been searching for this country for a long time. A home country where she could settle, where she could close the too heavy and too noisy book of days, of all those days, thousands of days, spent fleeing and begging. So it mattered little that this home was no bigger than a man, as long as there was a place for her. A genuine place that was quiet and out of the way. A place fashioned of desire and tenderness. Besides, countries that boasted vast areas, glory, and power meant nothing to her anymore. She knew that such countries could suddenly start shrinking until they were no bigger than a veil of mourning. She was born in the heart of one of the greatest of empires, had grown up amid its already nonchalantly festering splendors; yet in the end she had left what amounted to no more than a few acres of distressed land. It all began over a matter of blood shed, blood loss. The empire had started shuddering like an enormous and very old wounded animal — it had just been shot, somewhere in the back, in a place called Sarajevo — and on the same day her own body had started to stir: somewhere in her belly a strange wound had opened, had bled. Blood was spilled there, and the empire declared itself at war. A little blood flowed from inside her body, and she had been declared a woman. That doubly blood-bespattered day had deeply engraved upon her a confused memory, of bewilderment and pain — and violence, too: the end of peace and glory, the end of childhood. The empire had crossed the threshold of war, her body the threshold of womanhood. And the more she became a woman, the more men became corpses. Of her three brothers who went off to fight, only one returned, and this sole survivor did not even come back whole. He left his two legs and the best part of his reason at the front. Then, balking at the ruins and grief, her woman's body had also become a warring body.

For she suddenly fell prey to fantastic images, beset with garish colors, and hundreds of other bodies began to crowd through hers, demanding existence through her. So, in response to these appeals, she had armed herself with pencils and brushes, paints and knives, and she had captured forms on canvas and paper, in clay, stone, and wood. But these forms kept writhing, trying to bare their strength, to show it in the raw. She had stripped these bodies naked, unhinged their limbs, opened wide their mouths, slashed their eyes. She had done violence to their faces, making them gaunt and distraught — a violence to match the pity and madness that sapped them.

It was then that her father had come between her and those hordes of distorted faces and bodies. Her offense was great, he had told her, for she had dared to violate the Law by flouting the ban against depicting the human figure, and in addition she had also taken the liberty of outrageously mutilating these representations, already sacrilegious enough in themselves.

The memory she retained of this scene was seminal and dichotomous to the point of being self-contradictory. Her father suddenly appearing in her room, his shoulders so tall and massive they had obscured all the light when he stood with his back to the window. Her father dressed entirely in black, like a denial of all color and light. He had kept twisting his beard that was blacker than his suit, while he lectured at her in his hollow voice, at once forbidding and plaintive, his eyes moist, as much through anger as distress. He had started banging his fist on the table, overturning paintbrushes and saucers, then beating his chest as though trying to overturn his heart as well. A dull thud resonated from his black suit, from beneath his inky beard. And her father's beard had never looked to her so long, so thick, like the hair on a woman's head, upside down.

Then she had seen flash into her father's face the face of an upside-down woman whose eyes were two mouths, and her mouth two eyes shining with tears and fury. A woman hanging head down, with her disheveled hair lying loose over her father's chest. So which woman's head had he cut off like that and robbed of her hair? Her mother's: it was surely her mother's hair — with her bald head beneath her married woman's wig. And now he wanted to take away Ruth's hair as well, to rob her of her strength, of her images, and her multiple body, in order to reduce her to a single body under tutelage. But that could not be, for she belonged to another, more powerful than her father; she belonged to the power of an immense dream peopled with human images vibrant with color and violence. And this dream had invested her, the only daughter and youngest child of Joseph Aschenfeld, god-fearing trader of gloves, hats, and muffs, with a tutelary body, holding under its protection and inspiration these tribes of men and women with barbarous forms and anguished faces.

That same evening with a bold brush she had painted a portrait of her father. She had painted his face the color of plaster and marked out his eyes, mouth, and nostrils like cracks of scorched earth or rusted metal. Then she had cut off her hair — right up to the nape of her neck — and stuck it onto the still-wet canvas, like a great whiplash across the face. After that, she had run away, leaving behind that portrait of her derided father, cankered by the most vivid trace of herself. And since then she had not stopped running away, moving from town to town, living on virtually nothing, on luck and fresh air.

She had crossed Europe this way and that, she had lived in Berlin, Zurich, Moscow, Rome, Prague, London, and Vilnius. It was not her father she fled; besides, he made no attempt to find her. When he discovered the scurrilous portrait left standing there in defiance in the empty bedroom, he had registered his daughter's disappearance in the most extreme way: he had torn his clothes and covered his brow with ashes, and he had sat, stooped and bare-footed, on a small bench in the middle of her room, only getting up now and again to recite the Kaddish, as he had already twice done for his sons.

It was the portrait of her father that she fled, that dual and terrifying portrait, in which there was mingled as much violence and intransigence as grief and pity.

Even more than the portrait of her father, it was the portrait of her entire family, of herself, her people, that she fled. A plural face comprising the faces of men and women, the living and the dead, faces always set against the sky and against the earth. Faces raised very high toward a sky that was hard and bare like a great stone wall; faces bent very low toward an intractable and inhospitable earth. Faces that were never averted, although always engaged in struggle and hounded by fear and bereavement.

She had known the loneliness of friendships with no tomorrow, of love affairs with no memory, but with yesterdays fraught with shadows and noise. She had darned and mended, washed floors and dishes, read to old women and given dictation to children; she had modeled for painters and sculptors, and occasionally sold some of her own drawings and paintings on café terraces. And then Alma had arrived, so discreet and tiny she had made the want of a father weigh lightly. And this child, the chance result of a passing relationship, had changed Ruth's life.

It had been a slow change, inconspicuous but decisive. Ruth had gradually lost her rebelliousness and her impulse to flee, had shed her violence and fear; and those hordes of tormented images that for so many years had been ensconced in her heart and eyes had at last quit her. Sometimes some fleeting trace of them still returned, like laggardly cries lingering in her dreams.

She had been living in Paris for three years now, still doing all kinds of jobs in order to scrape a living and continuing to draw, from time to time. Her stroke had become finer, her colors lighter, to the point of transparency. Now she did little more than sketches, always incomplete, of trees, avenues, statues, and rooftops against big pale skies — but she drew no more portraits. And then Night-of-gold-Wolf-face had appeared and opened his arms to her, like a country that against all hope opens its borders to take in refugees. A free country. He was almost thirty years older than she, but he had kept a strange, untamed, and naive youthfulness of heart, which she herself had lost a long time ago. And it was this simple strength, forged of uprightness and endurance, that she had loved in him. Here, with him, she would find peace and be able to safeguard her daughter's happiness, whatever that grim woman with white hair might have said, who had fulminated against them from the doorstep on their arrival. For her trust in Victor-Flandrin was total.

And that was why she was smiling now, with her elbows on the windowsill, watching Victor-Flandrin put her cases on the bed. The time for flight was finally over, and her loneliness a thing of the past.

"Yes," she said again, turning back to the fields and woods that stretched below the window as far as the eye could see, "I like it very much here. It's so quiet . . ."

7

And Ruth did find the peace she had so much sought after. She even anchored her wandering self so well in Night-of-gold-Wolf-face's love and land that she became firmly settled there, and of this deep grounding four children were born. In the first year after coming to live in Blackland, she gave birth to two sons, Sylvestre and Samuel, who were joined the following year by two sisters, Yvonne and Suzanne. None of them bore any resemblance to that portrait she had fled for ten years, nor any trace of it; that affiliation was broken, another was established. The four children had the mark of the Peniels in their left eye. Only Alma remained fatherless and unmarked; her eyes, too big and slate colored, were a legacy only of her mother — and, perhaps, beyond that, her mother's mother, gentle retiring Hannah, whose features remained indistinct at the back of a shop selling all kinds of gloves, hats, and muffs, on a street corner somewhere in Vienna. But she had found in Benoît-Quentin a brother so loving, so devoted, that through him she had made this land her own. He had made her a wooden elephant, painted white, as he had promised her, and equipped it with wheels. For a long time he had taken Alma for rides on her elephant, along all the winding paths around the farm. Of all the children living on the farm, she remained for him the most beloved. He regarded her as his, at once sister and daughter, and sometimes in the confusion of the night he already dreamed of her as his wife.

With Ruth's arrival, a little of the outside world entered Upper Farm, and Night-of-gold-Wolf-face's fortress, for so long and so fiercely cut off, where time stood still, finally allowed access to outside sounds and activity. Newspapers and magazines, and above all the radio, slipped Blackland from its forgotten back-water moorings at the outer reaches of the country, if not of the world, and for the first time launched the Peniels on the tide of history. Only the older ones remained aloof and set their faces against this launching, which they deemed as futile as it was mis-guided. And indeed, what did Two-brothers care about hearing the distant murmur of history in the making at the four corners of the earth, when everything might all at once fly to pieces and burst into a discordant din without anyone having the time or the power to shout, "No!" As for Mathilde, history had come to a standstill for her upon Margot's death; it was now and forever too late.

These days, the magic lantern slowly gathered dust in the attic, while other boxes, more magic still, resounded with music and song, and caught on paper the everlasting smiles of family portraits. Ruth had gradually forsaken canvases and paintbrushes to devote herself to the art of photography. The tribes of grimacing images that had for so long obsessed her had completely receded and melted into oblivion. She had given birth to real beings, of flesh and blood, rejoicing in health and childhood, all play and laugh-ter. And it was now upon the faces of those around her that she fo-cused her gaze and all her attention, trying to track down through the portraits she made of them the buried traces of other images and imponderable likenesses.

Michael, Gabriel, and Raphael very quickly assimilated all this new energy that was relayed to them from the outside world and they became fervent devotees of the radio and phonograph. Michael and Gabriel became particularly keen on jazz; in its rhythms they found at last a cadence and verve to match their bodies, in their perpetual desire and movement. But soon the crazy need for speed, space, and violence that had spurred them since childhood exceeded all bounds. They ended up by leaving their kin, though they had never really considered them as such, and wandering off to live in the depths of the forest. They preferred to any other the company of wild animals, whose language they spoke and understood, and on whose flesh and blood they also fed. They themselves spoke little; they communicated more by sounds and gestures than by words. Never did they formulate the love they felt for each other; it was a love too absolute, too violent, to find any place among words. This love, too, they expressed through their bodies' vigor, and they became lovers even before they became men.

As for Raphael, though he did not follow his brothers into the heart of the forests, nor did he remain on the farm. He, too, went away, and it was his voice, a voice even purer than the whiteness of his skin, that tempted him into exile; it needed other spaces and other songs. He went off to the city and applied himself to perfecting his talent. He was only ever married to his voice, which was dearer to him than life, his sole love, and this mistress voice made him one of the most extraordinary countertenors ever known. But it did even more than that: it allowed him to pierce the silence and mystery of the dead. While his brothers understood and spoke the language of animals, and thrived only amid the indistinct resonance of blood, he learned to perceive the silenced voices of the departed — to respond to them, and even to call to them. And it was from this secret dialogue with the dead that his own voice acquired that absolutely unearthly tonality that none could hear without loss of reason for one breathless moment. For his voice had attained more than utter perfection — it had become a miracle of metamorphosis.

Not all the Peniel children became strangers to their land and kin. Elminthe-Presentation-of-the-Lord-Mary's two sons remained attached to both and did not leave their home. Their only extravagance was simply to fall hopelessly in love, one of them with a girl, the other with the sky. And the two of them lost their hearts on the very same day, in their sixteenth year.

On that day they had both cycled into town. The passions that were to ambush them were lying in wait at the corner of the main street, in a shop painted blue on the outside, with a sign that read Borromean Booksellers, where Ruth had asked them to buy a few coloring books for her children. Baptiste opened the door of the shop only to be left with the doorknob in his hand, and the sound of the shop bell made a fearful jangling inside Thadée's head, who was completely bemused by it. So they just stood there, on the threshold, at a complete loss, not even knowing any more what they had come in for.

"Can I help you?" asked a voice that emerged from the back of the shop. A young girl with braids pinned up around her head came toward them. She had a half-open book in her hand. Still clutching the broken handle, Baptiste glanced at the cover of the book but could not read the whole title: *The Princess of . . . .*

Then he looked up at the girl; she had almond-shaped eyes the color of dead leaves and a beauty mark over her right eyebrow. He fell madly in love with her, then and there, and immediately lost what little composure he had saved.

"Well?" she said, by way of encouraging them to say something, but both clients remained speechless.

Baptiste's sole response was to hold out the broken handle.

"Never mind," she said, "it happens all the time. I'll put it back again."

Since she seemed hampered by her book now, Baptiste finally

regained the power of speech and offered to take it while she fixed the doorknob. Thadée wandered off and began to rummage around the shop, while Baptiste opened the girl's book at the page she had marked. The passage he chanced upon so disquieted him that he began to read it out in a hushed, as it were confidential, tone of voice.

"Monsieur de Nemours was so taken aback by her beauty that when he came to her, and she curtsied to him, he could not help but show his admiration. When they began to dance, a murmur of praise was heard in the room. The king and the queen remembered that the two had never set eyes on each other before and found it somewhat curious to see them together, not knowing with whom they were dancing. They summoned the couple when the dance was over, without giving them a chance to speak to anyone, and asked them whether they would not like to know the other's identity, and if they had not some inkling."

Then he closed the book and held it out to the girl, who was still standing by the door, with her hand on the knob, as if she was about to go out.

"That's exactly where I'd got to when you came in," she said, taking the book. Then she added, "But the way you read it!"

"It's because I'm as much taken aback as that Monsieur de Nemours," replied Baptiste.

"And why's that?" asked the girl, trying the catch. "This isn't the Louvre and there's no ball here."

Baptiste thought she blushed slightly, and this emboldened him a little.

"There's you and . . ." he began warmly, but his voice immediately dried up and he did not go on.

The girl gave him sidelong glances, twisting the handle more and more nervously until it eventually came away again. They both bent down simultaneously to pick it up. They were now so close together they dared not move or even look at each other, and they remained crouched there, motionless, their eyes fixed on the doorknob.

Thadée had paid no attention at all to this scene; as he leafed at random through the books displayed on a big table in the middle of the shop, he had been arrested by a photograph of an eclipse of the sun and remained completely absorbed in contemplation of this image. It was only when he began to turn the pages of the book again that the other two gave a start, as if this quiet rustling had sufficed to rescue them from their embarrassment, and thereupon they both reached out to pick up the handle. But all they ended up with was the other one's hand, and again they froze, victims of increasing confusion. Baptiste squeezed the girl's hand so hard he must surely have hurt her, but she did not breathe a word nor try to release herself from his grip.

"Hey, Baptiste!" Thadée suddenly called out, still deep in his book. "Come and see this! It's fantastic!"

Baptiste abruptly stood up, and the girl, too.

"Come and see," insisted Thadée, all excited, "I tell you, it's fantastic!"

Since his brother was still not answering, he turned around, impatiently, and saw Baptiste standing stock-still in front of the door, beside the girl, holding her hand.

"Well!" he said simply, surprised at his brother's sudden intimacy with a stranger.

The girl, too, seemed surprised, as if she had only just noticed the twins' astonishing similiarity, and she began to look from one to the other and back, several times. At that point all three of them burst into gales of uncontrollable laughter.

"Well," Baptiste finally said, "tell us what you've seen that's so fantastic, then."

"It's true," said the girl, "it's your turn now to read out something."

And Thadée launched into a complicated account involving eclipses, moving planets, and shooting stars; a fabulous castle standing on a scarlet island where a huge astronomer with a silver nose held sway; an antelope that died from drinking too much beer; a big bronze globe on which the sky was inscribed; journeys, through snow and forests, made by princes, kings, and sages; a street paved with gold on the battlements of Prague; and the antics of a dwarf wise in madness and gifted with second sight.

From that day forward, Baptiste and Thadée often came back to town, making straight for Borromean Booksellers, one brother coming to court the girl in the bookshop, the other to further his acquaintance with Tycho Brahe.

Night-of-gold-Wolf-face let all his children follow their fancy. Time had less power over him than ever before, and he bestrode the days with giant steps. His lands extended so far now that his shadow could go wandering around, lightening any path, without risk of sending the dogs of some other master into a frenzy.

His memory was long and ran deep — there was not one of those thousands of days that constituted his life of which he did not retain a clear recollection. Many of those days had been full of pain and grief, but Ruth brought such intense brightness, such powerful joy to the present, that all of the past was thereby redeemed. And far from making him forget those he had once loved, Ruth's presence brought their faces into focus and captured them not in portraits but boundless landscapes. Melanie, Blanche, Blue-blood — they were all there, part of him, infinite expanses at last salvaged from the night, their blood in his blood, and their love forever in his heart.

Melanie, Blanche, Blue-blood — their names rang dear once more, like the names of fertile fields, of forests and seasons. Names and faces reconciled with life and with the present, thanks to that alchemy Ruth had been able to effect in his memory.

Though the world was no longer in the sight of God, it had nevertheless settled into a new position: Ruth was its fulcrum and point of equilibrium, or to be more precise, the focal point on which all things, all places, all faces converged, to take respite in comfort and happiness.

⤛ V ⤜

Night of Ashes

BY THAT TIME the Peniels had become totally landspeople, people of a land that was discreetly hilly, deeply penetrated with mists and rain, darkly forested, and with the very gray winding waters of a river cutting through it. An untamed land from which, come nightfall, rose the murmur of ancient legends about wizards and fairies, indomitable vagabonds, and wandering spirits. A land so often traversed by wars that it remained ever vigilant — land-memory on the alert, the blood of its past still pulsing through it.

But the sky above them was the same as in the days when they were still freshwater people: a vast windswept sky, of a gray slate color, dappled with luminous clouds, like the belly of some fabulous horse galloping on and on, over the earth's surface.

This grayness of the sky they carried deep inside them, ever and always. It reverberated even in their blood, their voices, and their gaze. Their hearts, too, were slate colored, fretted as much by the brightness of day as the shadows of night.

They had long washed their hearts in the terribly sweet waters of the canals, then they had brought them far into the fields and forests, and buried them under the earth among the stones and roots. And their hearts in turn had taken root, even flowering like wild roses, which were all of the same blood red.

Blood red.

The names of things and of roses acquired ever newer and stranger endings until they even became unpronounceable. There were men who actually manipulated the license to give names and the pattern of similarities, to such an extent that they completely perverted them. In fact they renamed everything and coated all things with a layer of black blood in which only a pattern of dissimilarities was now discernible.

They made blood rhyme with ashes and annihilation.

Blood red.
The names of roses and of men rent in cries and fell silent.
Blood-ash, blood-night-and-fog.
Then man made himself unnameable — and consequently God also.

Blood-god, no god.
God of ashes
Ashes and dust.

I

But the world according to Night-of-gold-Wolf-face, which Ruth's gaze had brought into the light, was to experience a gigantic and devastating eclipse. And it was not Ruth who detected the premonitory signs of this eclipse, any more than Thadée, the apprentice astronomer who spent his nights studying the stars in the sky. It was someone quite different: she who had renounced everything to such a degree that she had abjured her own being by surrendering her name to a terrible two word nomenclature — Violette-of-the-Holy-Shroud.

A letter came, written by her sister, Rose-St. Pierre.
"... It occurred so suddenly, in such a strange way, that no one here can understand what happened, and is still happening. It has been going on for more than three weeks now; that's why I finally decided to write to you. Several doctors have been to see her, but they don't understand it either. There's no explanation for the ail-

ment she has, and it's apparently incurable. But how can an illness be treated if the cause is unknown?

"She doesn't complain, as she has never in her life complained. And yet her suffering is infinitely great. But this is a suffering she feels in her heart. Only in her heart; that's what I believe. It's as though God wanted to wound the heart of the one who, of all us here, is the most devoted, the most loving. The blood, which on several previous occasions when she was a child had trickled from her temple for no reason at all, started to flow again. But not just a few drops, like before; it really is like blood from a wound. It's continuously pouring from her, her face is always covered with blood. She's so weak she has to stay in bed all the time, she can't go to prayers anymore, and she no longer has the strength even to eat or speak. The communion bread our chaplain brings her every day has become her sole nourishment.

"Yet sometimes she says things, but so faintly you have to bend right down and put your ear close to her mouth to hear her words. What she murmurs is so obscure it's difficult to understand. Anyway, they're not even sentences; she repeats words, always the same words, like: evil, God, world, ruins, ashes, agony. Her eyes have become almost impossible to look at there's so much anguish and pain in them. She has the look of someone who sees appalling things, things that cannot and ought not to be seen. I'm with her as much as possible. But I don't think she sees me, she doesn't recognize anybody now. She has this vision inside her, which is all-consuming, and which bleeds on her face like an open wound..."

Rose's letter went on, covering more than five pages with close tight handwriting. Never before had she written such a long letter to her family, never had she broken the rule of silence to such a degree since entering the convent. But something else was now breaking up inside her, irreversibly.

Night-of-gold-Wolf-face could not make any sense of this letter, except that his daughter was seriously ill, and undoubtedly to blame was the enclosed life she had imposed upon herself, for the love of an imaginary God — that God who only pretended to exist in order to abuse, humiliate, and afflict mankind. And his past anger, toward that God who had already proved his cruelty and violence only too well, returned to him. He was ready to go and remove his two daughters by force and bring them back home to the farm.

But Two-brothers remembered. He remembered Blanche, Violette-Honorine's mother, and the way she had died, what it was that killed her — what insane vision had killed her. And he understood what the others refused to understand, with the exception of Ruth, whose memory suddenly began to reverberate from the depths of so many centuries she could not count all the spectral faces that once more crowded her dreams — haggard flocks driven by a gray wind through emptiness and night.

The memory of her own people began to well up inside her like turbid water seeping from the depths of the earth, soaking through and altering the image of all things. It seemed to her that her children's faces, as well as the portraits she had made of them, became ghosted with superimpressions. Photographs, especially, exaggerated this phenomenon; the outlines of other faces, of another age, that had sometimes even been thought forgotten, began to show through these portraits wrested from time. All those photographs she had for years been taking and developing, so as not to forget what she saw then, now surprised her. For when she came to look at them, what she found in these photos was not so much the fleeting expressions of her children that she had wanted to capture as they grew up, but rather expressions that were much more prefigurative and ancient.

She saw the very thing she had forgotten, all her own people, the people she had had to leave, to flee, to deny. She saw that she had forgotten, and that such forgetfulness was no longer possible. Her forgetfulness had turned back on itself, forcing infinite undiluted remembrance on her. All those moments she had pinned down in her photograph albums, like little specimens of eternity, began to stir, to murmur. Something inside them was dissolving, altering; they were receding, carrying away her family's time-present toward obscure vastnesses opening more and more on time-past.

In the faces of her two sons, still so full of childhood roundedness, she glimpsed the faces of her brothers killed at the ages of eighteen and twenty, for the glory of an empire that disappeared with them, and the face of Jakov, the youngest brother, who had gone mad. Was he still alive, was he still living in her parents' house? But no, she knew very well that he could not be there now, any more than her parents. In the whole of her country there was not one house left to shelter her people. They had all had to flee, with their unlucky star sewn to their chests like a yellow target, a poor rag heart to tear. But then where had they gone, had they at least had time to get away? Was it even possible that her mother — whose morbid fear of her own albeit frail shadow had always kept her in the rear gloom of the family shop — had found the strength and courage to take to unknown roads? Her mother, whose excessive gentleness was reflected in every feature of Alma's delicate face. Really, she had hardly known her. It was only now that Ruth felt she was reestablishing contact with her mother, if not actually getting to know her, through her own daughter, who would soon be the same age as she was when she had run away from her family, her country, her history, and her God.

Her family, her history, and her God — it was all these things that resurfaced in the photographs she kept taking, retouching, enlarging, trying by these efforts to recover a memory that all of a sudden was pursuing her; a memory startled from its slumber and secretly scared by Rose's letter telling of Violette-of-the-Holy-Shroud's extraordinary agony, as if the young nun's blood fell on everything and everybody, even dyeing red the face of Ruth's father, which haunted her more than any other.

Her father, whose beard now seemed to her to be but a long weeping night. A night that after all these years had surely turned ashen. A sleepless night of vigil and unrelieved waiting.

It was as if the young nun's blood was welling up in everything and everybody, an inundation of the present suddenly muddied with the past and desecrated by the future.

". . . Isère, chief town Grenoble; Jura, chief town Lons-le-Saunier; Landes, chief town Mont-de-Marsan; Loir-et-Cher . . ." A schoolboy's voice inside Two-brothers's head chanted this off, imperturbably, buoying him up through long hours of insomnia. For he got no sleep now, as though he had to remain vigilant day and night so as to be ready to save his son, his one and only, as soon as the alarm rang out from St. Pierre's bell tower. Only Benoît-Quentin's deformity reassured him; the army would never make a uniform for a hunchback, he kept telling himself. Meanwhile, Benoît-Quentin was suffering a completely different torment — his boundless love for Alma. For it was his constant regret that his misshapen body was hardly one meant for desire.

Jean-François-Iron-rod was the only person not to be told what was happening to she who had been, and still was, the joy of his infinitely simple heart — she whom he called his little angel. Old age so lingered on in him that he seemed to have dropped out of time. He still liked to bring a chair to his door toward evening and to sit there, looking out over the land he had worked for such a long time, although his eyes were completely extinguished now and he saw nothing more than memories. Similarly, he was virtually deaf to the sounds rising from the earth, the cries of animals, or the voices of those around him. He caught only the song of his two turtledoves. He had always kept a pair, in memory of Violette-Honorine. Indeed, it seemed to him that he was himself turning into the cage in which his birds nested, and that they were perched there, on the very edge of his heart, gently cooing.

And when the bell tolled, he did not hear it. Death could find no access to his heart, nor any echo there, where his turtledoves dwelt. They protected him from all evil, from all alarm.

Yet this time the chimes were very loud, for there was no crack in St. Pierre's new bell; this bell had been cast in the consummation of victory and restoration of peace.

However, the crack had not entirely disappeared. It had simply been displaced, and it now appeared not in the bronze anymore but in the peace. It was for this reason that the bell rang out across the fields with such a full firm sound, proclaiming the great news to everyone: that the days of the energy had returned, the days of blood and fear, and this time they were gaining ground fast.

It rang so loudly that Gabriel and Michael heard it all the way off in the forest and they returned to the village, not to come home to their family, but to make another departure. A great departure, a real departure. For what the two brothers — these two blood-brothers and lovers — had instinctively felt was that at last the time had come for them to bring to the full light of day their passion, their violence, and the call of their blood, and to give battle all over the world.

And the camp they chose in order to accomplish their work, their great work, was the enemy camp. The blood work could only be achieved by that side, the side of the most intense hatred, of arrogant and destructive brotherhood. For they had a compulsion to kill. To kill, kill, kill. Until they made themselves breathless, until their bodies and their fury were exhausted, the fury that had clawed at their hearts and flesh since the very beginning.

2

The days of the enemy had returned with a vengeance, and there had been no one watching out for their arrival. But this time there was no prevarication; the enemy had come to stay. It must be said, it was still spring and everything happened so quickly that the summer months remained as delightful as ever, despite the ruins and the first dead bodies already strewn across the countryside.

The little village of Blackland, perched on its hill overlooking the Meuse, was not affected. It had simply slipped its moorings, drifting further from the rest of the country, and it seemed totally lost in the depths of its forests, like a hunted animal hiding in its lair, holding its breath. Actually, the whole country was dislocated and broken up into an archipelago. There had always been three Frances, but these were not quite the same as those; France was now divided, within its own borders, into three zones. One was called Unoccupied France; the other was declared Occupied; and the third was a prohibited zone. There were even more zones besides: some people sailed away on ships with other bits of territory in their pockets, to go and plant them elsewhere, in temporary greenhouses, in England, or Africa. And the city, the big city with parks and gardens, where Night-of-gold-Wolf-face had met his latest and greatest love, was held prisoner, in shame and grief, over there.

Over there. Here no longer existed, nor even today. There was nowhere anymore but over there, places that could neither be situated nor reached, and nothing but tomorrows gaping with fear. This new hastily drawn-up map kept springing surprises: a little town that nobody knew of, apart from people with liver complaints, was suddenly propelled to preeminence in this cataclysmic landscape.

The whole region of Blackland, by falling into the prohibited zone, seemed to have changed latitude. War latitude: the countryside was completely transformed by it. It was as though the land was hemorrhaging: crops, men, and livestock were rounded up and carried away over the border. Whole villages disappeared at the whim of a land register established from day to day by machine-gunning, fire, and bombardment. Weird forms of architecture sprang up all over the place: bunkers, air bases, camps, barracks, railway tracks — a concrete landscape with a barbed wire horizon.

Homes and fields underwent an abrupt change of ownership and function. The enemy reigned supreme in the best houses, driving out the population in great numbers, in order to settle in their stead colonists from distant regions in the east, and to send hordes of prisoners taken from every country to work over there.

At first, in the strength of its victory, the occupation force seemed to display some civility and even went out of its way to rally to its glory this scattered and defeated people lurking in the shadows of fear and resentment. But this did not last. In reality, the victory of might only gave rights and privileges to the victor; for the rest, it simply meant forfeiting their land and liberties, a state of affairs they regarded as temporary, to be reversed as soon as possible.

In the face of this intractability, the enemy openly declared its hatred and violence by means of red posters. The streets of towns and villages plastered with these posters became corridors of terror and death.

Blackland, which did not really have any streets, and whose only public building was the old washhouse, was for a while overlooked by the occupier, and the inhabitants of the little village almost forgot about the presence of the enemy they had only glimpsed through the windows of big black cars that now and again sped past them on the roads. But people had forgotten nothing of the enemy's former visitations to their part of the world, and they were well aware that death was no less on the prowl, that it must have been skulking in a corner, crouched, ready to pounce on them. It had always been so. Only they did not know exactly where, or when, or how it was going to strike. So they hunched their backs and kept silent.

The death they dreaded finally came. It manifested itself in the most bizarre way, striking not the living but the dead themselves. For war latitude meant this, too — surprise and derision.

A plane came down shortly before dawn, right on top of Montleroy cemetery. This time the church did not just lose its bell, it lost the whole bell tower along with it. As for the cemetery, it was three-quarters destroyed. Dawn broke to reveal, scattered among the ruins, the fragmented bodies of those the earth had actually been gnawing away at for a long time already. Faceless sexless bodies, sent flying higgledy-piggledy right up onto the rooftops of neighboring houses and into the branches of trees that were just beginning to lose their leaves.

For the parishioners of Montleroy such was the fruit picking of their first autumn in war latitude: they had to shake the remains of their long-departed dead down from the trees and bury them all in a heap in a communal grave dug under the armed supervision of the occupier, which for its part was only interested in one cadaver — that of the plane shot down.

This desecration of the cemetery, reduced to an anonymous ossuary, had a deep visceral impact on Night-of-gold-Wolf-face. It was his entire memory that had thus been ripped apart, violated. His entire memory, and his past loves.

Melanie, Blanche, Blue-blood, and his daughter Margot — all of a sudden their names pained him, and they started to darken and to burden his heart. His past, his entire past, lay in a common grave, snatched from history, deported from memory.

This time it was no longer possible to continue to ignore the fact: death and woe were well and truly back again. They had stopped prowling and had just made their first attack. And this attack had come in a surprising and crafty manner, from behind, targeting the past. But they were now going to assail the living, they were going to harry them at their flanks, then finally they would strike against them directly, head-on.

So it was that Blackland went further adrift, this time slipping straight into death latitude.

Benoît-Quentin thought he heard a very quiet moan coming from the other side of the fire, when the white elephant toppled onto its side in the midst of the blaze and burst into flames. He watched, to the point of distraction, Alma's delicate face, distorted by the flames dancing in front of her. Her eyes had never seemed so big to him. He did not even feel his father's fingers clutching his shoulders. Two-brothers was standing so close he seemed to be trying to take Benoît-Quentin into his own body, to hide him there.

The fire burned for a long time. This was because it was enormous; it had a fantastic pyramid of furniture, household linen, and objects to consume. As the flames rose, the surrounding snow looked as if it had long pink shivers running through it. It was strangely cold and at the same time scorchingly hot around this pyre.

The two little girls, Suzanne and Yvonne, had buried their faces in the folds of their mother's dress, and they scratched her arms in fear. They did not want to watch, they could not watch. Ruth stood still and wept in silence. She saw faces and hands endlessly rising, then fraying, in the intense black smoke billowing from the heart of the flames. All her albums were burned. Tears and flickering flames — even blinded, her eyes could see. And this black smoke was like a big crackling beard ruffled by the wind.

Only Mathilde stood apart from the group of women, her arms crossed on her chest, her white hair catching the firelight.

Night-of-gold-Wolf-face stood among his sons, Sylvestre, Samuel, and Baptiste. He reeled slightly, like a sleepwalker wavering between dreaming and wakefulness. His eyelids were still shaded by Ruth's hands, with which she had covered his eyes that very morning.

"Guess what I'm wearing today!" she had said.

When she took her hands away and he turned around, he had seen the green dress, the one from their first night together.

"You remember?"

"Of course I remember. It looks just as good on you as it did that day."

And it was true that her green dress fitted her just as well, as if neither Ruth nor the dress had changed after nearly ten years. The dress even carried in its folds and pockets, still, that grim shadow that had once so panicked him when he woke. That green shadow that now glowed red before the flames, and in which the two little girls had buried their heads. The shadow of ruin.

Even old Jean-François-Iron-rod had been ousted from his hut and dragged there; supported by Thadée and the farmhand Nicaise, he tried to apprehend the fire with his trembling fingertips, which he held out in space, before him. He kept hearing the terrible squawks his two turtledoves had uttered when the soldiers tossed their cage into the blaze.

When the fire had finally died out, the officer in charge of proceedings, who sat, with his legs crossed, on the only chair spared in this operation, rose and issued further orders. A second grouping was then carried out, which did not this time separate men and women, but those who had to leave and those who could stay. Then there was yet a third grouping, dividing those who had to leave: Ruth and her five children were separated into one group; the young men old enough to go and work for the Reich, Baptiste, Thadée, and Nicaise, into another. The hunchback was left aside being too deformed. But he was nevertheless deemed fit to serve the glory of the occupation army at least once. The officer had him issued with a gun and ordered him to shoot old Jean-François-Iron-rod, who was guilty of having concealed two turtledoves: in other words, two cunning messengers capable of flying counter to the winds of history in its triumphant march forward, and for which, as it just so happened, the officer himself was fighting body and soul.

Benoît-Quentin held the revolver flat in both hands and gazed at it in a distraught manner. He was on his own in the middle of the yard, before the pile of still-smoking cinders. All on his own between the officer and Jean-François-Iron-rod, who was desperately groping for support, so as not to fall over. The officer had a chair brought for the old man and even helped him to sit down on it. All the others had been driven back against the walls of the farm buildings and the house; they were only allowed to be spectators.

The officer repeated his order. Benoît-Quentin seemed not to hear, or at least not to understand a word of what he said. He looked alternately toward the officer and Jean-François-Iron-rod, with the weapon still lying across his palms. His back hurt; he felt as if something was moving inside his hump.

"My back is going to crack open," he said to himself. "An arm will come out and fire." This idea both terrified and comforted him. "An arm will come out . . ."

"Go on, do it . . ." murmured Jean-François-Iron-rod at last. "Don't worry, I'm already so old. They've killed my turtledoves, I may as well die, too, now. What does it matter . . . Go on, son, shoot, shoot then . . . quickly . . ." He whispered, nodding his head slowly, smiling strangely, with a sad absent look on his face. Benoît-Quentin's eyes sought Alma. He saw her over there, so far away, with her back against the cow shed wall, among her young brothers and sisters. Her eyes were so big they cast a blue reflection over the entire cow shed wall.

The officer repeated his order for the third and last time. His patience was running out; he warned Benoît-Quentin that if he did not within the next minute carry out the task entrusted to him, he, too, would be executed, for insubordination. The blueness of Alma's gaze was now reflected on every wall, and even on the snow, as far as the eye could see. It was all Benoît-Quentin could see, neither could he hear nor feel anything else. Only that: pouring from Alma's eyes, until all around was steeped in it, the slate blue color that trembled inside his own body like a long silent weeping. His back was sore, so sore he could have screamed. It felt as though a fist was trying to burst through his hump, punching with all its might from the inside.

He slowly slid the weapon into his right hand. It was heavy, and he did not know how to handle it. He raised his arm, took a few steps back, held his arm out straight in front of him, and very gently rested his finger on the trigger.

"Ha!" exclaimed the officer with satisfaction, and with his hands clasped behind his back, he moved a little closer to the chair to get a better view.

Jean-François-Iron-rod then began to utter a weird sound, a kind of cooing similar to his turtledoves'. He sat all hunched in his chair, with his hands crossed in his lap and his head bent forward, as though already preparing to topple off.

Benoît-Quentin cast a final glance at Alma, then adjusted his weapon, holding it with both hands. He pointed it at the condemned man, aiming right between the eyes, and fired. It all happened very quickly. He had found his mark, and the victim instantly fell on his face. Jean-François-Iron-rod was still cooing softly to himself, seated on his chair. Benoît-Quentin threw the weapon to the ground.

There were shouts on all sides, and a great scuffle over by the cow shed and barn walls. But order was quickly restored by means of blows delivered with rifle butts.

A few soldiers rushed toward Benoît-Quentin, who just stood there. They came straight at him, waving those bizarre devices with which they had set fire to the pile of furniture and things less than an hour earlier. Night-of-gold-Wolf-face wrestled with Two-brothers and pinned him face to the wall, so he could not see.

There was a low hissing sound. Benoît-Quentin saw three jets of liquid fire come whistling toward him. He only had time to catch one last glimpse of Alma's eyes, then everything was engulfed in a blaze. His body instantly caught fire; he was streaming with flames from head to foot. Jean-François-Iron-rod's cooing sounds expired in a shrill squawk. He, too, had just caught fire, and was being burned alive, sitting in his chair.

Benoît-Quentin wanted to shout out Alma's name, to call to

her and tell her at last how much he had always loved her and how much he desired her, at that moment more than ever before. But instead of Alma's name — the name of his sole wonderful love — it was something else that he cried out just as he dropped to the ground, consumed by the flames.

"The chair attendant!" he screamed.

Behind his burning eyelids, he had just seen the old chair attendant in the Parc de Montsouris drawing a flamethrower from the big pocket of her money apron, with which she was setting fire to all the people sitting in chairs and all the white elephants.

> "*Sheyn, bin ich sheyn,*
> *Sheyn iz mayn Nomen . . .*"★

Alma had started singing in a very little-girlish voice. She had the look of someone not in her right mind. She was ordered to stop, but she went on singing regardless.

> "*. . . Bin ich bay mayn Mamen*
> *A lichtige Royz.*
> *A sheyn Meydele bin ich,*
> *Royte Zekelech trog ich.*
> *Gelt in di Tashn,*
> *Vayn in di Flashn . . .*"†

She was brutally hit in the chest with a rifle butt, which left her winded, but she immediately continued with the same song in an ever reedier voice.

> "*Shrayen ale sheyn,*
> *Sheyn, bin ich sheyn . . .*"‡

★ Pretty, I am pretty,/Pretty is my name

† A pretty little girl am I,/I wear red socks,/There's money in our pockets,/Wine in our jugs . . .

‡ Everyone calls me pretty/Pretty, I am pretty . . .

The next time it was a bullet that hit her, in the throat. Her song ended in a gurgle of blood, while she very slowly sank to the ground, amid her brothers and sisters, whose shoes were soon dyed red.

The children and Ruth had no time to react; they were already being herded into trucks, with much bullying and shouting, together with Baptiste, Thadée, and Nicaise. Hurried along by these shouts, only little Suzanne murmured, but so low that nobody could hear it, ". . . *Bin ich bay mayn Mamen a lichtige Royz . . .*"

3

There were only Mathilde, Night-of-gold-Wolf-face, and Two-brothers left in the yard. The convoy had long since departed and they had been standing there, rooted to the spot, for quite a while. Night-of-gold-Wolf-face still held his son pinned to the wall; he dared not release his grip, Two-brothers's heart was beating so violently. He was afraid that if he let go of his son's torso, it might burst like an unhooped wooden cask. Yet all of a sudden strength and thought drained from him, and his arms dropped like two bundles of rags. Everything inside him went limp, gaping imbecilely. He had just heard the hollow sound of the heartbeat in his son's body suddenly stop. And on the instant came that sharp pain in his left eye.

Two-brothers slowly crumpled, his forehead scraping the wall, and he sank down on to his knees.

With his arms dangling, in a complete daze, as though just emerging from a dream, Night-of-gold-Wolf-face gazed around the yard, at the big pile of ashes in the middle with the two charred bodies beside it, and Alma huddled against the cow shed, her head haloed with a huge nimbus of blackening blood.

"So . . ." he said in quiet and surprised voice, "it's all over? That's it, then?"

Even the day was drawing to a close and the evening shadows

were slowly climbing the hill. It was perhaps to these shadows that his question was addressed.

He pointed to the children's bypath and said, "He came along there. I didn't even recognize him. It seems like only yesterday..."

But in fact everything seemed like only yesterday — Melanie, Blanche, Blue-blood, and all his children, the fifteen children he had fathered, and Benoît-Quentin. Yesterday.

In any case there could be nothing but yesterdays now, nothing else. Time itself had been consumed by the fire, along with their possessions, furniture, and bodies. There was no present any more, there would be no future. All that remained was a fantastic dream, caught in a time warp.

Night-of-gold-Wolf-face turned to his son, knelt down beside him, and picked him up in his arms.

He recovered his strength, he recovered his memory — a memory stricken with as much sorrow and grief as love. He carried Two-brothers to the steps leading to the house and sat down there, with his son's huge body lying across his thighs.

"It's all over," he repeated. "It's all well and truly over . . ." And he talked for a long while, in an undertone, almost smiling at times. He talked to his kin, to all his dead, to all his departed ones. He talked on like this until it was dark, imperceptibly rocking his son on his lap and stroking his face. He also talked to the night, to the wind, that began to blow again, and the snow that began to fall.

"Father," Mathilde suddenly asked, "what are we going to do . . . with all these bodies?" Then she added, "The earth's completely frozen. Impossible to dig . . ."

Although so simple, these words she used were difficult to say, so weighty had they become, and her speech was ponderous, hesitant. It was as though her mouth had silted up.

All these bodies. To dig. These words were so heavy, so black, and yet icier than the ground. She paced around the yard, with her arms hugged against her chest, not even knowing which cold she was fighting against in this way, the coldness of the night or the coldness of the words. Nor dared she return to the farmhouse; she knew it was empty, its windows and doors smashed, the floorboards ripped up. She could not go in, for there was no house left; there was only outside now.

Father. All these bodies. To dig. These words kept drilling their unintelligible sounds into her head, which was as empty as the house. They slammed against her temples, like unhinged doors swinging in the wind. One word detached itself and began to bang louder than the others: Father. Father . . . father . . . .

But her father was not looking at her, maybe he did not even see her. He was talking to the night and to the dead. She was colder than all those dead people and felt infinitely lonelier. Father, father, father . . . Would she, too, have to die before her father took her in his arms and comforted her in this immense pain that hurt her so much? Did she have to die?

And she was overcome with the desire to lie down in turn with all these broken bodies, just like them. She walked straight up to the pile of ashes covered with a thin layer of snow, and threw herself on top of it.

"Underneath," she said to herself, "underneath the fire may still be smoldering. Underneath it must be hot . . . hot . . . ."

She began to dig in the ashes, rummaging through the charred remains, searching for embers. She only succeeded in grazing her hand on a piece of iron. This wound, something vital at last, roused her from her torpor and immediately took away her taste for ash.

The object on which she had just grazed herself was a long iron box, all oxidized by the fire. She recognized it at once, and that is why she did not open it. It was the box Two-brothers had brought back from the other war. It did not much matter now knowing whose arm — Mathurin's or Augustin's — was fossilized inside it. She buried the box under the ashes again and stood up.

"What am I doing?" she thought, dusting down her dress, which was covered with ash. "My place isn't here. I'm still alive.

Alive. I'm alive. My father and I are both alive. Ash is for the dead. Yesterday's dead and today's. Not for me."

That already ancient arm in its corroded iron glove could rear up, for all she cared, it would not catch her. So let it grab those other bodies. All those lifeless bodies. Since the earth could not be dug, let them all go into the fire, every one.

"Father!" she cried, turning to Night-of-gold-Wolf-face. "We can't just sit here! We must burn the bodies. Otherwise wild beasts will come. The earth's too frozen, we can't dig it."

"The earth . . ." Night-of-gold-Wolf-face reiterated, like a very distant echo, "the earth . . ."

He was not even answering Mathilde; he was simply talking in his sleep. For he had fallen asleep, sitting on the threshold, with his eyes wide open, still clasping Two-brothers. He was now holding him like a very small child — this his firstborn son, yet with such a big body, and such heavy feet.

He was sleeping and dreaming. He was dreaming of the earth — this earth that was not the land on which he had been born. And this could well be the reason why it had never really wanted him, and why now, in addition, it was rejecting even his dead. So he remained a freshwater man — all that he had ever been was someone passing through, who had only strayed among landspeople. The truth was, it was impossible to penetrate the land, impossible even to inhabit it. Of course he had dug it for a long time, for seven years he had even descended into its black bowels, and for nearly fifty years he had worked it, plowed it, made it fertile. But all this now proved to have been just scratches on the surface, which immediately closed up again, leaving no trace. Having been a boatman rejected by the rivers, now all he was was a peasant rejected by the land, a lover and father rejected by love, a living being rejected by life, yet without being accepted by death. He belonged nowhere. For this reason he was in no hurry to rise from the threshold on which he sat sleeping.

He dreamed of the earth. Its copper and golden heads of grain, its green and blue grasses, its springs and forests, its flowers the color of fingernails, eyes, lips, or blood. Of all this, nothing remained. Frost and ashes.

"The earth . . . the earth . . ." murmured Night-of-gold-Wolf-face as he dreamed.

Dawn was beginning to break; hazy pinkish-white glimmerings touched the horizon.

Yet it was not this increasing light of day that woke him, it was the red glow of the flames. Mathilde had lit a big fire in the very same place where the soldiers had built their bonfire the day before. She had gathered straw from the cattle sheds, long since emptied of their livestock, and had piled up all the pieces of wood she could find. Then she had dragged over to it the bodies of Alma, Benoît-Quentin, Jean-François-Iron-rod, and even Two-brother's body, which she had had to wrest from his sleeping fathers's embrace. All these bodies were heavy, with the terrible weight of death and coldness, but also very tractable. And besides, Mathilde drew a renewed and fierce strength from having so abruptly come to her senses, finding herself still alive, at the very moment when she had thought of giving up. She contemplated this second fire, a purifying and beneficent fire this time — a good fire, which brought together again what yesterday's fire had sundered and freed the dead from their mortal frames, committing them to the wind.

Night-of-gold-Wolf-face rose and slowly advanced toward the fire. He said nothing. He, too, watched those peculiar flames in which the remains of his children and his old companion crackled and gradually disappeared. He did not even rebel; he had no anger or hatred against God left in him. What purpose would it have served, since heaven was as forsaken as earth, as empty as his house? There was no other God but all those he had so dearly loved and who were now burning in peace before his eyes. He watched the slow metamorphosis of God into ashes and said nothing.

It was completely light now. The sky was the same silky gray, verging on white, as the pile of ashes; as though it, too, had been burning all night. The wind had risen, as day broke, skimming across the snow and already scattering the ashes.

Night-of-gold-Wolf-face and Mathilde finally entered the deserted house. The wind blew in through the broken windowpanes, whistling along the walls. The silence and emptiness of the place gave a sharp resonance to these whistling sounds and carried them from room to room. They were like speechless, rhythmless voices, reduced to a mere breath. Disembodied voices, voices emanating from no mouth, which shot off in all directions. A host of toneless voices scared by their immense inanity.

Mathilde turned to her father. He was standing with his back to her, in the middle of the room, his arms hanging loose and his head bowed toward the ground.

"After all these years, all these tribulations, only to return to this!" she inwardly exclaimed, her heart all of a sudden seized with astonishment. For her father had just appeared to her exactly as she had seen him twenty-five years before, as he stood facing her mother's bed. His shoulders were simply broader, and also more stooped. Was he going to burst into sobs as he had that day? The love she bore her father was nothing but violence now, and infinite pity, battling so much inside her it wrung her heart.

She clasped her head in her hands. The room had started to spin and the walls to pitch. Yes, she had kept her promise, she had remained absolutely faithful, always at her father's side. She had never left him, neither for love nor death. Of the fifteen children he had begotten, she was the only one to have remained with him, through thick and thin. But in the end, what had been her reward for such loyalty? Nothing but indifference and betrayal. She felt violence overtake pity and turn to anger. Then everything blazed into an implacable sense of derision. She chewed her fist so as not to scream, and fell in a heap on to her knees. Then she burst out laughing. After all these years, all these dramas, of love, jealousy, and grief — to come back to this, to return to zero! She drummed the floor with her fist and shook her head, shrieking with laughter.

Night-of-gold–Wolf-face went up to her and said, "Mathilde! Mathilde! What's the matter with you? Stop it, please, I beg you! Get up, stop it!"

This laughter caused him pain, so false and wicked did it sound. He knelt down beside her and took her hand.

"I'm here," she started shouting in the midst of her laughter. "I'm still here. Me! Me! When all the others have gone, I'm here! But why, tell me, why? You've never loved me, neither you nor anyone else. Hah! I'm here, and there's no one to notice or to love me . . ."

Her hair had come loose and fallen over her face, into her eyes and mouth. Trails of her white hair glistened like tears on her face. She raised her hand to push her father away, but her hand dropped onto his shoulder and clutched it tightly. He took her in his arms and let her weep against him. Her scalding tears ran down his neck, under his shirt.

When she had stopped crying, she almost leapt up, briskly brushed her hair back, and declared in a firm voice, "We must set to work now! We'll have to make a fresh start."

Once again she had regained possession of herself.

4

And they set to work, with their bare hands, with no other motivation but the necessity to fight step by step against the encroachment of emptiness and the most terrible sense of tedium.

But they were soon given further motivation. It was a young girl who brought it to them. She arrived one evening, with nothing but the clothes she stood up in, and the child that was only just beginning to stir inside her. She came from town on foot and had walked all day to reach Blackland. For the town, too, had been burned. Bombers had flown over it and dropped more bombs than there were houses. There was not a single stone left standing in the

town, now turned back into an abandoned quarry. Nothing remained of Borromean Booksellers, with its fine blue shopfront —
neither roof, nor walls, nor books, not even the bookseller and his
wife, who were crushed beneath the ruins. Only their daughter
had escaped, and with her the child she was carrying, Baptiste's
child. This was why she came seeking refuge at Upper Farm.
Night-of-gold-Wolf-face took her in, as he had once taken in
Hortense and Juliette.

Pauline's arrival soon gave faces and bodies to all those mouth-
less voices that still lingered in the empty rooms, for she was so
keyed with expectation that Night-of-gold-Wolf-face was caught
up in the impetus of her feeling. She rescued him from the coldness of his immense loneliness. She was incapable of doubting
Baptiste's return. The war must end, she was always saying, just as
the other war came to an end. Besides, was it not already being
whispered almost everywhere that the occupation forces had that
depressed and harassed look that always comes upon them when
they sense their defeat is imminent? Was it not being said that the
enemy was running out of steam in its endless push into the desert
wastes of snow that extended way over there in the east, and that
the farther they advanced, the closer they marched to their down-
fall? Baptiste and Thadée were not at the front, they had only been
deported to a labor camp, somewhere in Germany. So it was best
to wait, willing their return so strongly that their desire might at
last, and quickly, become a reality.

While failing to force destiny and bring the exiles back home to
the farm, Pauline's stubborn hope infected Night-of-gold-Wolf-
face like a fever of the heart that was to persist until the war was
over. His loved ones had been taken away, admittedly he did not
know where, or even really why, but it could not be in order to
kill them, too. What happened in the yard the day the farm was
searched, with fire and bloodshed, had only ensued from the insanity of one officer and a series of terrifying misunderstandings.
But it was not the rule; it remained a monstrous accident that could

neither continue nor happen again. Yet recently he had four times felt that searing pain in his left eye with which he was only too familiar, but he had ignored it and refused to attribute any significance to this phenomenon.

It might even be, he came around to thinking, that his wife and children would be safer from the war in those camps, guarded by the enemy itself, and perhaps they would suffer less deprivation and hunger than if they had stayed on his disaster-struck farm.

While he could just about imagine what a prison camp or a forced labor camp might be like, he could not at all picture to himself the camps where the Jews were taken. In any case, he had never really understood what it meant to be Jewish, and the anti-Semitic propaganda disseminated by the enemy had not illuminated him on the matter, one that he had never before considered. Ruth had told him one day when they first met, "I'm Jewish, you know." No, he did not know, and he had not even seen what there was to know. The sole difference between them that he noticed was the difference in their ages, and this was the only thing that had worried him at the time. But even this he had eventually forgotten. The happiness of his marriage had wrought a confluence of their ages, as of infinitely slow sweet waters. It was only now that earlier remark of Ruth's came back to his mind and really confronted him with the issue. Yet he could find no adequate response to this absurd issue, and in the end he always reached the same conclusion: Ruth was his wife, his beloved, and would return to him with their four children, as soon as the uhlan's great-grandsons had been buried in the snow at the ends of earth, which they were trying to invade.

Yes, Ruth truly was bound to return to him, with the children. And not just for their own sakes, but for the sake of the two whose deaths he was unable to accept. For it was on Alma and Benoît-Quentin that his thoughts dwelt, even more than on his son and Jean-François-Iron-rod. He could not believe what his eyes had seen that day: Benoît-Quentin, his fondest companion, to whom he owed his encounter with his last love, all streaming with flames. And Alma, the eternal child, with eyes of greater immensity than time, the girl with a heart yet bigger than her eyes; her singing like a weeping of blood.

For the sake of these two, now turned to ashes, he had to be re-united with Ruth, so that in addition to their own love they could live out the love their children had not the time to live. He was well aware that only with Ruth could he find solace . . . and re-dress. For they were the only ones now who could give faces, in defiance of death, to those who had been, and still remained, among the most wonderful parts of themselves. And the others, too, would come back to him: Blanche's daughters and Blue-blood's sons, and even the other sons he had fathered in the depths of Love-in-the-open Wood, although he had not received any news of them since the beginning of the war.

As autumn approached, Pauline gave birth to a son. She called him Jean-Baptiste. This new birth on the farm, like those of all the Peniel children over the past half-century, gave Night-of-gold-Wolf-face renewed hope. So it was not in vain that he had rebuilt the walls of his house, rehung the doors on their hinges, replaced the shutters on the windows. Within these walls, which after all enclosed not emptiness and the outside any more but an inside, a real inside, a new cry had just risen, a new body stirred, craving in all its flesh after life and time. He was even more overwhelmed by this cry than the cries of his firstborn sons, for he perceived in it as never before the bitter and vital beauty of this world that was endlessly starting over again. Truly, a cry marking a new be-ginning, bringing life-giving hope and strength to this insane waiting, this most taxing vigil. Now he no longer doubted the return of all his loved ones. The cry of the newborn baby was none other than the as yet unformulated announcement of their return.

•

Pauline, even more than Night-of-gold–Wolf-face, saw her son as the bearer of this stubborn hope to which they both clung. He was the child of her youth, conceived on the very brink of dreamland, on a day of rain and nakedness.

How well she remembered that day! She and Baptiste had set off on their bikes. They had left town and cycled straight toward the very dark and luminous gray patch lying on the horizon, flush with heaven and earth, as if it were waiting for them and they had no time to lose in getting there. But before they reached it, the patch had suddenly spilled over the whole sky, which the wind started to buffet, like some vast gray awning, sending crazed and screeching birds scattering.

"It's going to rain. We'd better turn around and hurry home," Baptiste had said, resting his foot on the ground.

But the first drop of rain had fallen at that very moment. A very big, very cold drop that splashed onto his forehead and trickled down to his mouth, leaving a taste of stone and tree bark on his lips. And this taste immediately traveled through his whole body, lashing his flesh and his heart with deliciously violent desire.

"No, let's stay here!" she had suddenly said in a low and determined voice. "The rain will be so heavy, so beautiful! And besides, it's already too late."

She had then seized him by the hand and led him over to the embankment. The downpour had finally started, and the rain was pelting their shoulders and faces. They had dropped their bicycles at the side of the road. They had slid down the bank and rolled to the bottom of the ditch, where the grass was already turning muddy. Her skin was so thirsty for rain, for cold and the heat of passion combined, for caresses and kisses, that she had stripped naked in order to surrender herself totally to Baptiste and to the water. One of the wheels of the bicycles left lying on the edge of the bank had spun in the air for a long time. Looking over Baptiste's shoulder, she had watched that wheel spinning in the rain, like a steel sun, until it made her dizzy.

It was there, at the bottom of that ditch, silky with rain, moss, and mud, on a day of extreme nakedness, that she had conceived her son. He was the living and daily-growing memory of that wonderful day of insane love — her love, her desire, reaching out to all the earth around in the endlessly teeming rain — with the sky above them, inside them, like a gigantic drum rolling with deep hollow resonances.

Indeed, it was for this reason that she nicknamed her son Little-drum. And even more than being the bearer of hope and the keeper of her love, Little-drum was the forerunner of the victory to come and the happiness that was to return. Was not the first time he uttered that magic word of childhood, "Mama," the very day the world had learned of the defeated enemy's surrender, in the snow and the cold, on the far-off Eastern front? And had he not taken his first steps the day the enemy, defeated once again, on the other side of the world, had quit the African territories? A little while more and the child would be talking, would start to run and sing, then it would be the turn of their own lands to be liberated at last from the enemy. And Baptiste would come home.

The more time passed, the more the child grew up, and the more their hopes rose. At the same time, however, the occupier sensed that the ebbing away of its glory, which it had thought would surely last a thousand years, was gathering pace, and strove desperately in consequence to reaffirm its presence by means of extensive raids, lootings, and executions. A number of villages, and even towns, had become no more than hamlets, so many houses had been burned down and the streets emptied of their inhabitants. The war was not content anymore to creep along the ground; it had taken on wings and was sweeping through the sky as well. All those planes that flew upon the night really did seem to be an integral part of the sky — clouds, of a kind, that had dropped from the heights in order to rain down their steel and fire, or sometimes even strange white birds that got caught in the trees. One of these birds had actually landed right on top of the roof of Upper Farm one night, injuring a leg in his fall. Night-of-gold-Wolf-face had hidden him in the house, where he was looked after until he recovered from his injury. He spoke a language that no one at the farm understood, yet he managed to convey to them what he had come for. As soon as he was better, Night-of-gold-Wolf-face took him, by night, to Dead-echoes Wood. For in those days the forests harbored not only wild beasts and a lasting memory of wolves, but also hordes of men at odds with history who had come to take refuge there. It was no use the enemy's hunting them down and occasionally capturing them, and then executing them; they could never catch them all. There was no end to the number of trains in the area that were derailed, bridges blown up, convoys exploded, and soldiers killed. In war latitude, the fate of everything was always being disrupted like this, and nothing was achieved except by destruction.

Only the earth remained inalterably the same, an immemorially age-old body endowed with fantastic vigor, all set to continue, without fail, its eternal cycles.

This is what became apparent to Night-of-gold-Wolf-face, within the very limits of his stationary exile. It was borne in upon his mind all of a sudden, in a terrific flash, one day when he was coming home across the fields with a load of wood on his shoulders. He had halted, so struck with amazement it had taken his breath away. The unthinkable thought of God had just reentered his heart. But it was no longer that God who had for so long been seated directly over the world, far, far above, like some giant firebird perched beyond all light, and beyond time, raining down on men's brows once a year. Nor was it the God in whom Pauline believed, that God of flesh and mercy she prayed to every day on her knees at her son's bedside. It was a faceless, nameless God, immanent in the earth, made of stones, roots, and mud. An Earth-God that rose up in forests and mountains and flowed in rivers, and even abounded in winds, rains, and tides. And men were nothing but the more or less ample flourishes of this most recondite body wrapped in its perpetual dream. After all, what was he, Victor-Flandrin Peniel, but a heavy-handed flourish slowly dropping back into the depths of night, having sketched a few incomplete parabolas and scattered a few reflections of that dream in passing — a dream infinitely vaster and of longer duration than his own life?

He was only one flourish among thousands of others. And the war, the war that kept returning — like the harvest, the equinox, and women's menses — that, too, must have been divine; for, just like him, it was one of this Earth-god's flourishes, made in the continual stirrings of His troubled sleep. But the dead were even more divine than the living, than love, forests, rivers, or war, because although still imperfect, they were flourishes already accomplished, flourishes furled in the earth's bosom. They were part of the Earth-god's sleep, of the incredible sweetness of His dream.

Night-of-gold-Wolf-face had dropped his load of dry branches and just stood there in the middle of the field, aware only of that extraordinary combination of heaviness and lightness whirling around inside his body. A combination, too, of derision and gravity. He had gazed around for a long time and taken immensely deep breaths, as though to get a better appreciation of all this space around him — this space from which he would one day disappear, leaving no more trace than a gust of wind blowing through the leaves of a beech tree. And then he had experienced that strange sensation of his whole being rushing to his feet. For, after all, his presence in the world would never exceed the limited surface area of the soles of his feet. And he had started stamping his feet on the ground with heavy thuds as if to call to witness all his dead, now homogeneous with the mud, and to shake that Earth-god from His unseeing slumbers for a moment.

Then he had continued on his way, rearmed with hope, aware at every step of the sovereign weight of his body, the body of a living man still infinitely full of desire. He no longer felt rejected by the rivers, the earth, and love, as he had at the beginning of this recent spell in war latitude, but simply deflected to the very far edge of this mysterious and crazy dream of which he had just had an intimation, and which he wanted to waken.

5

Was it Night-of-gold-Wolf-face's stamping or Little-drum's light-footedness as he gamboled around the farm that got the better of the Earth-god's long sleep; a sleep made sluggish by His brutal flourish that for years had given the world the name of war and doomed multitudes of men to death? Once again people dared to expose themselves to the strong light of summer. For they felt strong in those words that reechoed from every corner of a country that was gathering itself together again: "They've landed!" "Paris is liberated!" "They're coming . . ."

The days of the enemy were numbered. The occupier was in hasty and disorderly retreat toward its own borders, at last recognizing its true limits. But as its army fled, it made a few more random halts in villages on the way and took pains to obliterate both the buildings and the men inside them.

So it was at Blackland. A fleeing convoy suddenly decided to stop there. The trucks parked in a neat row, soldiers got out, formed ranks, then improvised with absolute rigor and a sophisticated sense of staging an opera performed in three acts.

An opera of blood and ashes. Act one: having searched every house with total thoroughness, from the cellar to the attic, they cleared out all the inhabitants, whom they then directed to stand in the street around the well. Once they had these chance extras in place, they moved on to act two. They caused exceedingly red and raucous voices to burst forth from all the houses, by throwing a plethora of incendiary grenades into them. The stage was thus magnificently set, and with the choir of red voices in full song, they brought the heroes of the drama to the front of the stage.

The men, all either very young or old, were taken to the wash-house. They were ordered to kneel in the little wooden boxes, stuffed with straw, that stood around the basin, and, using wash-erwomen's beetles, to strike alternately on the water and the edge of the washboard, in rhythm. Act three was now reaching its cli-max. Outside, the scenery was still throwing up its tall flames. The women, congregated around the well in a single shapeless body, listened distraughtly to the strange cadence their men were bang-ing out, down on their knees in the washhouse. Only one small group of women stood apart. There were six of them, stiff and silent, with their arms crossed over their black shawls. It was a long time since these dry-eyed widows, their bodies crackling with loneliness, their hearts starched with grief, had had any men to weep for. They watched coldly as the curse of their house of wid-ows extended over the whole village.

There was a sudden change of tone. The rattle of machine-gun fire had just broken in on the drumming of the wooden beetles, almost instantly silencing it. The sound of bodies falling into the water was at once counterpointed by the immense cry of the women, sharply off pitch.

The last act over, the soldiers, still orderly and perfectly silent, withdrew and continued on their way. They did not get as far as Upper Farm, for they had not a lot of time; they had only arranged this brief impromptu opera in order to add a last minute footnote to history, now on the turn, signaling their most sovereign con-tempt for the conquerors.

When the liberators arrived, there was nothing left to liberate. All they found, in the middle of the village that had been reduced to ashes, were demented women floundering around in the wash-house, fully dressed, trying to drag out of the sticky red water heavy bundles of clothes ridiculously encumbered with bodies. Among these liberators was Nicaise. He had never reached the labor camp he had been dispatched to, after the raid on Upper

Farm. He had jumped from the cattle train taking him there, along with a few other companions, hurling himself headfirst into the night. And he had immediately started running, straight ahead of him, and not turned around when the train stopped with a long-drawn-out whistle, and guns began firing repeatedly behind him. He had run with the energy, stamina, and instinct of a wild dog tracked by hunters, as if he had drawn animal strength and intelligence from traveling in a stock car. A wild dog more vigorous and cunning than the dogs trained by these manhunters who had abducted him. When one of these dogs caught up with him and got him by the leg, in order to reveal his whereabouts and deliver him into the hands of its masters, he in turn had rounded on the beast, grabbing it by the throat, and strangled it.

He had run for all he was worth, all night long. Indeed, he felt he had not stopped running since that day, as if thousands of other dogs of death were continuously on his heels, day after day. And even when he had at last reached the sea and set sail with other companions of darkness encountered in his flight, it was as though he was still running on water. And when he returned, parachuted into the heart of these forests in the middle of the night, he seemed still to be running through the sky. The war had turned him into a perpetual runner who never looked back, never stopped. This extraordinary stamina for running that he had developed had saved him from every ambush laid by the enemy.

But now at last he was running in the opposite direction, not before the enemy any more, but behind. He had become the hunter, the pursuer. And it was as such that he entered Blackland, his native village. Yet he had to admit the fact that he had not learned to run fast enough, for this time the enemy had outrun him. Before even setting foot on the ground, he realized he had come too late, irretrievably so. Of Blackland's seventeen houses only one was left standing — the most isolated: the big farmhouse perched high up on the skirts of the protective forests. Of all the others, there remained nothing but smoking ruins. For once he had lost the race and would not be entering his parents' house as the triumphant liberating runner. And he felt himself become suddenly heavy, so very heavy and painfully encumbered with his living body — the body of a man who had escaped with his life more than a hundred times. So very heavy and derisory.

He stood rooted to the spot, by the well, incapable of taking a single step toward the old washhouse that rang with cries, wailing, and the sound of splashing water. His body no longer obeyed him. He was totally incapable of doing two things at the same time: seeing and walking were two irreconcilable acts. He watched; he could not move. Some soldiers had gone into the washhouse only to come straight out again and start vomiting against the wall.

Then the women came out. He knew them all and yet could not recognize a single one. All had faces distorted by a common madness, and dresses soaked and stained with blood, as if they had all risen from some dreadful collective childbirth. Among them was his mother, or at least a grotesque and terrifying double: a fat old woman, her hair all disheveled, dripping with red water, who convulsively flailed the air with her hands, reeling and groaning. He felt such violent disgust that he staggered and had to reach for the wall of the well to support himself. What on earth had this old and crazy mother of his just given birth to?

She went straight past without even noticing him. Had seeing and walking become irreconcilable acts for everyone? She was walking and could see nothing. He tried to call her, but no word issued from his throat, only a cry. A weird cry that frightened him, like the cry of a newborn baby. His cry was caught by the well, into which it dropped, resounding with a vast gloomy echo, distorted with emptiness.

His mother heard not the cry but the echo. She stopped, turned, and finally recognized her son in the body of this young man hunched against the well. She rushed up to him and shook him by the shoulders, then forced him to raise his head, shouting his name in his face.

"Nicaise! Nicaise!" repeated the well in its gray voice.

He opened his eyes and saw her again. This time he recognized her. This was indeed his mother, with her kind eyes and loving smile. She had regained her face, her real face. He clung to her, burying his head in her bosom. His mother's soaking wet dress exuded a stale and nauseating smell — the mingled blood of his father and younger brother. But he staved it off, receptive only to the very sweet warm smell of his mother's throat.

Upper Farm had been spared. Night-of-gold-Wolf-face opened his house to the women survivors who had nowhere else to go. He turned the barn and the cow shed, still empty of tools and livestock, into dormitories where the women moved in with their children. Apart from Nicaise, he was the only man left in the village. He still had no news of his other five older sons, or of Ruth and her children. Yet, a patriarch ruling over a flock of mad women, he felt even more dispossessed than all these widows and orphans. Having waited so long for the return of his family, and waiting for it still, he felt his heart lose patience and his desire rise up in revolt.

The return started in the following months, but rapidly dried up. The first to come home was Baptiste. He had not found the courage to jump from the train, like Nicaise, or to try to break out of the camp where he had been imprisoned. Thadée had escaped when they were very first interned, and no one knew what had become of him.

Baptiste had endured his long detention and carried out his forced labor with total submission. But why, and where, could he possibly have fled? There was only one place in the world for him to live — and that was with Pauline.

Pauline, his place, his land, his boundless space. Beyond her, there was no space — no time, even. Escaping to get back to her would have been completely pointless since she was living in the zone where the enemy reigned supreme; he would right away have been recaptured and separated from her again. He had preferred to suffer a stationary exile, rather than worsen the pain in wandering, for then his craziness for her would have lost all proportion. He would have sought her everywhere in his flight, behind every tree in the forest, on every street corner. And, even more important, he would have run the risk of being killed, and that he could not do, for it would have meant losing her for all eternity. So, since he was just as incapable of living or dying away from her, he had taken refuge in waiting, gutting time of all duration and forcing on himself a total absence from his own being. He had not even been aware of that part of himself that had suffered from hunger, cold, exhaustion, and illness. This had occurred somewhere in the forsaken and barren regions of his body, without impinging on his thoughts that were solely obsessed with Pauline. His companions had ended up calling him Crazy-for-her, since he talked so much about her, even in his sleep. In fact, he not so much talked in his sleep as cried out — her name. He cried her name in pain as much as in desire, for night brought into his every dream Pauline's naked body, offered to the rain, to love, to pleasure. It was this body, with its skin so bare and streaming wet, and now untouchable, that obsessed his heart and flesh, until he had to cry out.

And here he was, home at last, with no other glory than of having been absolutely true to his love, with no other wartime nickname than Crazy-for-her. He returned like a shadow for a long time separated from its body, that upon finding it again and recovering flesh and life starts to quiver, terribly, with joy.

But it was a twofold body that he found. Pauline came toward him carrying a little boy in her arms.

"You see," she said, holding out the child to him, "there were two of us waiting for you! I knew you'd come back. Thanks to him, I never doubted it, I never lost hope. Our son looks so much like you! I watched him grow, and saw you coming back to me, through him."

•

Thadée did not get back until a long time afterward. Yet he had announced this tardy return with a postcard bearing these simple words: "I'm alive. Although I have to learn how to live again. I'll be coming home. But I don't yet know when, for I have to make a long journey before I can return. And anyway I need to recover. Love and kisses — but how many of you are there left to kiss?"

For a long time the card was passed around among Night-of-gold-Wolf-face, Baptiste, Pauline, and Mathilde. Each of them in turn was arrested by some part of this message and wondered at it. Why must he learn to live again since he said he was alive? What was this detour he mentioned, and what illness did he have to recover from? And then what was he doing on Lake Constance? The card had been posted from Lindau.

But other questions tormented Night-of-gold-Wolf-face. He was still without news of Ruth and the children. Why did she not come home now that peace had returned? Why did she not write a postcard at least? The detour that Thadée spoke of, perhaps it was to go and fetch her? Ruth.

Baptiste and Pauline decided to wait until Thadée returned to be married. He had been witness to their first meeting; they wanted him also to be witness to their marriage. And Little-drum, too, got caught up in this waiting game. He imagined this uncle, who said he had to learn to live again, as a man who had turned back into a very small boy, as small as himself. His uncle would be his companion.

The man Little-drum saw arrive was not very small; he was the same size as his father and looked the very image of him. But he came with two children at his side: a little girl of twelve and a little boy of about five. Their names were as peculiar as their appearance. They were called Tsipele and Shlomo; they spoke, or rather whispered, some incomprehensible language, and they never let go of each other's hand, as if they were afraid of losing each other. Their eyes, kept shyly lowered, seemed to fear the light of day and the sight of faces.

"I promised their father that if I found them I would take them home with me to look after them and bring them up. They have no one left in the world," said Thadée, introducing the two children.

Their father had been his companion. They had slept on the same mattress, eaten from the same mess tin, worn the same garment woven in shame and cold, and suffered the same slow agony for more than a year together. But whereas he was still alive, his companion had died. He had died on his feet, one morning at roll call. His number went unanswered and had dropped into the register of lost ciphers. It was at Dachau. Thadée had then armed himself with his promise, in order to hold out against that other roll, called in the camp every day, at every hour, by death.

While the war had wedded Nicaise to running and Baptiste to stasis, it had wedded Thadée to detours. As soon as he escaped, he had joined a resistance group and fought with them until the day when they were denounced by some traitor and the enemy had surrounded them. Nearly all of them had lost their lives, but in his case death had taken a very long detour. He had been deported. And there had been so many detours, death had finally forgotten him, at least losing sight of him. Death was distant now — but life, too, remained yet almost as distant. He had had to go all that way to find it, in an isolated little village on the shores of a gray sea. And he had found it, although very fragile and still scared; it was there, flickering in the lowered gaze of both these gray-eyed children who had spent more than two years hidden in the depths of the cellar of an inn, behind a wall of sacks, boxes, and barrels.

It was the maid, who had been in their family's service since time immemorial and had suddenly found herself prohibited from continuing to serve masters now declared impure and cast into slavery, who had hidden them in the subterranean depths of that inn where she had then found employment. She came down every evening to bring them food filched from plates when the tables were cleared. So they had fed on leftovers, fear, and silence, too. For in their damp gloomy hideaway they had forgotten how to play, laugh, speak — and in the end even how to suffer and desire. They had forgotten how to be children, how to live.

As the months went by, they in turn had become shadows, gifted with the vision and hearing of night birds. And they still retained from that long seclusion infinitely slow and groping gestures, frightened eyes, almost silent mouths. They, even more than Thadée, had to learn how to live again.

Little-drum, who was radiant with childhood, did not find in them the companions he had been hoping for. But these chilly shadows, who scarcely murmured and had been bereft of everything including their childhood, had an immense privilege over him: they were brother and sister, absolutely united in a fierce love that he had no part in at all, nor even any access to.

This very deep love that bound Tsipele and Shlomo was a mystery to him and a source of fascination. He did not care that he had regained a father, and an uncle as well. What he wanted was a little sister. He imagined this little sister with his mother's features, both miniaturized and magnified. And all this little girl's beauty and love would have been attached to no one else but him.

He was soon pestering his mother continuously with his wish.

"Mama," he would beg with a kind of strangely gentle and vexatious bullying that astonished his mother, "I want a little sister!"

Pauline finally married Baptiste. At her wedding she was pregnant with the child her son had so greatly desired. Waiting was no game for Little-drum this time, but an attentive and jealous vigil. This child to be born was already his, and a sister.

As for Ruth and her children, their absence, redoubled with silence, was finally explained; their disappearance had a name. But a name so difficult to pronounce and to conceive that Night-of-gold-Wolf-face did not know how to deal with it. He turned it this way and that, even more than the card Thadée sent from Lindau.

But whichever way he wielded it, he merely kept tearing his heart on it ever more painfully.

For this name, like so many others, bristled with barbed wire, black smoke, watch towers, dogs' fangs, and human bones.

Sachsenhausen. A name of annulment, deleting in a single stroke the names of Ruth, Sylvestre, Samuel, Yvonne, and Suzanne. A name of finality.

6

Glory had been promised them, and they had vowed loyalty and valor. And they had set off for those vast plains, for the sake of that promised glory, that vowed loyalty. But only the wind swept those plains, only the cold awaited them there.

They had started out at the time when wild swans gathered in flocks in order to migrate, too, to other lands. And the men had never caught up with the swans, nor even reached the place from which they flew off, for over there everything always happened some place farther on. The cold wastes stretched away endlessly, endlessly extending their white zones — white to the point of madness — to the confines of the impossible. The men had been forced to stop well short of the great river that marked the boundary of the region of the most intense cold and the vastest wildernesses, beyond which the migrating swans gathered.

Yet men and swans were headed for the same cardinal point — due east — marching and flying to the sound of similarly deep-toned and raucous song. Their comportment, too, was the same, the men weighed down by their weapons and soon slowed by the cold and by their injuries; the birds hampered by their excessively large wings, clumsily beating the air in order to wrest themselves from the ground's terrible attraction. And they had similarly battled against the snow-spiked wind, and against frostbite, by huddling close to each other. But in the course of their long march the men had become more and more disfigured into terrible

ice-beasts, with stiff bleeding gestures and salt-eroded eyes, while
the swans, having finally broken away from the earth's embrace
after arduous efforts, had in the course of their flight — punctuated by stops on the frozen water of lakes, which they had to
break with their beaks — kept turning into wonderful, half-aer-
ial half-aquatic animals. Ungodly angels with hearts infinitely
blued by sky and sea.

The men had marched. They had sung and killed. Their youth was
the color of blood, and their hearts knew only one love — the love
of wrestling, bare fisted, with the angel of all violence. And their
love, so light-heartedly run wild, was so arrogant, so cruelly spell-
bound, that they had forgotten they were men. They thought
themselves more than men, whereas they were just warriors, their
hearts strapped with pride and insolence, their brows decorated
with black badges, and their bodies caparisoned with weapons.

They marched beneath the sign of the death's head and sang the
Song of the Devil, laughing uproariously.

> *SS marschiert im Feindesland*
> *Und singt ein Teufelsleid . . .*
> *. . . Wo wir sind, da ist immer vorne*
> *Und der Teufel der lacht noch dazu.*
> *Ha, ha, ha, ha, ha, ha, ha, ha, ha!*
> *Wir kämpfen für Freiheit,*
> *Wir kämpfen für Hitler . . .* ★

But neither the man in whose name they were marching to sow
death, nor the devil whose fraternal laugh they invoked, had any
care for them. The name of this man, manically bolstered with a

---

★ The SS march in enemy land/Singing the devil's song . . ./Wherever we are,
it's always forward/And that's where the devil's ever laughing/ Ha, ha . . .
etc./We're fighting for freedom/We're fighting for Hitler . . .

title as inordinate as it was absurd, was beginning to turn sour and sound hollow. The devil's laughter was at the expense of their own, and erupted behind their backs as death scythed through them.

They thought themselves armed with glory; they were just killers abandoned by their own people and reviled by everybody else. But they did not know it, they did not want to know. They advanced, proclaiming to empty space their meaningless honor and loyalty.

> *Wenn alle untreu werden*
> *Bleiben wir doch treu*
> *So dass immer noch auf Erden*
> *Für euch Fähnlein sei.* ★

But soon their flag flew only in the wind of a rout and kept furling up. Turning their backs on the cities in the east, cities that held out fiercely against them, even though they set fire to them, they fled westward. But they did not retrace their steps; they were not the kind of soldiers to retreat, and in any case such a retreat was not possible for they had so erred in love and battle that every trace of their footsteps was hopelessly lost.

They made for the sea. There was no country left they could call their homeland. For them, the name of every place was now wilderness and war. Only one city still cried out its name to them and was able to find an answering echo in their hearts. A city where they had never actually been before, lying in the middle of nowhere and already part of history: Berlin, the shrine of their faith, honor, and loyalty.

But their indirect return march went on and on. The plain around them was endless and implacably bleak. The wind that whipped them with snow swept across it, its strident whistling

---

★ When all become traitors/We remain true/So that here on Earth/There's always a standard flying for you.

only marking the silence more, and making the emptiness more limitless.

They marched for a long time, so long they slept on their feet, a drove of shadows loaded down like pack animals with weapons and snow, stealing through dark and foggy woods. They walked in their sleep like this for days and nights on end without uttering a word. But what on earth could they have said in such an infinity of coldness? Their faces were so icebound that their mouths, cracking with frost, could only produce whitish mists and cotton-wool rattles. Their eyes bled pink tears in which their gaze grew oblivious. They no longer remembered that there could possibly be any other landscapes on earth but these colorless expanses glistening like lakes of shale, or any other trees but firs and birches.

In fact, these were more than just trees; they were giants of changeable moods, sometimes deadly, sometimes protective, and it was with equal indifference that the firs closed in upon them, in order to shelter them or to shoot at them. For the trees did occasionally amuse themselves by shooting at them from the depths of their dense foliage, where their enemies were lodged.

They reached the seashore by the time the wild swans, sensing that the cold was slowly losing dominion, were gathering with great cries upon the islands in the Levant, upon lakes turning blue again with the return of spring. And the clamor of their calls, marking the terrible effort of their latest migration, once again resembled the clamor of the men, who persisted in singing their song of utterly futile valor and loyalty.

Men and swans, straining westward, were both returning to their country of legend, or of instinct.

The taste of the wind changed, and so too did its whip, but not its violence and coldness. It took on a taste of salt and whipped the survivors of that long march with lashes of rain twined out in the Baltic's swirling icy waters. The wind also carried the haunting cry of low flying sea birds.

They crossed sandy plains, dotted with lakes, woods, and marshes, and scattered with villages, with thatched roofs, and very straight narrow streets. But spring, whose return the swans, over there, were already celebrating by taking to the freedom of the skies, was slow in reappearing here. The plains were deserted wildernesses on which the snow lingered, and the villages, too, were deserted. There was no smoke from the thatched roofs, the streets rang empty, the windows were all closed. Dampness rotted the tables and beds in abandoned farmhouses, and also the wood of clocks, whose pendulums hung still. Cows left neglected in dilapidated cow sheds bellowed their pain, swinging their enormous udders, aching with milk. Nets hung useless on the walls of fishermen's houses, like great clumps of dead algae rejected by the sea. The sea, the earth, the town — everything rejected life.

The peasants and fishermen, the villagers — everyone had fled. But the townspeople were even more in flight, and especially those from the city toward which the devil's little soldiers were so valiantly heading, against the crowds in exodus, against the tide of history, still singing.

> *Wo wir sind das ist immer vorne*
> *Und der Teuful der lacht noch dazu.*
> *Ha, ha, ha, ha, ha, ha, ha, ha, ha!*

The city. The big city they had so much dreamed about — at last they were entering it. And perhaps, some of the soldiers, who marched bent under fire, began to hope, perhaps they would have the opportunity and the honor of seeing him, the little man to whom they had vowed loyalty and valor. He was said to have descended into the bowels of his gutted city, into the depths of his concrete palace.

Among those who nurtured such a hope in their hearts were Obergrenadier Gabriel Peniel and Obergrenadier Michael Peniel. They knew their adventure was coming to an end. And they were glad.

They had marched for such a long time, and killed and fought, and defied the cold, fire, and exhaustion, simply to reach this place, this time. To come and die here, among the fantastic ruins of the city — the city they had made their crossover homeland. To come and die here, near him, their prince with eyes illuminated with egregious hatred and nihilism. It was for him they had left their Blackland forests, denied their own people and country. It was for him they had marched for so long, their faces streaming with sweat, snow, fever, and rain. Now their faces were going to stream with blood, exult in blood. That most violent blood that had scalded their hearts and flesh from the very beginning. It was for him — the alchemist of this great enterprise of blood and ashes, whom they knew to be hopelessly doomed — that they entered the city singing.

Their final battle lasted less than a week — a battle through streets now without cobblestones, among devastated houses, from the tops of half-collapsed roofs, from the depths of ruined cellars. A battle during which the city burned down like a huge library of books made of stone, until every memory, every trace of its glory was consumed and there was nothing left to see, to read, but defeat and injury. The sky was the color of bricks and dust, the streets the color of flames, the walls the color of blood, and the men the color of plaster, rust, and smog.

The two Obergrenadiers Peniel ran from one barricade to the next, from door to door, from roof to roof, without taking time off any more to sleep, drink, or eat. All they had time for now was to shoot, to keep shooting, to destroy and set on fire. The end of their great dream of glory and triumph was approaching, so they had to hasten the rhythm of the final images, intensify the dream, make it blaze, crackle, explode.

Already they were not even soldiers any more, but guerrilla fighters maddened by conflict and fire, playing at destruction. For they were driven to destroy, and destroy, endlessly to destroy, like a sculptor who strikes at the stone and shatters it in order to release from it a yet unknown form, a magic power. They were driven to destroy, quickly, so as to release from the walls of the city, from the muddy sky, from these final hours of their youth and their battle, the pure form, the brute strength of their love. Stone of lightning. Arrow point planted in their innermost hearts since birth, and even before their birth. Stone of lightning, the color of blood, sidereal and tellurian — millenarian. Stone of blood.

Dawn was about to break. Michael and Gabriel, who had taken refuge on the third floor of a building in Prinz Albrecht Strasse, which they were defending alone against the enemy's constantly reinforced attack, suddenly stopped firing. They had just heard something, something indefinable, through the thundering of shells and the opacity of a purple soot sky. Something that was like an incredible silence, pure transparency. It came from nowhere, traveling toward them — straight toward them, only them, through the city, through the war.

And something else was coming toward them. It was a tank, an enormous tank. It advanced slowly, forcing its way with difficulty through the street blocked with heaps of rubble and the burned-out shells of vehicles, its huge gun nosing at the walls like the trunk of some prehistoric animal. The tank was at their mercy, all they had to do was fire. Fire, once again, once more.

But the two Obergrenadiers Peniel did not take aim. They laid down their weapons simultaneously. Their hands suddenly felt a great desire for emptiness and silence. They held hands and stood there, motionless, watching the great steel beast lurching very slowly among the ruins in the street, feeling that dazzling transparency and silence pour over their faces, wash their hearts. In the big deserted apartment where they were, every sound spoke to them, even the most tenuous. Especially the sound of water seeping from the cracked walls. They closed their eyes for a moment and smiled. Such sweetness penetrated their hearts. This transparency, this silence — they recognized them now. It was the voice of their brother.

The other one. The one whom they had robbed of his blood. The brother who was completely white, so delicate, so solitary. It was his voice, that marvelously high-pitched voice, which kept rising even higher, piercing the silence, soaring toward the purest light. A white light, silky with cold, with emptiness. They smiled and smiled, wonderingly, at such calm, such sweetness. They felt deliciously taken with shivers, taken with tenderness, with white passion.

The voice of their little brother, the other one, finally raised up what all their violence, all the blood they had spilled, had not yet succeeded in bringing to light — this stone of lightning buried in their hearts' core. This stone of blood, of cries, of earth. This stone of death. Now at last it was surfacing, in all its brilliance. Now at last it was breaking out of the shadows, out of their fury, to give them, as it cut through their hearts, the gift of smiling and of tears.

The voice of their brother, the other one, coming from the other side of the war, the other side of hatred. And the dilapidated walls around them, all sweating with dampness, became faces. Faces like tears, tear faces. Sweat and tears running imperceptibly in the plaster's, the skin's, filth. And the walls opened like great bay windows onto the city. This insane city, this doomed, fallen city. All the ruins assumed faces, all the dead regained faces and names. Raphael's voice kept soaring higher and higher, imploringly — like a song of atonement and absolute consolation. The voice of their little brother, the pure strains of mercy. At the very moment when all was lost, consummated.

Michael and Gabriel were no longer soldiers or guerrilla fighters. They were not anything any more. They became children again, two children lost in the city, lost in history. Two children trembling with reverie and tenderness. They stood facing the blown-out window, squeezing each other's hand so hard it was painful.

Stone of tears and smiles. It was no longer a matter of destroying but of disappearing. Into their brother's voice, with their brother's voice. Of becoming transparent. Voice of metamorphosis. Of slipping over to the other side, of entering the mystery of disappearance. Of accepting and renouncing.

The explosion was terrible. The big beast, by nosing around, had located its prey and loosed its fire. The façade shattered like a huge pane of glass and the roof caved in. Everything came crashing down. The two Obergrenadiers Peniel were caught in the avalanche and hurled down into the cellar under beams and rubble.

No trace of their bodies, crushed beneath the ruins, was ever found. They were lost in the ashes of the big city, in the ashes of history and oblivion, like the man whose name they had so loyally praised and served, utterly ruinously, utterly deluded.

7

There was no world left according to Night-of-gold-Wolf-face. No world left for him. The disappearance of Ruth and of their four children had cast the world down lower than earth, lower than anything. There was not night and silence any more, but gloom and muteness. Sachsenhausen. This word hammered in his mind, night and day, without respite, to the exclusion of any other. No thought, no image managed to form within him, especially not to take hold. Sachsenhausen. It drummed like the inscrutable sound of his own heart — with a similar blind rhythm. Weeks, months went past, and nothing availed, the dull cadence, the terrible monotony of the drumming persisted. Sachsenhausen. Sachsenhausen.

Night-of-gold-Wolf-face spent his days sitting on a little bench, facing the wall, in a corner of his bedroom. His days and nights. He held his head in his hands, with his elbows resting on his knees. His head was so heavy, so heavy with emptiness, and with that perpetual internal hammering, it could not even hold itself up any more. As soon as he let go of his head it started swaying backward and forward, slowly, like the pendulum of a clock that nothing can stop. He had ceased to experience hunger, or sleep, or thirst. He was not even in pain. It was as if he was beyond pain, or fell short of it. He had toppled into a zone of nothingness. He endured the terrible passage of time, hour by hour, second upon second. A time warp outside of time, drained of duration — void. Sachsenhausen. His mind was at breaking point, everything inside him was at breaking point, yet nothing gave way. Even his body, deprived of nourishment and sleep, held out. He was like a tree trunk, planted in the corner of his empty bedroom, a fossilized tree trunk.

In any case, he was incapable of doing otherwise. He had no control over himself any more, no longer thought, or felt. He endured. Sachsenhausen. Sachsenhausen. He endured the ordeal of total night — night in which everything has disappeared, night of annulment. And he was assigned to pure insomnia, to an insane presence steeped in absence. It was impossible for him not to be there — nowhere, keeping vigil hour by hour — in time that never was, never could be. It was impossible for him not to see, to see the very thing that was not visible — to see the very antithesis of all seeing. He saw the Night, of simultaneously opaque and translucent inkiness, an ink predating, or postdating, all writing. Black Night-of-ink where nothing more is written, said, read. Illiterate Night-of-ink where nothing more occurs.

In fact, perhaps it was not even he who thus kept vigil in the Night, it was the night itself keeping vigil through him, in him. He was no more than an empty space, an abandoned shelter of bones and skin that Night itself had entered as sentry, to mount guard over its own immensity, its own silence. Sachsenhausen. Night. Night, the Night.

Mathilde, her two half-brothers, and Nicaise worked to repair the damage to the farm, to restore life to the fields, and to the village. Once again Blackland was picking itself up. A few men had returned from the labor camps, and slowly, tentative efforts were made to rebuild, to start afresh. It had always been so at Blackland.

Tsipele and Shlomo seemed to grope their way back to life — they learned to be children again, to love, to trust, but still with such hesitation and shyness. They followed Thadée around like two silent shadows, not daring yet to go near the others, to mix with all these strangers, not yet. And always they held hands, silent and terribly grave. Their slender figures haunted Little-drum incessantly, appearing even in his dreams, against the backdrop of night. Inaccessible. But another face also appeared to him now, and this one smiled at him, to him alone, to no one else but him. The face of a little girl with blonde braids, with almond-shaped eyes the color of dried leaves, watching him through the windowpane. For his little sister always appeared to him in his dream on the other side of a window with misted glass. No sooner did he approach the window to open it, or at least clear the glass, than he would awaken with a start. But he did not lose hope in her, however. He was waiting. She would soon be with him, all his, his alone.

There was a letter from Rose, a very short letter.

"Violette's agony has come to an end. It lasted for five years. Five years of suffering, of blood. She died very peacefully, smiling, as if nothing had happened. For she was smiling in death, and nothing was able to efface that smile. The blood suddenly stopped flowing from her temple, and the most extraordinary thing happened: even the mark disappeared. It fell off — the birthmark fell from her temple like a dead rose petal. The sisters here speak of a miracle and are filled with wonder. But I don't believe in miracles any more; it's meaningless. It's come too late. I don't believe in anything anymore. I only entered the convent to be with Violette, I only stayed so as not to be parted from her. Now she's dead, I don't want to stay any longer. I've asked to be released from my vows. Soon I shall leave. I don't yet know when, or what I shall do when I get out of the convent. But it doesn't much matter anymore."

It was Mathilde, cold haughty Mathilde, who was the most affected by the news of this death. She had brought up Blanche's two girls; and above all, she knew what it meant for a Peniel child suddenly to be robbed of her twin, her double. She alone understood the despair Rose-Eloise must be suffering, having herself endured for more than ten years that insane inconsolable grief of being left forsaken, all alone. Violette-Honorine had just died, at an interval of some ten years, at almost the same age as Margot. This reminder, this repetition deeply upset Mathilde. But once again she was able to regain her self-control, with a further hardening and greater loneliness. She was more lonely than ever before. The others would never gain admittance to her heart. All she was left with, as ever, was her father — her crazy father — her impossible love, her hatred, her frigidly jealous passion. Moreover, she would not let anybody go into Night-of-gold-Wolf-face's bedroom. Only she went up there, three times a day, to visit him. Well, let him stay there, huddled on his little bench, sitting with his head in his hands, his face turned to the wall. Well, let him stay there as long as he wanted, as long as he needed. She knew what he was like; he would recover. He had always recovered, like her, like the fields of Blackland. Their strength was inexhaustible, their endurance indestructible. He would recover and leave her again, betray her once more. She knew it. And it was precisely because of this that she hated him so much and could not turn her back on him. On her father, now, through grief, become her child, her thing; a dumbstruck crazy child, whose mind was elsewhere. But for a while, all hers, no one elses's but hers.

Nothing was ever heard of Michael and Gabriel again. No one knew, and certainly did not want to know, what had become of them. For everyone, it was enough to know of their joining the Charlemagne Division, of their treachery to their country, to their people. No one ever spoke of them again, their names were rooted out from family remembrance, their memory cast into the ashes. They were banished forever to the obscurity assigned to the damned. As for their brother, Raphael, all trace of him, too, was lost.

There had certainly been rumors about him, but these came from very far away, carried by the newspapers. It was said that one early May evening, in New York, he had lost his voice, and his mind, during a performance of Monteverdi's *Orfeo,* in which he was singing the part of Hope. Never, it was claimed, had his voice been so pure, so marvelous, above all so overwhelming, as on that evening. So much so that the people in the hall, including the musicians and other singers both on stage and in the wings, had for a while been left breathless, allowing an almost terrifying silence to fill the place. So much so, they said, that Orpheus, almost driven to madness with the passion of his part, in a voice crazed with tears had cried rather than sung when he came to rendering *"Dove, ah, dove te'n vai . . ."* ★ after Hope had delivered those last words before vanishing:

> *Lasciate ogni speranza, voi ch'entrate.*
> *Dunque, se stabilito hai pur nel core*
> *Di porre il piè nella città dolente*
> *Da te me'n fuggo e torno*
> *A l'usato soggiorno.* †

And everyone in the audience had seen the countertenor actually fade away before their very eyes, and sensed that he was abandoning his role and even defying Hope, whose part he played. Everyone had felt he was stealing a march on Orpheus, that it was he who was entering the city of woe and of ashes. But nobody would have been able to say what Eurydice he thus went in search of, or even in which region of the impossible and the invisible.

★ Where, o where are you going . . .

† Abandon all hope, you who enter./So, if you are still determined in your heart/ To set foot in the city of woe/I shall leave you and return/To familiar climes.

He had gone right through the place, right through the bodies of everyone there, and disappeared. For his voice, carrying too far, soaring too high, had left him. It was also said that since that evening, when he lost his voice and his mind, he had wandered New York, begging. He was the white beggar with soft pink eyes who walked the streets, open mouthed, mute, and always flanked by two big dogs, one black, the other straw colored, that came from no one knew where.

But Raphael's voice, too, had taken to begging. It trailed around the world, across seas, forests, plains, and towns, so colorless, so light of breath that no one paid any attention to it, except those who had a memory of ashes, a mouth wasted with silence, a heart depleted. A plaintive breath of wind.

> *Dunque, se stabilito hai pur nel core*
> *Di porre il piè nella città dolente*
> *Da te me'n fuggo e torno*
> *A l'usato soggiorno . . .*

Really, it was not even a voice any more, but the frayed ends of a voice, a trail of echoes. And what this frayed voice begged for was a heart that would listen, a heart to enter, where it might find rest at last.

> *Dunque, se stabalito hai pur nel core*
> *Di porre il piè nella città dolente . . .*

Those who gave shelter to this mendicant voice in the course of its wanderings were no better than it was. They were people who for a long time already had been exposed to every wind, to every emptiness and silence. People of ashes and dust.

It came all the way to Blackland. For days it lurked around Upper Farm, whispering, hugging the ground and the walls, and then one night it slipped under the door. It wandered through the

rooms, climbed the stairs, stole into the bedrooms. But it found
no way into the slumbers of the dream-engrossed sleepers. There
was, however, one person who heard it. True, this person was not
asleep, he was only keeping silent, sitting almost on the ground,
with his head buried in his hands.

The voice ran up his back, like a shiver, to the nape of his neck,
and then wound around his neck in an importunate murmur. The
man shuddered; he felt a great coldness spread from the small of
his back to the back of his neck, from his neck to his brow. He took
his hands away from his face and looked around, totally amazed,
like someone waking from a deep sleep.

Outside it was night. A beautiful translucent night of inky black-
ness, spangled with bright stars set high above. In the room it was dark.
He listened. But the voice had already penetrated his blood. However,
he thought he heard another sound. This one came from Pauline and
Baptiste's bedroom. A woman moaning. He slowly got to his feet,
steadied himself. He took off his shoes and quietly left the room. He
went downstairs, out of the house, and shut the door firmly behind
him. It was a truly beautiful clear and frosty night. He went inside the
barn to look for something. He saw in the dark better than ever. He
came out, stuffing a little paper bag into his pocket. He then made his
way to Dead-echoes Wood. His shadow circled around him, very
light. He walked barefoot, bareheaded, wearing only a light pair of
trousers and a shirt.

He was not cold. The cold ran in his blood, was his blood. He
entered the forest. The darkness here was total, but he saw every
detail of grass, bark, insect. The night was in his eyes. He came to
a clearing. There he sat down on the ground, against a big jutting
rock. He took the paper bag from his pocket, opened it and began
to eat fistfuls of the red wheat seed it contained, until his mouth
was clammy and his gorge rose in disgust. He fell onto his side, his
head rolled in the moss, in the damp leaves, the dry branches. His
brow was streaming with sweat.

✛

Night of Night

A woman rises from among the tree roots.
She wears a dark red dress. Blood red, raw.
She sways her hips as she walks.
He sees her from behind.
He sees only her, she blocks his view entirely.
He sees only that — those truly magnificent buttocks of hers, gently swaying beneath the blood red fabric that gives a fluid rhythm to the swaying of her hips.
She stuffs her hands into her pockets, rummages,
extracts things.
Loads of things,
which she throws away one by one.
There are ribbons, keys, silver forks and spoons, candlesticks, green and purple marbles, tresses of women's hair, gloves, fruit, women's shoes, bill hooks.
There are so many things, and yet
the pockets of the red dress seem as empty as ever.
The woman keeps throwing things away,
and blocking his view.

    The wind has risen. A terrific wind.
    The sky is black, streaked with long horizontal clouds of saffron yellow.
    A man — very tall, stooped — walks on the horizon, against the sky.

He carries another man
or perhaps it's a woman
on his shoulders.
They have to struggle against the wind.
The woman in the red dress has reappeared.
Still with her back turned.
This time they are photographs
that she throws from her pockets
and little stone statuettes.
And then lamps as well,
lamps made of glass and colored paper
that cast feeble glimmers of orange light
in the dark grass.
Like will-o'-the-wisps.

> A railway station. At night.
> An ordinary little country railway station.
> A train arrives,
> with a long tail of cars.
> The train is so long
> it even extends beyond the platform.
> The rear cars
> are stopped in open countryside.

These are old wooden cars, closed with big iron bars. Cattle cars
or freight cars. The engine puffs and whistles, expelling whitish
ashy clouds that undulate along its sides. There is smoke everywhere coming out from under the belly of the train, from the rails
in the grass. It floats just above the ground on the deserted platform and the engine wails plaintively/The sides of the cars have
started moving like the flanks of breathless beasts panting/ The
worm-eaten wooden slats lichen-covered soot-blackened quietly
quiver and creak/Eyes thousands of eyes glisten behind the slats All
have the same look A unique look completely rounded completely
hollow completely fixed

He runs alongside the cars
in the whitish smoke
his hands touch the damp sides
the wood is so rotten so soft
it smells of moss of cowpats
he tries to get into the cars
but finds no door or window
he peers between the disjointed slats
but what he sees is always
the same thing
faceless looks
bodiless gestures
lost in emptiness darkness
all the same
he does not find what he seeks
those he seeks
his own

He enters the City the big City he enters it by river on a kind of
raft so flat it is completely level with the water a black viscous water
in which nothing is reflected all around there are just ruins and
ashes sides of houses lean strangely and then suddenly collapse
without a sound total silence reigns on a bridge over there he
catches sight again of the man carrying another man or is it a
woman on his tall thin shoulders they are both bowed their limbs
are long and bony and swing gracelessly in space black rugged figures soon followed or passed by other similar figures his raft drifts
gently in the slightly pungent smell of the cold dirty water from
bridge to bridge he sees the same man again the same scene
From bridge to bridge night deepens
and his pain increases
There, in his torso, in his belly
a burning pain

a searing pain
>The small grains of red wheat
>have set fire

to his blood

to his flesh

>He rolls on the ground
>violent tremors jerk his shoulders
>Now he is seized with convulsions

The raft spins around caught in an invisible whirlpool all of a sudden umpteen noises arise from the city bells pealing shutters slamming at every window the noise of trains crossing iron bridges the screech of trams descending narrow streets dogs howling at the moon children squalling men and women shouting hooters and sirens

but one sound soon dominates all the others

the footsteps of a woman in high heeled shoes walking hurriedly
>through a tunnel

tap-tapping echoes

his eyes are all misted with sweat

every image is distorted by it

images overlay each other, move, tear into each other

he feels himself growing heavier and heavier

weighted with the mud of night

with that fire of hell in his entrails

the earth lurches everything overturns

he tumbles hurts his shoulder on the jutting rock

all of his red wheat mash turned into incandescent lava rises in his
>throat and fills his mouth again with his forehead against the
>rock he starts to spew up

for a long time

his red wheat mash

Red the dress of the woman with swaying buttocks

who dances dances in a deserted square

sweat streaming all over her body
he digs his fingers into the soil
he is thirsty
he chews the earth
or his fist
he does not know which
the wind rises again with incredible force
but inside his body
only inside his body.

     He sees a book
     an enormous book
     with black leather binding
     a book as big as a man
     a book with man's shoulders
     a book seized with convulsions
     The book
     all sonorous with wind with whistlings
     now deep now sharp
     twists and writhes
     like a sick beast
     Its pages flap
     its words chafed by the wind
     come pouring out as saliva as black blood

It runs from his mouth. He groans. He is in agony. He thinks he is
    speaking calling naming. No nothing. He groans slavers spews.
    Sticky black blood.

He rolls over onto his back again completely suffocating tries
to keep his eyes open.

Night. Night, the night.

The clearing slowly spins around, a big carousel of trees and ani-
    mals ridden by crazy children fantastic figures.

With the water of his icy sweat mingles another water, scalding
    hot. Tears.

And now Night-of-gold-Wolf-face starts calling on his grandmother, weeping.

"Vitalie! Vitalie!"

he murmurs, as if only the oldest name had withstood oblivion, burial.

But the name is there, very close, very warm, answering,

"I'm here. Sleep. Sleep now . . ."

and the name spreads its light shadow over him, covers him.

And beneath the nape of his neck, just where he dug,

chewed the earth,

at the foot of the jutting rock,

water wells up.

A clear water, and very cool

that bathes his head

washes his face

refreshes his mouth

"Sleep, sleep, my little one, my darling little one . . ." says Vitalie's voice, over and over.

It was at the same time — just as a spring welled up, in the clearing in Dead-echoes Wood, under the neck of Victor-Flandrin Peniel, called Night-of-gold-Wolf-face — that, over at Upper Farm, Pauline gave birth to her second child.

It was a son. A fine boy full of strength and vitality, with a shock of hair the color of honey and amber. He gave a cry like the song of a tuba, and gaily waved his hands and feet in the air when his father lifted him up, as though dispelling all shadows in advance.

He was named Charles-Victor.

He was the last-born of the Peniel line. The postwar child. The child born after all the wars. The one in whom the Book of Nights closed — the Book of Names and Cries.

But the book did not close to end there, to fall silent.

The last word does not exist. There is no last word, last cry.

The book was turning back. It was going to flick through its pages in reverse, lie idle, and then start again. With other words, new faces.

Charles-Victor Peniel, the one everyone would later call Night-of-amber, was in turn destined to fight in the night. To the midnight of Night.

THE BOOK OF NIGHTS

was set in Linotron Bembo, a typeface based on the types used by Venetian scholar-publisher Aldus Manutius in the printing of *De Aetna*, written by Pietro Bembo and published in 1495. The original characters were cut in 1490 by Francesco Griffo who, at Aldus's request, later cut the first italic types. Originally adapted by the English Monotype Company, Bembo is one of the most elegant, readable, and widely used of all book faces.

Book design and composition by Elizabeth Knox, New Haven, Connecticut. Printing and binding by Haddon Craftsmen, Scranton, Pennsylvania.